Bouquets of **Rose's**

"This mystery is the story of Rose French, great screen star in the silent days, who had married and left five husbands, and who dies suddenly one day at the end of summer in a deserted garden. The coroner and others marked down her death as a natural one, but Frank Clyde, who knew something of her story and suspected more, was quite sure that it was not. ...amazing, told with suspense and wit."

—Long Beach Tribune

"A fast-moving tale of intrigue in a first-class job of heads-up writing."

—Birmingham News

D0951518

By **Margaret Millar**
available in Library of Crime Classics® Editions:

AN AIR THAT KILLS
ASK FOR ME TOMORROW
BANSHEE
BEAST IN VIEW
THE FIEND
HOW LIKE AN ANGEL
ROSE'S LAST SUMMER
A STRANGER IN MY GRAVE

Margaret
Millar
ROSE'S LAST SUMMER

INTERNATIONAL POLYGONICS, LTD.
NEW YORK CITY

To the Memory of
M.M. Musselman

ROSE'S LAST SUMMER
Copyright © 1952, 1980 by Margaret Millar Survivor's Trust
u/a 4/12/82
Cover: Copyright © 1985 by International Polygonics, Ltd.

Library of Congress Card Catalog No. 85-60548
ISBN: 0-930330-26-9

Printed and manufactured in the United States of America
First IPL printing April 1985
10 9 8 7 6 5 4 3 2 1

1

Rose was on the skids again. Everyone in the boarding house knew it. This was no great tribute to their powers of perception since Rose went on the skids as she did everything else, with noise, abandon and a fine sense of timing and style. Saturday night at supper she told several humorous stories, and when nobody laughed as hard as she expected, she insulted everyone and went upstairs to her room.

In the middle of the night she decided to sing some old folk songs, and when Miss Henderson, who occupied the adjoining room, objected by pounding on the wall, Rose pounded back so vigorously that she knocked a hole in the plaster. Rose was furious at Miss Henderson for causing the hole in the plaster, and reported the incident immediately to Mrs. Cushman, the landlady.

Mrs. Cushman woke up and looked sadly at the clock and then at Rose. "Rose, for Pete's sake, it's too early to get up. It's only three o'clock."

"I haven't been to bed."

"Then you better—"

"I can't sleep. Who could sleep with a crackpot like that pounding on the wall all night? Knocked a hole in it as big as your head. I've got a good notion to move out."

"Why don't you?"

"By God, I will."

She spent the next few hours packing her belongings and sipping a little wine now and then to give her energy. By breakfast time she was in an excellent mood. She unpacked all her clothes and replaced them in the closet, she

3

hung a calendar over the hole in the wall, and publicly forgave Miss Henderson for her lousy manners, rotten disposition, and lack of musical appreciation. For some reason Miss Henderson did not respond to this act of charity, and by noon she had left, bag and baggage, leaving the room next to Rose vacant again for the third time in as many months.

Rose couldn't understand anyone being so petty and she said as much to Mrs. Cushman.

"You're better off without her. We're all better off."

"She paid her rent."

"Money. What's money?"

Mrs. Cushman's plump face took on an angular severity. "Money happens to be what I live on."

"I used to throw the stuff away. God, did I!"

"It's too bad you didn't throw a little my way. In fact, it's too bad you—"

But Rose was beyond the sordid present. She lay back on the bed, careful not to bump her head on the wine bottle under her pillow, and gazed dreamily up at the ceiling and the past. "Did I ever tell you about the party I gave once, just after *Anguish* was released? There must have been four hundred people, and—you know what?—I didn't know a bloody one of them."

"Last time it was three hundred."

"I'm no good at figures."

"Rose."

"If I'd been any good at figures, I'd be a millionaire right now." She spoke with pride and only a trace of regret. "God, how I threw the stuff away. It was sheer genius."

"Rose," Mrs. Cushman said, "you're hitting the bottle again."

Rose stood up, looking very dignified and awesome, in spite of her shortness. "What a perfectly vile and offensive remark."

4

"I don't care. It's the truth."

"I swear, I swear by—"

"I don't care if you was buried in Bibles right up to your neck, I wouldn't believe you. You're hitting the bottle again and I'm going to phone Frank."

Rose was shaken, though she tried not to show it. "Call him. Who cares?"

"Maybe he can straighten you out like last time."

"Straighten me out." Rose snorted. "You talk as if I'm an old wrinkled pair of trousers and this crude and callow youth can—"

"Come off your high horse, you're not going anywhere."

Rose looked around the walls for reassurance. They were covered, from floor to ceiling, with photographs of herself, smiling, sultry, coy, gay; in period costumes and bathing suits; stills and action shots; Rose being kissed, strangled, rescued, fed to the lions, lighting a cigarette, toasting a lover, dancing a polka. All Rose's, all magnificent, not in the least like an old wrinkled pair of trousers.

"You can't phone Frank," she said finally. "It's Sunday, it's his day off."

"I can get him at home."

"It's debasing, degrading. I won't talk to him. I'll lock my door. I'll *throw* things at him!"

"You do and he'll send for the butterfly net."

Rose was terrified by this expression. It made her feel like a butterfly, imprisoned, beating its fragile wings in futile struggle.

"He wouldn't dare," she said coldly.

"He would so, if he had to. You talk to him nice, now, won't you?"

"I think this whole business is completely revolting."

"You like Frank, you know you do."

"He stinks," Rose said. "Leave me alone."

When she was left alone, she locked her door, and, removing the wine bottle from under her pillow, she poured 'some into a glass and savored its bouquet. It smelled a little like ketchup, but Rose didn't know the difference, and when the wine was gone she felt better. She changed into her best silk print, combed her short hair carefully, and put on some makeup. Surveying the results of this effort in the mirror, she decided that she looked pretty good considering that she had fifty-two years of assorted living behind her. Her features were quite plain, a fact that Rose herself was willing to admit had contributed to her past success; it had been easy for women to identify themselves with her and for men to consider her within their reach.

She had always got along better with men than with women, and her vanity was still powerful enough to make her want to look her best for any man. Before Frank arrived she sprayed a little cologne around the room, hid the empty wine bottle inside her bureau, and, with the image of the butterfly net in the back of her mind, made a solemn resolution to behave with extreme grace and charm.

"You dear boy," Rose said throatily. "You dear sweet boy to come calling on an old woman on your day off."

Frank was quite unsurprised by this cordiality. He had known Rose for over a year, ever since the day that Mrs. Cushman had brought Rose, slightly drunk and very belligerent, to the mental hygiene clinic where Frank was one of the psychiatric social workers. Since then he had had many talks with Rose, and after each one he was left with the disturbing impression that Rose was not maladjusted to the world, but that the world was maladjusted to Rose.

Frank was twenty-seven. He had a wife, two sons, a mother-in-law, a cocker spaniel, an orange-colored cat and very little money. He was absorbed in his job, and so was Miriam, his wife. His main difficulty, aside from money, was getting to bed in time at night, since he and Miriam

6

liked to discuss his cases and it was usually one o'clock when they retired. As a result, Frank always looked a little sleepy. This, too, served its purpose: most people felt relaxed with him and told him more than they intended because he seemed so inattentive that it was impossible to believe he was prying into their secrets. Rose was an exception. She wasn't easily fooled, and Frank had discovered, by trial and error, that the best way to deal with Rose was to be as candid as possible. He had a great deal of respect for her and believed firmly that she was neither a mental case nor a true alcoholic, but an ageing woman who needed a job and some new interests.

"You are a sweet boy," Rose repeated, "to think of me like this, on your day off."

"Mrs. Cushman called me."

"That old bat, if you'll pardon the expression. What did she say about me?"

"Just that you were kicking up a little." Frank sat down in the upholstered rocking chair beside the window. "Are you?"

Rose laughed heartily at this preposterous question. "My dear child, I never felt better in my life. The thing is that the old bat can't stand to see anyone else having a good time. That's the thing."

There was such a strong element of truth in this, as there was in so many of Rose's remarks, that Frank was tempted to agree with her out loud.

"She told me you disturbed the household," Frank said. "Is that true?"

"I didn't *disturb* anyone. I merely *sang*. Can't a person even sing? My God, you'd think this was Russia instead of California." For the past six months Rose had divided all blame for everything equally among the Russians, Mrs. Cushman and the mental hygiene clinic. "Are you going to write down what I say today?"

"No."

7

"Not even afterwards when you go home?"

"No. This is just a friendly chat. Tell me, when did you start this bout?"

Rose was silent a moment. "It isn't a bout. It isn't a bout yet, anyway."

"Think it's going to be?"

"Maybe not. I don't know."

"Let's try to stop it, the way we did last time."

"We?" Rose elevated her eyebrows. "*I've* never had to depend on anybody. I'm completely independent. I've supported three husbands in my lifetime, never took a cent from any of them. I'm a giver, that's what I am. I'm a giver, not a taker."

"What's on your chest, Rose?"

"Nothing."

"What happened? What started you off this time?"

"It's none of your business. Just remember, I'm independent. I don't need any help or charity from anyone. I'm expecting a long distance call from central casting any day now."

"Are you going to sit around drinking until it comes?"

"That's my affair."

"You're stubborn today, Rose."

"I intended to be charming," Rose said, "but you put my back up. Would you really send for the butterfly net?"

Frank smiled, he couldn't help it. "You don't need one."

"That old bat said you'd send for the butterfly net if I weren't charming. I could be charming as hell if I wanted to."

"I'm sure you could."

"The thing is, why bother? You know too much about me."

"I wish I did," Frank said. His report on Rose covered more than a hundred pages, but it was impossible to separate fact and fiction. About some things, like her three

8

husbands, she was devastatingly candid; other things, like her family, she refused to discuss—seemed, in fact, to have forgotten.

"You know, Rose, I used to go to all your pictures. I thought you were a great actress."

"Who are you kidding, I was a ham."

"You were great."

"Don't use any of your lousy therapy on me. Trying to make me feel good, baloney."

It was partly true and partly baloney, and sometimes she ate it up and sometimes she spat it out like a moody child.

"Have you anything hidden around the room?" Frank said.

"Not any more. I drank it."

"Got any money?"

"Some. I could go on a good bun if I want to, if that's what you're trying to find out."

"I hope you don't."

Rose laughed. "I hope I don't too."

"Hold on for a while, will you? I'm still trying to get you a job. I have a couple of new leads."

"In a small city like this I don't stand a chance. Everybody knows me. If I could just get south again and start going the rounds."

"South" to Rose meant only one place, Hollywood. It was only a hundred miles away but to Rose it often seemed a million. When, on Saturday nights, she walked down the quiet main street of La Mesa, she became violently homesick for the lights on the strip and the big stores on Wilshire and the confusion of people at Hollywood and Vine. Wherever she went in La Mesa she could see the sea. Rose had no use for the sea; it was cold, dangerous, and smelled of fish.

"How's your canasta game coming along?" Frank said.

"Don't try to change the subject. So you think I

9

wouldn't make good if I went south, that's what you think."

"You're probably better off here."

"Bull. Bull."

"Quit trying to play the bad girl, Rose. It doesn't suit you."

"Bull." She flounced over to the window and looked out through the pink net drapes. There was the lousy sea again, leering at her. "Why'd you come here anyway?"

"To cheer you up."

"Well, you don't cheer me up," Rose said coldly. "You depress me utterly. *Utterly.*"

"Then I'll leave."

"Go ahead, leave."

"Why not leave with me? Come out to the house and have dinner with Miriam and me."

"I can't."

"Try."

"I can't. I'm expecting a call."

He took her at her word.

When he went downstairs, he found Mrs. Cushman posted at the front door. Mrs. Cushman had a great capacity for enjoying remote catastrophes like hurricanes in Florida or train wrecks on the New York Central, but petty annoyances at home sent her blood pressure up.

"Is Rose going to be all right?"

"Hope so," Frank said. "I'm not sure."

"Well, my goodness; you should be."

Mrs. Cushman, who was never sure of anything herself, couldn't tolerate this weakness in others, especially someone from the clinic. The clinic had had considerable publicity in the local newspaper during the past year, and Mrs. Cushman had somehow received the impression that it was omniscient and infallible. Frank was sorry to disappoint her.

"I think Rose will be all right," he said. "Don't exaggerate her condition. Compared to most of the people I deal with, Rose stands out as a shining light."

"Well, she don't stand out no shining light with me. Many's the hour I've spent regretting the day I opened this very door and there she stood and I recognized her right off. Rose French—I said it right out loud like that— Rose French. Little did I dream at the time—"

"I'm trying to get her a job."

"Huh. The day you get her a job and the day she keeps a job, that'll be the day."

It seemed like a good exit line, and Frank used it.

Before he got into his old Chevrolet, he looked up at Rose's window. Behind the pink net curtains he could see her small, still shadow. He lifted his arm and waved but the shadow didn't move.

By the time he arrived home he'd almost forgotten about Rose. Miriam had planned a beach picnic and the two boys were waiting with the cocker on the porch steps, loaded with equipment for the day like a couple of marines. The orange-colored cat was sitting on her haunches on the railing, withdrawn, despising the excitement. The cat's independence reminded him of Rose.

That night he and Miriam spent an hour discussing Rose, but the only conclusion they reached was that Rose had too large a personality to be squeezed into a small world.

He didn't expect to hear from Rose for a while. If she got drunk she wouldn't ask for his help, and if she stayed sober she wouldn't need it. But at three the following afternoon she phoned him at his office. She was in a cheerful mood.

"Frankie? It's me. Rose."

"Hello, Rose. How are you feeling?"

"Couldn't be better. I'm leaving town."

"Oh."

"Don't *oh* me like that. What a sourpuss. All you can say is *oh* when I've got good news."

"What's the news?"

"I have a job. I told you I didn't need any help, didn't I?"

"You told me. What's the job?"

"Nothing much really, but it should be fun. And I get paid with *money*. God, was the old bat surprised when I handed her the back rent. She damn near cried."

"You were paid in advance?"

"Some. I'm going to be a sort of housekeeper."

Frank laughed.

"What's so funny?" Rose said suspiciously. "I suppose you think I can't keep house. I've kept a dozen houses. All you've got to do is order the servants around."

"Are there servants?"

"Of course there are servants," Rose said, as if she would never have demeaned herself by accepting a job in a house without them. "Well, anyway, I just thought I'd phone you and say goodbye and thank you. I guess I owe you something. The old bat *says* I owe you something, damned if I know what."

"You don't owe me a thing," Frank said. "Just let us hear from you once in a while."

There was a minute's silence before Rose spoke again. "Well, I'm not much for writing letters and stuff like that."

"Just write your name on a postcard so we'll know you're all right."

"Sure. Sure, I guess I can do that."

"Good-bye, Rose, and good luck."

"Good-bye, Frank." Another silence. "You want to know something? Now that I won't have to put up with you any more, I think you're a pretty nice egg."

She hung up before he could answer.

The postcard arrived in the next morning's mail. The

message side contained nothing but a crude pencil sketch of a rose.

The postcard pleased him. He thought of it off and on all day, and kept it in his pocket to show to Miriam when he got home for dinner that night.

Miriam met him at the door. She had the evening newspaper in her hand and her face looked pale and stony as it always did when she was trying not to show her emotions in front of the children.

"Rose is dead," she said, and pressed her forehead tight against his shoulder.

2

SHE WAS FOUND by Ortega, the young gardener on the Pearce estate that had been rented to some summer people from San Francisco. Ortega went out early Tuesday morning to set out a flat of larkspur in the bare patch of ground between the patio and the garage. Rose was lying on her face beside the lily pool. A small, white canvas garden chair was overturned behind her, and just out of reach of her hand was a battered rawhide suitcase covered with scraps of labels.

That was all Ortega stayed to see. He dropped the flat of larkspur and ran toward the house, making little grunting noises of distress.

Willett Goodfield was at the table in the dinette whose windows faced eastward to the mountains. The morning paper was open in front of him, though he wasn't reading it. It was his habit to keep the paper there in case Ethel his wife should unexpectedly show up for breakfast; then, by staring at it, he could subtly show her that he preferred to be alone first thing in the morning until he became adjusted to the new day. This business of adjusting wasn't getting any easier. There were money difficulties, there was worry over his mother and the recurring pain in his back which Willett diagnosed as kidney stones if he was depressed, and imagination, if he wasn't. There was inflation, his new bridge which didn't fit properly, the exorbitant rent on this house he'd been forced to take for the summer, and the battery on the Lincoln which kept going dead.

Willett was pink and portly. He looked like a banker or a lawyer. In actual fact, he had never done anything in his thirty-five years except pay occasional and ineffectual visits to the doll factory which his father had built and which had supported the entire family ever since. At his father's death all the stock had gone to his mother, Olive. Olive had had a brief and glorious fling at being a business woman and then lost interest and went back to her hobby of raising begonias. Willett adored his mother and personally escorted her begonias to all the flower shows when Olive was unable to do it herself. For the past several years Olive had been very ill. She frequently discussed her approaching death, not in an effort to get attention or pity, but to accustom her children to the cold fact.

Mother, Willett thought, and had to blink his eyes to keep back the tears.

Ortega blew into the room, his heavy work boots crashing over the waxed concrete floors.

"Sir, sir," Ortega said. "A lady lying down dead, sir, oh my golly."

"You should learn to knock before—"

"A poor old lady—my golly, sir, come quick."

Ortega was grinning broadly, out of nervousness, and his face was the color of ripe limes.

Ortega went with the house—his services were included

in the rent—and Willett had never spoken to him before or even noticed him particularly.

"A dead woman, you say? Well." Willett cleared his throat. "Well, I'll tend to the matter immediately."

He got up, glanced at the hall door in the faint hope that Ethel would appear so that she could accompany Ortega while he, Willett, phoned for the police. More authoritative that way.

Ethel did not appear. Breathing hard from annoyance, not exertion, Willett followed Ortega around the side of the house to the lily pool and Rose.

Narrowing his eyes so as not to get too clear or vivid a picture of anything, Willett glanced briefly at the woman's body and returned to the house to call the police. He was trembling all over and the pain in his back was intense.

After a while Ethel floated downstairs in a long silk robe.

"I was watching from my window," she said.

"That was a big help."

"What could I do?"

She sat down at the glass-topped iron table and gazed, chin in hands, at the blue ridge of mountains. She had a wide, milk-white forehead and dark, deep-set eyes so that she always looked as if she were thinking great thoughts. The truth was that she rarely thought at all; she was afraid to. When she spoke she spoke softly, and when she asked a question she lowered her voice at the end of it as if she didn't expect or deserve an answer. "Aren't the mountains pretty in the morning."

"Mountains. I've got more on my mind than mountains."

"Why get excited." She reached slowly for the cigarette box in the center of the table. All of her motions were very slow and graceful; she seemed to move under water.

Ethel floated in and out of rooms, and up and down stairs; her hand floated out for a cigarette and floated back to her pale, full mouth. She was pale all over as if the water had washed out all her color. "Why get excited. Everything's going to be all right, isn't it."

"You haven't any feelings."

"Well, isn't it."

"Everything's going to be fine!" Willett shouted.

"You'll wake your *mother*," Ethel said, very softly.

Willett's face purpled like a ripening plum and his chubby little hands curled into fists. "You'd better watch your tongue."

"What did I say."

The front doorbell rang and Ethel made a slight move as if she intended to answer it.

"I'll get it," Willett said. "You go upstairs and see if she's all right."

"She's sleeping. I looked in on my way down. She had all that sleeping stuff last night, didn't she."

"Go upstairs and stay with her."

"I can't just sit there and watch her sleep, can I."

"You can stay out of sight, can't you?"

The doorbell rang again. "They might want to ask me some questions."

"*Ethel.*"

"Well, all right, only it won't be much fun watching somebody sleep. I wouldn't mind answering questions."

"There's no reason why they should want to see you at all."

"Why not. I live here, don't I."

"Ethel, for God's sake, don't argue."

"Who's arguing," Ethel said. But she went upstairs. When Willett swore, it meant that he was at the end of his rope and it was better to avoid him. Poor Willett. She wished she didn't hate him so much. It would make life easier for both of them.

16

She opened Olive's door, saw that the old lady was still sleeping, and went on to her own room. Here, curled up on the upholstered window seat, she watched the people below moving around the patio and the lawn, or standing in small tense groups near the lily pool. As the news spread the crowd grew. There must have been over fifty people already, but Ethel recognized only three of them: Ortega in animated conversation with a policeman, Willett wiping his forehead with a handkerchief, and Ada Murphy, the maid, just returned from town with a large bag of groceries which she clung to with both arms.

They all looked quite absurd, yet Ethel envied them. She would have liked to defy Willett and go down and mingle with the crowd, talk a little, listen a great deal, and experience that sense of excitement and comradeship which sudden death arouses in the living. But she didn't have the energy to move until the old lady called her name.

"Ethel?"

"Coming." She crossed the hall and opened the door.

The old lady's eyes were open and glared like twin glass marbles among the pillows. Her voice was husky with sleep. "Have they found her yet?"

"Yes."

"Have they found out who she is?"

"I don't know. Willett wouldn't let me stay down."

"I hope everything will be all right."

"Willett said it would be."

"I'm hungry."

"I'll make your breakfast. Murphy's back with the eggs."

The old lady turned and coughed into her pillows. "I had a bad dream, a hell of a dream, but I feel pretty good now."

To the very young people the name Rose French meant

17

nothing. In the older ones—Captain Greer, Willett and the photographer from the local paper—it evoked a certain nostalgia and regret. Rose was part of the good old days, and the good old days were gone.

Whispers went around the crowd that Rose had been attacked, drowned, strangled, shot; but when Greer turned her over he found no marks of violence at all except for the abrasions on her nose and forehead where she had fallen on the flagstones. The dark areas around her neck and head were not bruises, Greer assured Willett; they were usually present in normal deaths. Rose did not look normal, though. Her mouth was open, the jaw loose, and her cheeks were sunken and gray as putty.

Identification was not immediate or positive. No one said, at the first sight of her, "That's Rose French." Greer found her purse underneath the body, and there were some letters in it, a Bank of America checkbook, a driver's license that had expired seven years before, a religious pamphlet, and half a dozen penny postcards all of them addressed to Mr. Frank Clyde, 321 Montecito Street, La Mesa. There was no message written on any of them. Greer drew only one conclusion from the postcards, that Rose hadn't expected to die. In his opinion, the cards plus the fact that the suitcase was packed for a trip, with several changes of clothing, toothbrush, aspirin tablets, comb, and a pint of bourbon wrapped carefully inside a pink boned corset, ruled out suicide. Obviously Rose was going somewhere. Perhaps she had taken a short cut to the railway depot, which was only a quarter of a mile farther on, and coming upon this pleasant little garden, she had stopped to rest a while.

"Why here?" Willett kept saying. "Why in *my* garden? There are signs up, No Trespassing."

"I don't imagine a woman like Miss French would pay much attention to signs." Greer had taken an instant dislike to Willett and was rather pleased that Rose, with a choice of gardens, had chosen Willett's.

Greer was a large, quiet man whose face people could never remember. The most conspicuous thing about him was the broad-brimmed Stetson he wore, winter and summer, year after year. These hats were not uncommon in La Mesa. Quite a few men wore them—doctors, businessmen, brokers—as a sign that they lived on ranches out of town and had half a dozen lemon trees, a couple of avocados and a horse. Greer wore his because it was comfortable, kept the sun out of his eyes, and made people like Willett undervalue him as a hick.

"The least you could do is send all these people away." Willett's eyes were bloodshot and trickles of sweat slid down behind his ears and soaked into his hard, white collar. He seemed ready to pop his skin, like a sun-swollen tomato. "My mother's a very sick woman. She can't stand any excitement. Send all those people away."

"I would if I had a couple of divisions of marines," Greer said.

"You're supposed to have some authority."

"I have the authority but I haven't the men. It's impossible to keep people away from fires, accidents, murders—"

"Murders! Good God, you're not implying that this woman was murdered?"

"I simply don't know. I'm not a doctor."

"But that would be terrible, terrible. My mother's a very sick woman. This sort of thing might easily—"

"Mr. Goodfield, why don't you go back to the house? I'll talk to you later."

It was noon before the last of the crowd disappeared and Ortega was left to survey the wreckage. The lawn was littered with cigarette butts and gum wrappers; orange peel floated in the lily pool; the bed of Marconi shastas was trampled into rubbish, and the flat of larkspur had been overturned and split down the middle as if a heavy man had used it to stand on to get a better view of Rose.

Ortega was in an agony of self-recrimination. He had been careless—it was the wrong time to set out larkspur—he should have waited till evening or a cloudy day. But no, he had not waited, and he had paid for his carelessness by finding a dead woman and having the daylights scared out of him and the shastas ruined.

His picture in the evening paper did little to console him. In the picture he was grinning (from sheer nervousness) and his family and friends told him it looked disgusting, him grinning like that when a lady just died.

3

THERE WERE two pictures of Rose in the paper. One Frank had seen before on the wall of Rose's room, a glamorous still taken when Rose was about forty. The second was a scene from an early movie showing Rose virtuously resisting the advances of a sleek young man identified as Dwight Hamman, the second of her five husbands. Rose had mentioned only three of her husbands to Frank; the other two came as a surprise.

He experienced an even greater surprise when he read the account of her death. According to police estimates, Rose had died about noon on Monday.

He phoned Greer immediately, and after dinner he drove down to the white stone building that contained the police offices and the city jail. The grounds of the building were kept immaculate by a volunteer jail crew made up mostly of petty thieves, drunks and non-support cases. Frank knew a great many of these men, particularly the repeaters. Some had been referred to his office for help; others he had met at the meetings of Alcoholics Anonymous which were held once a week at the jail and which Frank attended sometimes for information.

Frank had known Greer for two years. There was a considerable difference of viewpoint between the two men and disagreement over techniques, but they were moderately friendly. Frank believed that Greer was a just man if not very bright, and Greer was willing to admit that the clinic occasionally did some good, however slight or impermanent.

Greer's office was a big square room with dazzling fluorescent lights that gave everyone a prison pallor.

"Sit down," Greer said.

"Thanks."

Greer sat down too, rubbing his eyes. "Those damn lights give me a headache. And don't kid me it's psychosomatic, either."

"I won't."

"You psych boys are a funny bunch. A guy falls down an open manhole for instance. Does he fall because he needs new glasses? No. Because he's thinking of some dame and isn't watching where he's going? No. He falls because he was rejected by his old lady or something."

"We won't argue," Frank said. He knew Greer was touchy on the subject because he had a duodenal ulcer.

"Jesus, next thing you know you guys will be trying to cure death by psychoanalyzing everybody."

"Don't worry about it, Greer."

"I never worry," Greer said, stroking his forehead in an unconscious attempt to erase the worry lines. "This is a funny business about Rose French. This morning I thought I had it all figured out."

"And now?"

"Now it doesn't make sense." Greer took a pipe out of

his pocket and put it in the corner of his mouth. He didn't light it because there was no tobacco in the pipe. He used it as a prop, for chewing on, tapping his desk, scratching the side of his neck, or emphasizing a point he was making. "You knew Miss French fairly well?"

"I knew her as well as she let me know her. I have no information on her that she didn't volunteer."

"You mentioned over the phone that you'd seen her recently."

"On Sunday, late in the morning, I went to her boarding house. The landlady, a Mrs. Cushman, had called me and said Rose was acting up a little, so I went to try and straighten her out."

"You're quite a boy scout."

"Helping other people helps me. It's the same principle as A.A. They stay sober by helping other people stay sober."

"Some of them."

"Some of them."

"So you straightened Rose out."

"No, I didn't get anywhere with her. She wouldn't communicate."

"So?"

"So I took Miriam and the kids to the beach."

"And that's all you wanted to tell me."

"Not quite all," Frank said. "At three o'clock on Monday afternoon Rose called me on the phone and told me she had a job and was leaving town."

"That's impossible."

"It happened."

"It couldn't have happened," Greer said. "By that time she'd been dead for three hours or more."

"Some mistake's been made."

"Perhaps by you."

"Perhaps, but I don't think so. Take a look at this."

22

He brought out the card Rose had sent him and tossed it on the desk. "It's postmarked 6:30 P.M."

Greer tapped the card with his pipe. "Why the picture and no message?"

"One of Rose's little jokes. When she told me she was leaving town to take a job, I asked her to keep in touch with us so we'd know she was all right."

"What kind of job?"

"As a housekeeper. That was her story anyway."

"Didn't you believe it?"

"I did yesterday. Now I don't know what to believe. Maybe it wasn't Rose on the phone yesterday afternoon. I'm no specialist on voices, but it certainly sounded like her and things she said were typically Rose. And if it wasn't Rose, who was it?"

"A close friend, a woman who knew her very well and knew, too, about her connection with you."

"What would be the point of such a call?"

"I can only guess," Greer said. "Rose was already dead and the woman didn't want it known. Perhaps she intended merely to falsify the time of death, or perhaps Rose wasn't meant to be found at all—it was to be a disappearance."

"Why did she phone me?"

"Your office has a habit of following cases through. If Rose had suddenly left town without notifying you, you might have started a search for her."

"But there was no attempt to hide the body. She was found in somebody's back yard where she couldn't possibly be missed."

"I know that," Greer said heavily. "It's a damn funny case. If there was money involved, maybe I could find a reason for all the shenanigans. But there's no money, not that I know of. Rose had one dollar in a savings account, checking account overdrawn as of last Saturday, and the only jewelry she hadn't pawned or sold was the wedding ring she was wearing when she was found, a plain gold band initialed RF, HD."

"I know the ring. It was from her first marriage, when she was sixteen."

Greer was silent a moment, tracing letters on the blotter in front of him with the mouthpiece of his pipe. From where Frank sat they looked like initials, RF, HD.

Frank said, "Who did the autopsy?"

"Severn."

"He's competent."

"Of course he's competent," Greer said irritably. "The woman died of a heart attack yesterday around noon. The heart was badly damaged and half again normal size."

"There's no question of murder then?"

"There wouldn't be if she'd been found dead in bed. As things are—" he spread his hands—"as things are, I don't know. It would be easy enough to kill someone with a bad heart condition—a shock, a soft pillow over the face —there are lots of ways it could have been done. But *was* it, that's the question."

"As far as I'm aware, Rose had no intimates during recent years, friends or enemies."

"And before that?"

"She must have had hundreds of both. She was aggressive; it was easy for Rose to make friends, and just as easy to drop them. Lately she'd made a fetish of independence. I think probably Miriam and I were the closest thing to a friend she had in this town, except perhaps her landlady, Blanche Cushman."

"Mrs. Cushman identified the body this afternoon. She did quite a bit of weeping and wailing, but I got the impression she wasn't too sorry."

"Rose caused her some trouble now and then. When Rose was drinking she could get pretty noisy."

24

"Was she a drunk?"

"I don't think so. I may be a little prejudiced, though. I liked Rose. She didn't like me in return very much. She frequently accused me of prying and so on."

"How much did she confide in you?"

"Just what she wanted to. I had no idea, for instance, that she had a heart condition. She never mentioned her health, her age or her family. She talked freely about three of her five husbands, but I didn't even know about the other two until I read tonight's paper."

"There were five, all right. I had one of the boys check with the publicity department of her old studio. She divorced three of them, one was killed in a sailing accident and one of them committed suicide."

"Poor Rose."

"That depends on your viewpoint," Greer said sharply. The telephone on his desk buzzed and he leaned forward with a grunt of annoyance and picked it up. "Greer speaking."

"Greer?"

"That's right."

"This is Malgradi. I'm down at the F.P."

"Did you get her fixed up again?"

"Sure. That's what I called about. There's a man in my office that wants to see her."

"Who is he?"

"Claims to be her husband. I got her looking pretty nice, but I thought I better check with you first before letting anybody see her."

"What's his name?"

"Dalloway. Haley Dalloway. Think I should let him in?"

"Keep him around until I get there. I'll be right down."

"I haven't had any dinner yet."

"I'll bring you a bag of popcorn." Greer put down the

25

phone and turned to Frank. "Dalloway's showed up, her first husband. Want to come along and meet him?"

"Not particularly."

"Come anyway. I'd like you to take a look at Rose."

Frank shifted his weight and the chair squeaked in protest. The noise sounded almost human. "That's not my line of work."

"Once they're dead you're finished with them, eh? What's the matter, Frank, you afraid of nice, harmless, old dead people?"

"I haven't had any experience."

"There's always a first time."

"Anyway, I promised Miriam I'd take her to a movie."

"I'll call her and tell her you'll be late," Greer said. "What's the number?"

"You don't have to bother."

"What's the number?"

"23664."

Greer called Miriam while Frank went over to the window and looked out through its iron grillwork at the city lights. Even from there he could hear Miriam's clear, firm voice coming all too distinctly over the phone. It was the first she'd heard of any movie date, Miriam said, and besides she was washing her hair.

Greer hung up, looking very pleased with himself. "You could have done better than that, Frank."

"Miriam's only fault is a habit of pushing the truth out in front of her like a wheelbarrow."

"It's a nice way of taking people for a ride. Are you ready?"

"I guess I am."

Greer laughed. "You'll be O.K. If you get to feeling queasy, Malgradi will give you a couple of slugs of embalming fluid."

4

MALGRADI'S FUNERAL PARLOR was in the east end, a new white stucco building with rows of fluted columns like a Greek temple and a flashing neon sign like a theatre. This incongruity was carried on inside. Malgradi was a showman, but he also possessed a deeply religious feeling about death, and the biggest collection of organ records in town. All of Malgradi's clients got a fine send-off, and always (since Malgradi was a confirmed optimist) in the right direction. He felt that when he had made each of them as pleasing to the eye as possible and bade them farewell with the finest organ music available, he had done his duty. His conscience was clear, he was devoted to his family and they to him, and he was, in spite of his rather lugubrious profession, a happy man with excellent digestion.

Malgradi had a working agreement with the police. He was not qualified to do autopsies himself, but his back room was used by the pathologist of the local hospital to perform autopsies on all people who died suddenly without apparent cause or under suspicious circumstances. Rose was no longer in the back room.

"I've been getting quite a few calls," Malgradi told Greer. "Seems like a lot of people are curious; they want to know about the funeral."

"Is that right?"

"So, as a matter of fact, do I. Think it'll be county?"

"It'll be county if nobody shows up who wants to foot the bill. Where's Dalloway?"

"In my office."

27

"By the way, this is Frank Clyde, a friend of mine."

Malgradi and Frank shook hands heartily and Malgradi said, as the three men went down the corridor, that any friend of Greer's was a friend of his.

Malgradi's office at first glance seemed like a somber room dedicated to sorrow. A more careful study revealed a camouflaged television set, a portable bar discreetly draped in gray velvet, and a large bowl of potato chips on Malgradi's desk.

The room smelled of cigar smoke. The man who was smoking the cigar rose and looked around nervously for an ash tray. Finding none, he transferred the cigar to his gloved left hand. He was tall and erect, a man in his sixties, with clipped white hair and wide-spaced brown eyes that looked naïve and trusting as a boy's. He had trusted, perhaps, too often and too well. The rest of his face bore the marks of bitterness and pain.

The hand holding the cigar remained motionless and Frank realized that it was artificial.

Dalloway took a hesitating step forward. "You're the police?"

Greer nodded.

"I'm Haley Dalloway. This is terrible, a terrible thing. Rose was always so full of life and energy. I can't believe that she—that she—" He turned away for a moment, fighting for control.

When he recovered his composure, Greer introduced Frank and himself. There was more handshaking and murmurs of condolence, and then Malgradi pressed a button behind his desk and organ music poured into the room, soft and thick as syrup.

"For God's sake, turn that thing off," Greer said.

Malgradi glanced at him reproachfully. "Well, I only thought it would be appropriate, under the circumstances."

"Under the circumstances I'd rather listen to coyotes howling."

"Can I help it if some people are tone deaf?" But he turned the record off. He had a good deal of respect for Greer. Greer had gone to Princeton for two years and his opinion on what was appropriate was not to be taken lightly.

"Thank you," Dalloway said. No one could tell from his expression whether he was thanking Malgradi for the snatch of music or Greer for the silence.

Greer was studying Dalloway, not subtly, the way Frank had to observe his cases, but openly and directly the way Miriam sized people up. "You live here, Mr. Dalloway?"

"No. No, I don't. I live in Belmont, that's a suburb of Boston. I came out here for—for a vacation."

"Where are you staying?"

"At the Rancho del Mar. It's a motel down near the beach, East Beach, I believe they call it. If there's anything you want to discuss with me you can reach me there. Right now I—I'd like to see Rose."

"Certainly," Greer said politely. "Do you mind if Mr. Clyde here goes along?"

"Well, I—no."

"Mr. Clyde was a friend of Rose's. He's been trying to help her this past year."

"Help her?" Dalloway's eyes focused on Frank. "In what way? Are you a doctor?"

"I work for the mental hygiene clinic," Frank said, wishing there was some simple way of describing his functions. "Rose was brought to my attention a year or so ago."

"You mean Rose was insane?"

"No, indeed I don't. The clinic does preventive work, not as much as we could do if we had enough money and trained help. But we do some. I gave Rose an appointment whenever I felt that she was getting too depressed or too high."

"Rose was always like that," Dalloway said quite brusquely. "It's nothing new or serious. One day she'd be so low she hated everyone and the next day she was the life of the party." He raised his chin in a gesture of pride. "I'm glad, I'm glad she didn't change."

But she had changed, she'd changed so much that Dalloway, when he saw her, backed away from the satin-lined casket and covered his eyes.

Frank gazed stonily down at the dead woman. He was appalled. She didn't look like Rose at all. In life Rose had been rather careless. No matter how often she combed her hair it always looked a little wild, her makeup was never quite straight, and her clothes gave the impression that she had just come in after a fuss with a high wind.

Now Rose lay in her borrowed casket, meticulous, not a hair out of place. Her cotton-stuffed cheeks were symmetrically rosy, her mouth rigid and straight as if she didn't dare to move it for fear of disturbing the lipstick. There were no more high winds for Rose.

"It is," Dalloway said finally, "it *is* Rose?"

"Yes," Frank said.

"I'd never have known her, she's aged so much." He spoke as if the years that had aged Rose had passed him without a glance. "She's still wearing my ring."

"I've never seen her without it."

"That's funny, isn't it, after all that's happened to her. So much, so much happened to Rose. I used to read about her in the papers from time to time, after she left me." Except for his breathing which was labored and irregular, Dalloway seemed under control. "Did she ever tell you how she left me?"

"Once. She ran away with a circus."

"That's right. The circus was in town—we were living

in Boulder Junction then—and when it moved out Rose moved with it. After the divorce I married again. I had to give Lora a home."

"Lora?"

"Rose's child and mine."

"She never mentioned a child."

Dalloway was not surprised. "How like Rose, to forget the inconvenient things. I—well, there's no point in staying here, is there?"

"No."

"I'd like to hear more about Rose, how she's been living the last while. I hate to impose on anyone, but perhaps you might consider coming down to my motel for a drink or two? Would you?"

"I might."

"The fact is, I'm alone in town. It's rather depressing."

"Your family didn't come with you?"

"I no longer have a family. My wife died several years ago. And Lora—" Dalloway's face tightened like a fist, and for the first time Frank saw, behind the innocent trusting eyes, a shrewd, hard, obstinate man. "My daughter, Lora, disappeared two months ago."

The Rancho del Mar was one of a dozen luxurious motels that edged the beach. Thirty-foot palms rustled frantically in the offshore wind while the ivy clung motionless to their bone-gray trunks. The patio was strung with colored lights and crammed with garden furniture, chaises and gliders and canvas chairs. None of them was occupied. The nights were too cold, even now, toward the end of May. When the sun vanished so did the people, and the sea fog took over the patio and hung in wisps under the big umbrellas and the redwood tables.

Dalloway had a corner room that overlooked the sea. He had left the windows open and the air in the room was damp and cold.

He turned on the panel heater and stood in front of it, warming his right hand until the bellboy appeared with a pitcher of ice and a bottle of Scotch. The bellboy acted with the extreme deference of someone who has been well-tipped in the past, and Frank wondered how much money Dalloway had and how he'd made it. Rose had always claimed that she had supported him.

Dalloway mixed the drinks. It was obvious, from the deft way he managed with one hand, that the loss of his other was not recent.

"You're a restful young man," Dalloway said suddenly. "You don't talk much."

"My job is to listen."

"And observe."

"And observe, of course."

"What are you observing about me?"

"Do you want the truth?"

"Naturally."

"I was wondering how you lost your hand."

"Oh, that." Dalloway laughed. "I lost it in the most un-heroic way possible. Caught it in a buzz-saw, very careless of me. Is your drink too weak, too strong?"

"Just right."

"I'm not a drinking man, but there are times." He paused. "I suppose Rose died penniless?"

"Yes."

"She was a fool about money."

"She didn't think or care much about it," Frank said. "There's a difference."

"The results are the same."

"Rose wasn't bitter about lack of money. The only thing she wanted was something like a job to get interested in."

"She had a job once, looking after her own child. But that wasn't quite good enough. She preferred the circus."

Dalloway stared grimly into his glass. "Like mother, like daughter. It's a peculiar thing: though they were separated all these years, the resemblances were strong, right down to the final one. They both ran away from me without any reason at all."

Frank wasn't so sure about the lack of reason. "You've heard nothing from Lora?"

"Not a word, in two months. There's not much I can do about it. Lora's a grown woman of thirty. At least she's grown in years. Actually she's quite immature like most of her friends, though they call it being 'creative.' She fooled around with painting and sculpture and little theatres, things like that. She talked a lot about expressing herself, but as far as I could see the only thing she really expressed was an antipathy to good honest work."

It was a familiar cry to Frank: the too-strict and unimaginative parent and the child who escapes into dreams or illness. "She wanted to be an actress like her mother?"

"Yes. She had the lead in a few experimental plays that were put on back home and it went to her head. Possibly she has talent—I wouldn't know, the plays seemed extremely silly to me—but she's over thirty. She's too old to begin a career like that. I tried to explain this to her last March, the twenty-fifth I believe it was. When I returned home for dinner that night she was gone. I telephoned some of her sorry crew of friends, but they professed to know nothing about it. After two days I reported her as a missing person. The police were unconcerned, even a little amused, I thought. Their assumption was that Lora had eloped with a man, and they advised me to go home and wait for a letter. I did. I'm not a waiting man, but I waited a whole month. Then one day in the subway station at Cambridge I happened to pick up a New York paper. There was an article in it about a proposed television program that was to feature some old-time movie stars. Rose's name was among the ones mentioned as possible. The article said she was retired and living on a big estate here in La Mesa."

Frank thought of Rose's room in the boarding house and wondered whether Rose herself had given out this misinformation.

"I came here," Dalloway said, "to see her. Not for old time's sake, but to find out if she knew anything about Lora."

"Why should she?"

"For a long time I've had the idea that Lora intended some day to try and find her mother. During the past year she talked about Rose a great deal, and once she even mentioned the possibility of a reunion with her. I told her it was ridiculous, and the subject was dropped. I'm afraid Lora picked it up again."

"You have no proof of that?"

"None. Yet the more I think of it, the more obvious it seems. Lora believed—and, as a matter of fact, so did I— that Rose was well provided for after her career and her series of husbands. We had no idea she was on her uppers."

"So you came here to see Rose."

"Yes."

"And did you?"

"I tried to. She wasn't listed in the phone book or city directory or credit bureau, and she wasn't at either of the hospitals here in town. I intended to make further inquiries, but as it turned out, I didn't have to." He set his empty glass on top of the radio. It came down with a decisive thud and a sharp impatient clink of ice. "How did she die?"

"Apparently of a heart attack."

"She was strong as an ox."

"People change with time," Frank said. "Rose lived pretty high, I guess."

34

"These people, the Goodfields, in whose garden Rose was found. Who are they? What do you know about them?"

"Just what Greer told me while we were driving down to Malgradi's place. Goodfield and his wife and mother are from San Francisco. The mother is in bad health, and they've spent the last few months or so traveling around the country to find a climate that would agree with her. They finally decided on La Mesa, rented a place, hired a maid, etcetera. They've only been here for two weeks, but according to the maid and the next-door neighbor, Goodfield is a devoted son and his wife Ethel is a devoted daughter-in-law, and that's about all there is to the Goodfields."

"I wonder."

So did Frank, though he didn't say so. Instead, "It seems to be just an unfortunate accident that Rose was found on the Goodfields' premises. It could have happened anywhere."

"Perhaps it could. I merely wanted to check. Life has taught me to be suspicious."

It had taught him well, Frank thought.

5

WILLETT SHOWED the effects of a bad night. His eyes were rimmed with pink, and his breakfast stuck halfway between his stomach and his throat and refused to budge. When the front door chime sounded he dropped his spoon. Leaning over to pick it up, he bumped his head against the table, and then clutched his heart dramatically.

Ethel watched these maneuvers with her customary detachment. "Did you hurt yourself, dear."

"For heaven's sakes, how many times do I have to remind you to get those chimes fixed? They're loud enough to wake the—they're too loud. They've got to be toned down."

"What do I know about chimes."

"You can wrap a handkerchief around them or something."

"Your handkerchiefs are bigger than mine," Ethel said, sounding very pleased at her ability to score a point, however small.

Willett could not allow this triumph to go unchallenged. "What's that got to do with it? Couldn't you use one of my handkerchiefs?"

"You know I never pry into your things."

"It's *impossible* to *talk* to you any more."

"Then why try."

"We can't live in total silence."

"I can." To a large extent this was true. Ethel could go for days without talking. It drove Willett, whose satisfactions were almost entirely verbal, to distraction. "Anyway we shouldn't quarrel at a time like this," Ethel added. "It's disrespectful to the dead, isn't it."

Willett looked furious, but he didn't say anything because Murphy had come into the room.

Murphy was a very thin, arrogant young woman with short, black hair and a great deal of what Willett described as class. Murphy's right to this description was unassailable. She knew her place, which was high, and her duties which were few. From a practical viewpoint she was the worst maid Ethel had ever had; but Ethel, who was raised on a farm in Wisconsin, was impressed by Murphy's niceties and quite willing to do most of the work herself as long as she was addressed as milady.

Murphy was, in her way, a jewel, and like most jewels

she showed off well in the drawing room but was of little value in the kitchen.

"Captain Greer to see you, sir," Murphy told Willett, making the *sir* sound like *your lordship.* "I took the liberty of showing him into the drawing room."

"Thanks, I'll see him right away."

"I believe he also wants to talk to Mrs. Goodfield."

"Me?" Ethel said.

"No, milady. The older Mrs. Goodfield. I explained to him that she wasn't well but that I thought he might see her for a few minutes."

"What in God's name did you do that for?" Willett said, forgetting his lordshipdom. "I'm surrounded, surrounded by imbeciles."

He went storming out of the room, and Ethel and Murphy exchanged glances.

"What'll we have for lunch?" Ethel said.

"I'm very fond of shrimp, milady."

"All right, I'll make a shrimp salad. Willett's an awfully hard man to live with, isn't he? I mean, you know what I mean."

Murphy knew what she meant. His lordship was hell on wheels.

"What I mean is," Ethel added, "you can't take him seriously, and yet you can't take him not seriously either. You know?"

"Quite."

"It would be nice, wouldn't it, if people with bad tempers could just take a pill or something and become quite cheerful and sunny."

"Hot rolls would go very well with the shrimp, milady."

"Would they? Yes, I guess they would." Milady sighed. She hated making rolls but Murphy refused to eat the bakery kind.

All of his life Willett had been immobilized by self-doubt, plagued by uncertainty over the most trivial matters like whether or not it was proper to shake hands with a policeman like Greer. When he finally decided that it was proper, he performed his duty with nervous reluctance and afterwards he unconsciously wiped his hand on the side of his trousers. Greer noticed the action and misinterpreted the reason for it. And so Willett was once again in the position of having incurred animosity without knowing why. The self-doubt, the action finally taken, wrong and late, and the ensuing unpopularity which bred more self-doubt—it was a circle of errors and Willett ran panting around in it wondering where the end was.

"I thought this business was settled yesterday," Willett said. "The poor woman's dead and all that. What more is there to do?"

"This." Greer handed him a subpoena and Willett looked at it with grave suspicion.

"What is it?"

"A subpoena. The coroner's inquest will be held tomorrow morning. You're to testify, just tell the jury what happened."

"I don't want to. I've never had anything to do with this sort of thing before. It makes me nervous. I'm not a well man by any means. I have a kidney stone."

"Be reasonable, Mr. Goodfield."

"Reasonable? Is it reasonable to drag an innocent bystander into court? I have a good notion to break my lease and go back home. Surely I have grounds for breaking the lease—having a dead woman found in—"

"I wouldn't know. I don't have much to do with leases." Greer didn't argue about the subpoena. He just put it down on the glass coffee table while Willett stared at it as if he expected it to come alive, grow wings or legs or teeth.

"I hate sordid things," he said finally. "Do you—do you suppose it will be very sordid?"

"Oh, not very."

"No question of suicide or murder, anything like that?"

"That's for the jury to decide."

"I see." Willett coughed. "Well, I suppose I have my duties as a citizen."

"That's a good way to look at it."

"The poor woman who died—my wife and I were discussing it last night—I hope she'll have a proper burial with flowers and all that?"

"I don't guarantee the flowers, but she'll be buried according to regulation. The county will foot the bill if no one else does."

"It seems so cold-blooded, having no flowers."

"Rose won't know the difference."

Willett turned quite pale. "I wonder—my wife and I were wondering—we feel a certain sense of responsibility in this affair. We're not wealthy by any means, but we're comfortably well off and I thought—Ethel thought—perhaps a check for a hundred dollars—?"

"You're offering to bury Rose?"

"I—yes, you might put it like that. Ethel's very soft-hearted, you know."

Greer didn't know. "You'll have to take the matter up with the County Administrator."

Willett had no idea what or who the County Administrator was, but he nodded wisely. "I see. There's red tape involved. You think it might be better to forget the whole thing? I mean, I certainly wouldn't want my generous impulses to get me into trouble. It wouldn't be *fair*."

"There are lots of worthy causes to give money to," Greer said shortly. "Flowers are fine, but Rose can't smell them."

Willett took out a handkerchief and wiped his forehead.

He hated this callous policeman with such intensity that he felt nauseated. "I—if you'll excuse me—I'm not well."

"Sorry to hear it."

"We—we're not a strong family. Things upset us."

Greer believed it. "I just want to talk to your mother for a few minutes. I'll try not to disturb her."

Willett felt too weak and sick to argue. "Murphy will take you upstairs," he said and headed for the door, pressing the handkerchief against his mouth.

Greer sat down to wait for Murphy. The day was already becoming warm and the atmosphere in the room was depressing. From the open windows came a too-sweet scent of flowers which Greer could not identify. Greer was not an intuitive man but he had the impression that the Goodfields were concealing something, perhaps about Rose, perhaps only about themselves. He felt that, by talking to the old lady, he might have this impression confirmed or denied. It was obvious that she—and Murphy—dominated the household.

"This way, sir," Murphy said.

Greer rose. "How long have you worked for the Goodfields, Murphy?"

"Two weeks, sir."

"How were you hired?"

"I inserted an ad in the local paper."

"Many replies?"

"Certainly, sir. I chose the Goodfields because they didn't expect me to perform any menial duties. Ortega does the gardening, a cleaning woman comes in twice a week, the laundry is sent out, and Mrs. Goodfield does all the cooking."

"That must leave you with a fair amount of time to yourself."

"It might seem that way to a casual observer," Murphy said shortly, and led the way upstairs, walking very stiffly as if she were balancing a book on her head.

"It's a curious job for a woman of your talents, isn't it?"

"Is it, sir?"

"I think so. You've been to college, haven't you?"

"Certainly I've been to college. That's where I learned that good domestics make more money than good teachers, and they even have an opportunity sometimes to marry the boss. If you follow me, sir?"

"I follow you."

"When the Goodfields return to San Francisco, I will go with them. There are more, shall we say, possibilities in a larger city."

"I'm sure you'll explore them."

"Thank you, sir. I'll try."

Mrs. Goodfield was lying on a mountain of pillows in an old-fashioned four-poster bed with a ruffled pink canopy. The bed dwarfed her; she seemed no larger than a child, a pale and limp little girl strangely aged by a long illness. Her skin had the white translucence of paraffin, and even in the dim light that filtered through the closed Venetian blinds her short, black hair had the purplish gleam of dye. Her thin, slightly curved nose gave her a look of pride and arrogance. Even in bed she wore her jewels— diamonds and rubies on her fingers, a bracelet that tinkled with every move she made, and pearl earrings that matched the pallor of her small delicate ears.

"I have no use for the medical profession," she said, giving Greer a long, hostile stare. "You might as well pack up and leave."

"He isn't a doctor, milady," Murphy said. "He's a policeman, Captain Greer."

"A policeman, eh? I suppose Willett went through a red light. He never could handle a car, it handles him. Makes me wonder sometimes if I brought him up right. Murphy, you may leave."

"I think it would be advisable if I stayed, milady."

"I think it would be advisable if you got the hell out of here. And stop pulling that milady stuff on me. It makes me gag, understand?"

Murphy departed with an elegant shrug.

"Impossible, ain't she?" the old lady said cheerfully. "Lots of people think *I'm* impossible, but I don't agree. Did you ever play baseball?"

"Shortstop on the high-school team."

"Seems to me you're built more like a catcher. Course I can't see your legs. You got heavy legs?"

"Heavy enough."

"You should have been a catcher. But I don't suppose you came up here to talk baseball, did you?"

"No."

"Well, now it's your turn to say something. I talk a lot, but I'm very fair about giving the other fellow his chance. Go on, say something."

"I suppose you've been told what happened here yesterday morning."

She nodded. "Rose French was found dead in my back yard. It made Willett nervous."

"Did you know Rose?"

"Know her, I did not. But I used to go to her pictures. Never considered her much of an actress, myself." She thumped one of the pillows to emphasize her point. "What's all the fuss about, anyway? If she's dead, she's dead. Not much I can do about it."

"The possibility occurred to me that you might have known her personally."

"Well, I didn't."

"How about your son?"

"I've never allowed Willett to have any truck with actresses," she said with severity. "When the time came for Willett to spread his wings, I picked out Ethel for him. Good, sturdy stock, Ethel. Don't let those wispy airs confuse you. She's strong as a horse. Now let me see,

where were we? Oh yes, actresses. I explained all about
actresses to Willett when he was eighteen. Does that answer your question?"

"I think so."

"Now it's your turn to say something again. Go on.
Course if you can't think of something, I'll take another
turn and then you can have two turns next time. That
suit you?"

"I think I'd better take my turn now," Greer said dryly.
"There may not be a next time."

The old lady grinned and stroked her rings. She was
having a wonderful time.

"Would you mind telling me, Mrs. Goodfield, how
Willett makes a living?"

"By agreeing with me. That's how he makes a living."

"Could you be more specific?"

"I have no interest in business details. Why don't you
ask Willett or Ethel?"

"All right, I will," Greer said, and took a hesitant step
toward the door.

"You're not going already, are you?"

"I promised not to stay too long and disturb you."

"Disturb me?" She propped herself up on one elbow
and repeated, "Disturb me? Don't they realize I'm lonely?
I like to talk to people, *outside* people. Why don't you sit
down for a minute and we'll talk about baseball? I won't
cheat on turns, either. That suit you?"

"It would suit me another time. This morning I have
work to do."

Mrs. Goodfield flung herself back among the pillows
like a petulant child. "You won't come back. I bet you
won't. You think I'm an old crank. But I'm not. It's just
that I've had so many disappointments in my life. My
children were the worst. First Willett and then Jack and
then Shirley. They're not bad children, but they lack will
and spirit. They'll never amount to anything, not one of

43

them. Jack's a party boy, always the extra man at dinners and cocktail parties. Makes quite a fool of himself, falling all over other men's wives. You know the kind?"

"Yes."

"And Shirley, poor girl, she got married very young to a schoolteacher. He died of a stroke two years ago, leaving Shirley with four children to support." She added almost reverently, "Thank God for our little factory; it's kept us all out of the poorhouse so far."

"What do you mean, so far?"

"Things can happen, especially after I'm gone. Did Willett tell you that I'm supposed to be dying?"

"Not exactly."

"I'm *supposed* to be, but I'm not sure I'm *going* to. Not till after the World Series anyway. You don't happen to know any bookies in town, do you? I was wondering, maybe if I take up betting on the horses, it would give me another hobby besides baseball."

"Officially there are no bookies in town."

"And unofficially?"

"I'll see what can be done."

The old lady grinned again, and rubbed the palms of her hands together.

Greer departed with the strong conviction that he had been hog-tied by an expert.

THE FOLLOWING MORNING, Thursday, at 9 A.M., a coroner's inquest was held to determine the cause of death of Rose Elizabeth French, a human being.

44

Mrs. Cushman, the landlady, dressed elegantly for the occasion in flowered chiffon, identified the body. The pathologist, Dr. Severn, read his detailed report of the autopsy to the jury, and Ortega in a hushed voice described how he set out to plant the larkspur Tuesday morning and found Rose instead, lying in the sun beside the lily pool.

The Sheriff, Angell, doubled as coroner. "Did you touch her, Mr. Ortega?"

"No sir. I couldn't touch her, I had this flat of larkspur in my hands. It was heavy; I had my hands full."

"Yes, yes. What did you do?"

"I run up to the house and told the man what I found. That man." Ortega pointed at Willett, who was sitting in the second row. Everybody turned and stared at Willett curiously, and he tried to appear less visible by slumping in his seat. Noticing this, one of the jurors made a mental resolution to watch Willett like a hawk for further signs of guilt.

"Now I'd like you to think back to Monday," Angell said. "My reasons for this will become clear in a moment."

A male juror raised his hand and announced that he would like the reasons to be made clear right away, inasmuch as he was having trouble following the witnesses who wouldn't speak plain English a man could understand. He sat down, with a reproachful glance at Dr. Severn.

Angell faced the juror. "Dr. Severn established the time of Miss French's death as being eleven o'clock Monday morning at the earliest and one o'clock in the afternoon at the latest. Since she was not found until Tuesday morning, I want the jury to know why."

"I know why," Ortega cried with an air of triumph.

"All right, Mr. Ortega, tell us."

"On Mondays I don't work for that man"—he indi-

45

cated Willett again—"Just on Tuesday, Thursday and Saturday. On Monday and Wednesday I work for Mrs. Pond. She grows cymbidium orchids."

"Then you were not in the garden at 2201 Ventura Drive on Monday at all?"

"No sir."

"Describe this garden to the jury, will you, Mr. Ortega?"

Ortega merely looked baffled.

"How large is it, for instance?"

"It's not so large but there's always work to be done."

"Has it a fence around it? A hedge?"

"Oh sure, you got to have a fence and a hedge."

"Why?"

"Well, the road goes right past at the back, the road to the beach and the highway. People would be tramping all over if you didn't have a fence and a hedge."

"What kind of hedge?"

"Eugenia. Very old, very big. In the fall my mother makes jam from the berries."

"That's very interesting," Angell said, and one or two of the jurors laughed. "Is it possible for an average person to see over or through this hedge?"

"No sir, not without a ladder."

"Is there any break in this hedge, say from the road at the back?"

"Yes sir, where the gate is. There's a little iron gate back there."

"Is it kept locked?"

"No sir, I never saw it locked."

"Then it's quite possible that Miss French was walking along this back road, carrying her suitcase and heading perhaps to the highway, perhaps to the railroad station— and that she saw this garden, decided that it would be a good place to rest, and came in through the little iron gate. Would you say that was possible, Mr. Ortega?"

46

"Golly, I don't know. If *you* say it's possible, it's possible."

"All right, Mr. Ortega. Thank you." Angell consulted his notes. "Mr. Willett Goodfield, will you please step into the box?"

Willett gave his name, address, occupation, and explained that he was living in La Mesa temporarily for the sake of his mother's health.

"Yesterday's events must have been quite a shock to her," Angell said.

This approach was a great surprise to Willett. He had expected to be bullied, or, at the very least, roughly cross-examined, and this unforeseen friendliness threw him into such a state of confusion that he didn't know what to say.

"Were you acquainted with the deceased, Mr. Goodfield?"

"I was—not. No sir, I was not."

"Probably you were familiar with her name, however?"

"She was very well known at one time. But I didn't recognize her as Rose French when I went out with the gardener and found her. I had no idea what—who she was. It's been a dozen years or more since I've seen one of her pictures."

"Tell me, Mr. Goodfield, the extent of your household."

"There's my mother, my wife, myself and one maid. We're living very simply."

"You were all in the house at 2201 Ventura Drive on Monday?"

"Yes sir."

"All day?"

"Yes sir."

"Did you go out into the garden at any time?"

"No sir. My mother is bedridden, and my wife and I and the maid are still trying to get settled in the house."

"You recall the spot where Miss French was found. Is

this spot visible from any of the windows in the house?"

"I don't know. I mean, I've never tried to look out at one particular spot from one particular window. Never had reason to."

"That will be all, thanks, Mr. Goodfield. Please don't leave the room until the evidence is completed in case you are recalled to the stand. Captain Greer, you're next."

Greer told the jury that he was James Rudyard Greer, he had been a policeman for twelve years, and a resident of La Mesa for over twenty. On Tuesday, May 22nd, at 8:16 A.M., he received a telephone call from Willett Goodfield, 2201 Ventura Drive, stating that a dead woman had been discovered on his premises. Greer then proceeded to that address in a prowl car along with Sergeant Fiske and Patrolman Halderman, arriving at approximately 8:30. The dead woman was identified by means of the contents of her suitcase and handbag.

"You have a list of these contents, Captain?"

"Yes, I have a list and the contents themselves."

"Show the court, please."

The handbag and suitcase were brought out and emptied on the long mahogany table, and the members of the jury filed past one by one. Some hurried, some delayed, some were nervous; but they were all curious. When they returned to the box, fifteen minutes later, they wore an air of subdued excitement. Greer, watching them, knew they were anxious to get home to tell their relatives and friends and neighbors about their experience.

Silence settled on the courtroom like snow.

"Tell me, Captain, what is the significance of these half-dozen penny postcards addressed to Mr. Frank Clyde?"

"Mr. Clyde is in court, sir. I suggest you ask him."

"All right, we'll recall you later, Captain. Will Mr. Clyde please step up?"

Frank was an experienced witness at commitment trials

48

in Superior Court. This inquest was different; it was informal, there were no lawyers involved, and no arguments back and forth about points of law.

After the routine identification, Frank told the jury that he had known Rose French for over a year.

"She considered you a friend, Mr. Clyde?"

"I believe she did, toward the end anyway."

"When did you hear from her last?"

"On Monday afternoon she telephoned me to say that she had found a job as housekeeper to an old friend and was leaving town. I asked her to keep in touch with me now and then, and she agreed."

"That was on Monday afternoon at what time?"

"I thought it was around three."

"You realize that your thinking contradicts the facts as presented by Dr. Severn?"

"I realize that, but—well, I might be mistaken, I suppose. I receive a lot of calls and there are always people in my office."

"Have you usually a good time-sense?"

"Not particularly, but—"

"Do you wear a watch?"

"I have a pocket watch."

"Is there a wall or desk clock in your office?"

"No sir."

"Without consulting your watch, what time would you say it is now?"

"I suppose it's about a quarter to eleven."

"It's exactly seven minutes after ten."

Frank glanced at Greer. Greer merely shrugged his shoulders and looked up at the ceiling.

"You admit," Angell said, "that you could have been mistaken about the time of that phone call?"

"I could have been, but I don't think I—"

"That will be all, thank you, Mr. Clyde."

49

Frank stepped down from the box without argument. He knew—and Greer knew—that the verdict would be what Angell wanted it to be.

At three in the afternoon the jury made its decision. The deceased, Rose Elizabeth French, had, after over-exertion, died of natural causes, a heart attack.

On hearing the verdict, Mrs. Cushman, who had conducted herself with dignity and decorum for the whole day, burst into tears, and had to be escorted out into the corridor by Frank.

"With the evidence they had, no other verdict was possible," Frank said.

"It isn't the verdict that bothers me." Mrs. Cushman wiped her eyes on her flowered chiffon sleeve. "It's her poor heart, and her with never a word of complaint, and me badgering her the way I did sometimes."

"Don't let it get you down."

"And the way I spoke sharply to her about not keeping her room neat like Miss Henderson's, and her all the time ready to drop dead from a heart attack. I'll never forgive myself."

"Cheer up. Rose considered you her best friend."

"She did? Honest?"

"I'm sure of it."

"I'm not so sure. You know what she called me? An old bat, that's what. When I think of all I done for that woman and her turning around and calling me an old bat, it makes my blood boil."

"You were very kind to Rose."

"You bet I was."

"No one could have been a better friend."

"No one else would of been such a fool."

"Let me drive you home."

"All right." Mrs. Cushman glanced vaguely around the corridor as if she was trying to locate the guilty conscience she had temporarily mislaid. Frank knew what she was looking for but made no attempt to help her find it.

"I got a feeling," Mrs. Cushman said, frowning, "I got a feeling I forgot something. I better go back in and take a look around."

She went back in and examined the bench she had been sitting on, and the floor around it, but she didn't find anything except a discarded copy of the *Los Angeles Times*. She took that instead.

7

OVER A CUP of hot, strong tea in Mrs. Cushman's front parlor, Frank heard considerably more about Mrs. Cushman's trials and tribulations with life in general and Rose in particular.

It appeared that, for the entire week before her death, Rose had been acting secrety.

"Now if there's one thing I can't stand, it's secrety people," Mrs. Cushman explained, "people that go around all the time without telling other people what they're thinking or doing. To give credit where credit is due, Rose wasn't *always* secrety."

"Just for that one week," Frank prompted.

"Well, no. It began quite a while ago but the past week especially, I knew something was on her mind besides men and liquor. Men and liquor I could understand, knowing Rose, but this going out all the time and not telling a soul where she'd been, that worried me. And always dressed up too, fit to kill."

"She might have had a date with a man."

"I thought of that, first thing. Only can you imagine a woman like Rose having a date and not bragging about it all over the place? Bragging was Rose's worst fault, God rest her soul, except for vanity. Rose was vain as they come. Why, many's the time she's taken up the whole supper hour telling about how this man ogled her on the street and that man tried to pick her up at a bus stop. It was disgusting, at her age. And speaking of age, did you hear what that Dr. Severn said at the inquest? *He* said Rose was between 60 and 65. *She* claimed she was only 52. That goes to show, don't it?"

Frank wasn't sure what it went to show, but he nodded.

Mrs. Cushman took the nod as a sign of approval and encouragement. The fact was that, while Rose was alive, Mrs. Cushman had always been a little afraid of her. She had thought many nasty thoughts about Rose which she couldn't put into words because Rose was armed against attack not only by past prestige but by a present tongue as sharp as a razor. Now that Rose had no chance for a rebuttal or a return match, Mrs. Cushman for the first time felt free to speak her mind. Frank was the perfect audience, quiet, interested, and of the opposite sex.

"I'm not bitter, never've been bitter but when she started going out all the time and wouldn't play canasta any more—not that she could play canasta any better than a six-year-old child, she had no head for figures. I often had to let her win just so's she'd keep her temper and wouldn't walk out on the game."

Frank covered his amusement with a little cough. He had heard a good deal about these canasta games from Rose. In Rose's version Mrs. Cushman was an unmitigated cheat who would stop at nothing to win a paltry game of cards.

"I could beat her with my eyes closed and my hands

tied behind my back," Mrs. Cushman said briskly. "More tea?"

"No thanks."

"I'll take a drop more myself. Rose couldn't stand tea. One of her husbands was an Englishman and after that she couldn't stand tea."

"About these excursions of hers—"

"Well, like I said, she went out every morning after breakfast all dressed up. A couple of times I asked her, I said, Rose, are you going shopping? She said yes, she was, but when she came home she didn't have any parcels so I knew she hadn't been shopping. Besides, there was nothing new in her room when I went to clean it up." Mrs. Cushman flushed, but only slightly and momentarily. "Maybe you think I oughtn't to of gone through her things, but if I didn't clean up once in a while, who would? And anyway she was behind in her rent and I thought, *well*, if she's got enough money to go shopping she's got enough money to pay her rent. So I just checked to make sure. She had no new clothes, no new anything except a lipstick from the dime store and a whole bunch of maps."

"Maps?"

"Yes, maps, and I don't wonder you're flabbergasted. So was I. It was the first notion I had that she was planning a trip somewhere. There must of been twenty maps altogether, of different parts of the country and of different cities."

"Were they new?"

"Brand new, like she'd just suddenly decided to go away some place and got a whole bunch of maps from a travel agency."

"Did you ask her about them?"

"In a sort of way, I did. I said, Rose, are you thinking of going on a trip? And she gave me one of those sly secrety looks and said, my dear Blanche, one never knows what the future holds in store for one."

"Did she seem pleased?"

"Pleased as punch, but trying not to show it. The thing is, where would she get the money for a trip?"

That was the thing all right, but as yet it had no shape, size or identity. Frank said, "Rose was an impulsive creature. If she did decide to take a trip, I can't picture her planning it carefully with a lot of maps."

"Impulsive, that's the word all right. Whatever Rose wanted to do she did, and it always seemed right to her at the time she was doing it. Later when it was all over she could look back and see her mistakes and admit them. But *at the time* she always thought she was right."

"That's a good analysis."

Mrs. Cushman flushed and said shortly, "It's not mine. Rose said it about herself."

Frank was not surprised. Rose had admitted her faults with the cheerful unconcern of someone who has no intention of trying to change them. *This is me,* Rose said, in effect. *This is what I did and why I did it and tomorrow I may do it again.*

He said, "What did she do on Sunday after I left?"

"Stayed in her room for a while. About two o'clock she had a phone call and right after that off she went, looking kind of worried."

"Who took the call?"

"She did. When the phone rang, she came running down the steps like a bat out of hell, shouting, it's for me, I'll get it. That's not the first time it happened, either. You see now what I mean about her acting secrety?"

"Yes."

"There's more, too. Last week—Wednesday it was, I remember distinctly—Wednesday night Miss Henderson came home from work and said she'd seen Rose walking by herself out on the breakwater. Now you know Rose, she just hated the ocean, never had a good word to say for it. What was she doing out there?"

"Meeting someone, perhaps."

"Exactly what I thought. Exactly. So the next morning at breakfast I said to her, meaning to be funny, I said, well, I didn't know you was so fond of physical culture, Miss French, that you go prancing up and down the breakwater of an evening. You know what she did then?—told me to mind my own business. And that's not all. She said if a lot more people did a lot more walking, they wouldn't get fat as pigs. Meaning me. Real venomous she said it." Mrs. Cushman reached for her tea as an antidote. "I've taken a lot of things from that woman, but that was the unkindliest blow of all because it so happens that I've lost two pounds in the last month. If you're born skinny the way Rose was, it's no credit to stay skinny."

Frank, who was born skinny, agreed. He ate like a horse and Miriam gained weight.

"Well, I oughtn't to take up your time like this," Mrs. Cushman said. "But I just felt I had to tell somebody about how peculiar she was acting."

"I'm glad you did."

"I didn't want to go to the police, it's no place for a respectable woman."

"I suppose they came here to look at her room?"

"They did, Tuesday afternoon before supper. Rose had left a lot of stuff behind and they went through it. But it was all just junk that she was too lazy to throw away, left it for me to clean up."

"Did you clean it up?"

"No, they wouldn't let me. They said I had to wait till after the inquest. Well, the inquest's over." Mrs. Cushman rose, giving her skirt a decisive little tug. "I might as well get at it."

"Perhaps I could be of some help."

"You? Well, I don't know. It's real nice of you to offer."

"I didn't offer out of niceness. I'm more curious about Rose than you are."

"It's funny how she had that effect on people. You sort of couldn't believe she was real, and then she turned out to be realer than anybody, you know?"

"Yes, I know." It was the same conclusion he and Miriam had reached, put into different words. Frank preferred Mrs. Cushman's: Rose was realer than anybody.

He followed Mrs. Cushman up the stairs. She paused at the top and glanced uneasily over her shoulder, as if she half-suspected that the footsteps behind her were not Frank's.

"I don't relish the thought of going through her things," she said in a whisper. "It was all right when she was alive. But a dead person's things are creepy, they make you wonder what it's all about."

Mrs. Cushman didn't get her chance to wonder. Rose's room was locked, and the door was triple-sealed, across the keyhole and at the top and bottom, with identical printed notices: *Sealed by order of the County Administrator.*

8

ROSE'S FUNERAL—paid for not by Willett or the County Administrator, but by Dalloway—was held in Malgradi's chapel on Friday afternoon. The solemnity of the occasion was marred by several small incidents which Rose herself might have thoroughly enjoyed.

In the first place no one knew what minister to ask to conduct the services, since Rose's attendance at church had been limited to getting married, and she had left no will containing funeral instructions. Still no decision had been reached by noon, so Malgradi called a conference in his office. Malgradi liked conferences and he invited everyone he could think of who might be concerned with Rose's send-off: Greer, who declined without reason; the County Administrator, who said the estate was now out of his hands and he had no jurisdiction or interest; and Frank and Dalloway, who accepted the invitation.

Dalloway was in a difficult mood. He said that he thought a religious service was unnecessary, inasmuch as Rose had been an atheist when he knew her and probably still was when she died.

Malgradi made protesting little noises, like an alarmed rabbit. "If she was an atheist, all the more reason why we should give her a boost."

"You asked my opinion. I gave it."

"Perhaps, as a girl, she was baptized? Or confirmed?"

"Never."

It was finally decided, under Frank's guidance, that they choose the minister in a fair and impartial way, by looking through the yellow pages of the phone book until they found a likely-sounding name. The Reverend Pickering was selected because Pickering was the name of Malgradi's mother-in-law.

Pickering was sent for in a hurry and given a brief resumé of Rose's career and character. The choice turned out to be somewhat unfortunate. The Reverend was quite elderly, his eyesight was poor and the lights in Malgradi's chapel where Rose was resting were dim and flattering. Through this combination of circumstances, Pickering got the impression that Rose was a young woman, and having no time to prepare anything new, he fell back on his cut-off-in-the-flower-of-her-youth eulogy.

Sensing disaster, Malgradi immediately stepped up the volume of the organ music to drown Pickering out, or at least soften the discrepancies. Pickering was a hard man to drown. He had competed during his lifetime with epidemics of coughs and whispers, squalls of babies, giggles of choir boys, and even personal attacks in the form of spitballs from the gallery and peashooters from the vestry. He had no intention of giving ground to a mere organ.

By shouts and pantomime he indicated to the rather dazed audience that Rose was a flower and only the fairest flowers were plucked to grace the garden of the infinite.

Hearing this, Mrs. Cushman, who had arrived late and taken a seat in the back row, assumed that she had somehow come to the wrong funeral and she immediately rustled out again to look for the right one.

"Let us pray," Pickering said, and pray he did, for the soul of this lovely young woman to enter the eternal glory and eternal youth.

Malgradi did his best. He coughed, shuffled his feet, and under cover of his hand, made faces at a small boy on the aisle in the faint hope that the boy would become frightened and start screaming and all hell would break loose. The boy merely stuck out his tongue at Malgradi in a friendly way and re-focused his attention on Pickering.

Malgradi could stand the agony no longer. He slipped out into the corridor. Here he met Mrs. Cushman who had been wandering in and out of rooms finding out a good deal about the embalming business. The experience had unnerved her and left her quite unprepared to cope with this sudden meeting.

"Eeeee," Mrs. Cushman said, and made a frantic beeline for the nearest door, which happened to be that of the chapel. So she didn't miss Rose's funeral after all.

It was, on the whole, exactly the kind of funeral Rose would have liked, since it left everyone in a state of confusion. Pickering finally exhausted himself and sat down; Malgradi locked himself in his office and took two stiff drinks of the sherry he kept to revive female mourners attacked by fainting spells; and Dalloway remarked sourly to the man sitting next to him that the whole thing had been a farce.

The man next to him happened to be Willett. "I beg your pardon?"

"I said it was a farce."

Willett's eyes were rimmed with pink and a little swollen. Willett often cried on melancholy occasions and at sad movies, while Ethel chewed gum.

He gave Dalloway a cold look. "A farce, sir? I don't agree."

"You're Mr. Goodfield, aren't you?"

"I am."

"My name is Haley Dalloway. I was hoping I might meet you here today."

"You were? Well—that is—this is my wife, Ethel. Ethel, Mr. Dalloway."

Ethel parked her gum deftly beside a molar, and acknowledged the introduction with a dreamy smile. She knew who Dalloway was and she tried to warn Willett by kicking him quite smartly on the left shinbone, a gesture that produced no reaction from Willett except pain.

"The fact is," Dalloway said, "I'm not satisfied with the results of the inquest. Are you?"

"I—well, I haven't thought about it. I mean to say, it's not my business."

"Justice is everybody's business."

"Oh, quite, quite. But—"

"I have a strong suspicion that there's foul play involved and that it's being hushed up."

"Do you really think so?" Ethel murmured. "Isn't that interesting."

"It's more than interesting. I think something should be *done* about it."

"Willett would be just thrilled to do something, wouldn't you, Willett?"

Willett denied this with some vigor. "I would not. For heaven's sake, Ethel, I'm not a policeman, I'm a businessman."

"So am I," Dalloway said. "My business is lumber. What's yours, Mr. Goodfield?"

"Dolls. That is, we manufacture dolls. The Horace Goodfield Doll Corporation of California."

"Let me explain my interest. You see, Rose French was my first wife and the mother of my daughter. I came here looking for them." Dalloway paused a moment. "Do you know a young man called Frank Clyde?"

"I believe I—yes, yes, he was one of the witnesses yesterday."

"He has a curious story to tell. Would you like to hear it?"

"No," Willett said decisively. "I mean to say, this isn't the time or place—"

"Clyde claims he talked to Rose on the telephone a couple of hours after she died. Now Clyde seems to me to be a very sensible young fellow. It isn't likely that he was mistaken about the time, no matter what the jury decided. But it's quite possible that he was mistaken about the voice."

"Voice?"

"On the telephone. It's my conviction that he didn't talk to Rose at all, but to an impostor. Someone, for reasons I can't fathom, imitated Rose on the telephone."

"Isn't that interesting," Ethel said. "Well, we'd better be leaving now, everybody else is. It's been so nice meeting you, Mr. Dalloway, and we hope you'll come out to the house and see us sometime, don't we, Willett?"

Willett didn't answer.

"Don't we, Willett?"

"Oh, certainly, by all means." Willett reached underneath the folding chair for his hat. "Be delighted."

People had started to file out, talking quietly among themselves. In five minutes they were all gone. Malgradi cut the organ music, paid the Reverend Pickering off in cash and harsh words, and went in to see Rose. He stood beside the casket with his hands clasped and his head bowed.

"Please excuse the bungling, dear Lord, and accept this woman into your heavenly kingdom where she may see the light that she did not see on earth. Thank you. Amen."

⑨

DALLOWAY SPENT a restless night. The people in the adjoining suite gave a party and there was a woman in the crowd whose full, hearty laughter reminded him of the way Rose used to laugh.

In the morning he phoned Captain Greer at his office.

"This is Haley Dalloway, Captain."

"Yes, Dalloway."

"I may as well say it before you do—I have this Goodfield family on my brain."

"I hardly envy you."

"As far as you're concerned, I expect this business about Rose is finished."

"It's finished," Greer said, "because there's simply nothing to go on with."

"You could be wrong."

"I often am. You're at liberty to correct me if you can."

"That's the trouble. I have nothing definite except Clyde's statement."

"Which is hardly definite enough."

"I realize that. Call it a hunch, if you like, but I have a strong feeling that at some time or another Rose had a connection with the Goodfields."

"What if she had?"

"They deny it. That's suspicious in itself—if, of course, there was a connection."

"My own opinion is that the Goodfields are exactly what they seem. The mother's a tyrant, Goodfield is a mouse, and his wife has forty-eight cards in the deck. If I investigated every family like it, I'd be working seventy-two hours a day. The Goodfields are more along Clyde's line than mine."

"Then you intend to drop the case?"

"Officially it's dropped."

"What about unofficially?"

"Some time if I ever get up to Frisco I may drop in to see how dolls are being made these days. No pun intended."

"That's really very good of you," Dalloway said earnestly. "I appreciate it."

"Why?"

"Well, after all, Rose was my wife."

"You didn't see her for thirty years, the bonds couldn't have been too strong."

"Perhaps I'm getting sentimental in my old age."

"Perhaps, but I wouldn't bet a plugged nickel on it." There was a pause, and a rustle of paper. "We've had no word so far on your daughter Lora."

"I didn't expect any."

"To be perfectly realistic about it, the police don't break their necks on these voluntary disappearance cases unless a minor is involved. When a girl's old enough to vote and earn a living, she's old enough to leave home."

"She's never earned a living, but I suppose that's beside the point."

"What is the point?"

"I merely want to find out where and how she is. I have no intention of forcing her to return home or anything like that. But the fact is she's my only child, I'm no longer young, and I have a fair amount of money to leave behind. Before I make another will, I want to know just how that money's going to be spent."

"You mean if you find her married to a bum, no money, eh?"

"Not a cent."

"Those are hard words for such a sentimental man."

Dalloway laughed. "Money and sentiment don't mix."

"I wouldn't know," Greer said. "I've never had enough of either to try mixing them."

"I'll hear from you then, perhaps soon?"

"Perhaps soon, perhaps never. I haven't committed myself."

"By the way, I would like to look over the things Rose left behind in her room, but I was told by Clyde that it was sealed."

"Not any more. One of the boys from the County Administrator's office made a routine check through everything in case any money or valuables were hidden around. Nothing was found."

"I suppose they checked *thoroughly?*"

"That's their job. They examine every feather in the pillows, every book, magazine, picture, mattress, letter—"

"I get it. You wouldn't have any objection if I went and took a look around myself, though?"

"None at all. Just square yourself with Mrs. Cushman. It's her house, and if she doesn't want to let you in, no one can force her to."

Force was not necessary. Mrs. Cushman was flabbergasted by the appearance, in the flesh, of one of Rose's husbands. Until the moment when Dalloway introduced himself at the front door, Mrs. Cushman had viewed Rose's husbands as legendary creatures who might or might not have really existed.

"My land, I've heard Rose mention the name Haley Dalloway a hundred times." Mrs. Cushman's tone implied that each of the hundred mentions had been flattering; nothing could have been further from the truth.

"It's nice to know that Rose didn't forget me," Dalloway said dryly.

"Oh dear, no, she didn't forget you, I should say not. She often said—" Mrs. Cushman paused, trying desperately to invent something pleasant that Rose might have said, but the task was beyond her. "She spoke of you frequently. She was a great talker, Rose was. But look who's telling who. I bet she talked your arm off."

It was at this point that she noticed that Dalloway's arm was indeed talked off, or at any rate missing.

Dalloway touched his artificial arm, casually. "Rose didn't talk it off, she merely tried."

"I didn't mean—I—"

"Please don't be embarrassed. I'm not."

"It was real tactless of me. That's what my late husband used to say, that every time I opened my mouth I put my foot in it."

To avoid further marital reminiscences, Dalloway told her why he had come, and Mrs. Cushman led him upstairs explaining, as she paused on the landing, that she hadn't had the spirit to clean Rose's room and it was very likely a mess.

It was. The bed, the bureau, the chairs were strewn with old magazines, dresses, stockings, underwear, letters, sachets, empty containers of makeup, a discarded light bulb, an apple, and a flattened and distorted red rose that looked as though it had been recently pressed between the pages of a book.

Dalloway glanced around the room, frowning. It was a crude ending for a sentimental journey.

"A real mess," Mrs. Cushman said with considerable satisfaction. Cleaning up a real mess was more enjoyable than cleaning up a half mess, since the results were more startling.

"I thought Rose had given up this room," Dalloway said.

"She did."

"It seems odd that she'd leave so much stuff behind, especially clothing. I understood she was broke."

"Couldn't be broker. She was always behind in her rent. Impractical, Rose was—not wishing to speak ill of the dead, but that's the honest truth."

"When did she decide to leave? Did she give you any notice?"

"Not a minute's notice. Monday at lunchtime she comes in, hands me the money she owed me, and says she's leaving to take a job out of town. Inside of twenty minutes she was gone, taking just that one suitcase with her best clothes in it. Gone like that." Mrs. Cushman snapped her fingers. "Of course I knew she was up to something because of the maps."

"What maps? I don't see any."

"She must of took them with her. She had a lot of maps that she'd marked things on with a pencil."

"Things such as?"

"I didn't pay too close attention, but I remember one where she'd written some people's names on the top and some dates beside the names."

"Can you recall any of them?"

"Phil was one. And Baker, I remember that because it was my maiden name. Now let me think a minute, don't rush me."

Dalloway went over to the bureau and picked up the pressed rose while Mrs. Cushman thought a minute.

"Paul. That's another," she said finally. "And Byron. Or Bernard, was it? Yes, it was Bernard."

"Any women's names?"

"I can't recall any, but I think there was. Yes, I'm sure there was. Millie or Minnie, something like that."

"And a date beside each name?"

"Yes."

"What did you make of it?"

"I just figured she was making up a birthday list and didn't have anything else to write on. Isn't that reasonable?"

"It might be, if Rose had developed into the type of person who remembered anyone else's birthday."

"Rose could be very thoughtful at times," Mrs. Cushman said cautiously. "She gave me a nice Christmas present last year, five pounds of caramels. I thought that was real nice of her, considering she couldn't chew caramels herself on account of her dentures. For instance she could have given me peppermint patties and eaten half of them herself. Or maraschino cherries."

Dalloway began to circle the room, looking at everything but not touching anything except the pressed flower he had taken off the bureau. His feelings about Rose were stronger here in this room than they had been at the funeral. He was depressed by the sordid litter of stuff she had left behind her, and impatient at Rose herself. How like her to make a birthday list on a map (and that's all it was, probably) and then go off and die in somebody's garden. She had no sense of propriety, never had had any.

"Maybe you'd like to be alone with her memory for a while?" Mrs. Cushman suggested.

"No," Dalloway said. "No, thanks. I came here actually with the idea of finding something worthwhile to give my daughter Lora as a keepsake of her mother."

"Her mother?"

"That's right."

"Why, Rose never breathed a word—"

"She had a very faulty memory about some things."

"Well, my land, I just can't feature Rose as a mother."

"Neither could she." Dalloway smiled, trying to conceal his hot rush of anger. It was as powerful now as it had been thirty-two years ago, the day Rose had left him.

"Fancy Rose having a daughter and never breathing a word about it, not even when she was hitting the bottle. It's just a miracle, Rose being the blabber she was—not wishing to speak ill of the dead." Mrs. Cushman put her head to one side and glanced around the room like a plump, inquisitive robin. "There must be *something* here you could take home to the little one."

"Lora is over thirty."

"She is? Why, yes, I guess she must be. It's too bad Rose took all her pictures with her."

"Pictures of what?"

"Herself. She had the walls covered with them. I'm not so sure it was plain vanity either. She used to be very critical of them. Look at that silly pan, she'd say, or, look at that stupid expression." Mrs. Cushman wiped her eyes with the back of her hand. "We had many a good laugh together over those pictures, I can tell you. Nobody could be funnier than Rose when she was in a good mood. But I guess you know that."

"Yes." Nobody could be funnier, and nobody could be sadder.

"Which most of the time she was—in a good mood, I mean. Not lately, though. Lately she's been real touchy, fly off the handle at anything. I often heard her talking to herself, too, talk, talk, talk, like she was ordering people around. Except there *weren't* any people around. I asked her about it one day and she said she was just rehearsing because she expected a big part in a movie any day. Same old story, I heard it a million times. She couldn't get it through her head that she was finished."

"What finished her?"

"She finished herself. Too many good times and parties, they ruined her looks and her health. Rose dearly loved a party."

"I know."

"My, she must have been a lively one when she was young. I bet she led you a merry chase."

"Yes." The merry chase was over, the lively one dead.

Dalloway turned and walked out of the room, unaware that he still had the red rose crushed in his right fist.

Mrs. Cushman puffed along at his heels like a toy locomotive. "You don't have to run off so sudden-like."

"Sorry, I have an engagement. You've been very kind," he added, seeing her disappointed expression, "and very helpful."

"I was hoping maybe you'd stay and we could have a little chat about Rose?"

"Perhaps some other time."

"I wish there was more I could tell you, like the names on the map."

"There might be," Dalloway said. "Did she ever mention any of those people to you—Minnie, Baker, Bernard, and so on?"

"She knew a Minnie that's a checker down at the Safeway, but only in the line of business. Not likely she'd concern herself with *that* Minnie's birthday."

"It doesn't seem so."

"As for Phil, there's a Phil Dickerson lives over on Bagnos Street, but he's just a boy going to high school, delivers for Fred's Drugstore on the side. I don't know any Bakers or Bernards, not that I can recollect offhand. You know what I think? I think all those people were people she knew a long time ago, not ones she was associating with in the here and now. They were figures from her past, in my opinion. And there's only one person that Rose ever let down her real back hair in front of, and that's Frank Clyde."

"Indeed?"

"Indeed." Mrs. Cushman echoed the word lovingly. It was a good word and she intended to use it frequently in the future. When one of the boarders complained about something, Mrs. Cushman would say "Indeed?" raising her eyebrows just as Dalloway had done.

"Why?"

"Why did she talk to Frank, you mean? Well, first and foremost, she liked him. She never let on she did, she even insulted him, but you could tell that underneath she considered him a real good guy. Which he is."

"I agree. I've met him."

"Grade A, in my opinion, and I'm not the one to say that about everybody. I've met too many Grade C's in my lifetime and they look all right on the outside but just try cracking their shell, if you get my meaning."

"Quite."

"Quite." Mrs. Cushman beamed with pleasure. She liked the way Dalloway talked, the nice crisp words he used like "quite" and "indeed." A most distinguished man. She wondered if he was married.

Dalloway saw her wondering and edged toward the front door. "Thank you for your trouble, Mrs.—"

"Cushman. Blanche."

"Ah—yes, I believe I'll go and have a talk with Mr. Clyde."

He opened the door decisively, and Mrs. Cushman knew in her heart that he was walking out of her life forever. She made one final move to stop him.

Crossing her arms on her chest, she said ominously, "You know what I think? What I think is, Rose was murdered."

10

THE CLYDES' HOUSE was one of a row of identical almost-new stucco houses in the west end of town. Even the plantings were identical and had been chosen for their rapid growth: flowering maples less than a year old were already as big as trees and in full bloom, and castor beans the same age loomed above the flat roofs, their smooth red trunks glistening like oil in the afternoon sun.

Miriam came to the door, a pretty, dark-haired young woman with a demure smile and sharp intelligent eyes. She had on a T-shirt, denim pedal-pushers and a blue cotton apron that looked as if she had made it herself. She wore this strange costume with a certain style and self-assurance that seemed to say, *I can't afford to buy good clothes but with my figure I don't have to.*

"Mr. Dalloway? I'm Miriam Clyde."

"Very glad to know you."

"Come in, won't you? Frank will be back in a minute. After you phoned he decided to go down to the office and pick up the file on Rose."

"I didn't realize there was such a thing as a file on her."

"There is. I've read it."

"*You* have?"

"Surprised? Don't be. When a man is as wrapped up in his work as Frank is," Miriam added cheerfully, "I have to get wrapped up with him to survive."

The living room and the furniture in it were obviously new, but already they bore the marks of living: a child's handprint on the woodwork near the light switch, strands of dog hair on the loveseat by the fireplace, black scars of

70

rubber heels on the hardwood floor, and a deck of cards spilled over the piano like fallen leaves.

Miriam made no attempt to pick up the cards or apologize for the room. She accepted a certain amount of disorder as she accepted the weather and the quarterly payments of income tax. She was a fighter, but she never fought the inevitable or started a battle that she wasn't sure of winning. The main battle was money, and though it was still going on, Miriam was confident of final victory some day.

"I realize this is an intrusion," Dalloway said, "coming here on Frank's afternoon off."

"Frank doesn't mind."

"You must."

"Oh, I do, a little. I don't mind you personally, Mr. Dalloway—just the general idea of never getting any free week ends. Frank carries that office of his around like a turtle carrying his shell. It goes with us to the beach, the movies and down to the corner drugstore." Her sudden, bright smile took the edge off her words. "Sometimes I think my kids will get the impression that the entire world is populated by Frank's patients."

Dalloway returned her smile. He liked this calm, candid woman and he wished that Lora could have acquired some similar qualities, a sense of humor, perhaps, or a hard core of common sense. Lora was an idealist without ideals, a rebel without a cause, a woman who affected to despise money and yet was completely dependent on other people for support.

He said aloud, "It would be handy, anyway, having an office you can carry. And the turtle can't afford to despise his shell."

"I guess not." From the back yard came the shouts of children and the shrill barking of a small dog. "Frank's like a turtle in another respect. He's always sticking his neck out."

"Oh?"

"He has no time—no right, even—to go around investigating Rose's death."

"Is that what he's doing?"

"That's what you're doing, why you're here, isn't it?"

"More or less."

"Mostly more, though?"

"Very well, mostly more."

"Why?" Miriam said. "Why is everyone so suspicious about Rose dying?"

"You aren't?"

"No, I'm not. I think both you and Frank simply feel frustrated by her death. Frank didn't have a chance to finish his job on her, and you didn't have a chance to question her about your daughter."

"You seem to be full of both theories and information," Dalloway said, sounding amused. "As a matter of fact you may be right about my part of it. I *do* feel frustrated. I think it was extremely inconsiderate of Rose to die before I could talk to her. I'm not sure whether she would have been able to tell me any news of Lora or not. I believe she would. When Lora was in one of her sullen moods, she frequently toyed with the idea of a reunion with her mother. You get the picture?—one sensitive, artistic soul crying out to the other across the bourgeois wilderness."

"I'm afraid my imagination boggles at the idea of Rose being sensitive and artistic."

"Mine boggles even more, in Lora's case. She has the hide of a rhinoceros, as so many people do who confuse sensitivity with egocentricity. When she makes a childish fuss at the dentist's, for example, she always manages to convince herself that it's because she feels more pain than ordinary people."

"Oh, everybody thinks that, about feeling more pain than other people. That's my opinion, anyway. You don't have to agree. Frank says I make too many sweeping statements. But how else can you get a good argument started?"

"Do you want a good argument?"

Miriam laughed. "I wouldn't mind. Frank never argues."

"Choose your subject."

"That's easy. Rose."

"It's a wide field. Narrow it down."

"All right. Was she murdered or not?"

"I've never claimed she was murdered."

"Claim it now, for the sake of argument."

Dalloway rubbed the side of his jaw thoughtfully. "I'm afraid I can't. It doesn't seem very reasonable. No one gained anything from her death. She had no money, no securities, no jewelry—"

"Nothing tucked away for a rainy day?"

"Rose was living in the rainy days."

"I know," Miriam said, with a sober little nod. "We tried to help her as much as we could. We took her to a ball game one night—she was bored stiff by the game but she liked the crowds—and she came here for dinner a few times. At first I was afraid that she'd, well, you know, act up a little in front of the kids, especially if she'd been drinking. But Frank said she wouldn't, and she didn't. She was very reserved and sweet. I don't think she liked the children much, but she talked to them in a grownup way and she played with the dog. She was very fond of dogs. Are you?"

"Fond of dogs? Oh yes, moderately." Dalloway looked as if he was trying to keep from laughing. "Don't tell me you're one of these women who judge people by whether or not they like dogs."

"I certainly am. Frank says it's a very unscientific system and he's always citing cases of murderers who were doglovers, like Dr. Crippen. Naturally there are exceptions. But I do think that there's something outgiving and gen-

erous about people who are sincerely fond of dogs. Cats
are a different matter. Cats are for introverts, lonely people and rather timid people who are afraid of a dog's gusto
and his demands. Cats don't give or take, they walk alone,
and so do the people who own them." Miriam paused for
breath. "There. That ought to start an argument."

"Why do you want an argument?"

"To get rid of my aggressions. I have quite a few."

"Indeed?"

"Certainly. So have you. I get rid of mine—some of
them—not by spanking my kids or beating my husband,
but by talking. Oh yes, and once in a while I break a dish.
That's more expensive than talking, though."

A car stopped outside, its tire-savers screeching against
the curb. A moment later Frank came into the house carrying a manila folder under his arm.

He shook hands with Dalloway and grinned across the
room at his wife. "I see you've been entertaining Mr. Dalloway with a few theories."

"How can you tell?" Miriam said.

"You're looking smug."

"Oh, I am not." Miriam went over to the large mirror
on the mantel to see if she was looking smug or not.

Frank turned back to Dalloway. "I brought the report
on Rose. It's not complete, as I explained to you before.
We're seldom able to get a complete report on anyone
unless there's been a series of previous commitments. In
the case of Rose, I have only what information she volun-
teered, plus a few of my own interpretations which may
or may not be right. So don't expect much."

"I won't," Dalloway said.

"Actually I had no business taking Rose on as a patient.
I don't think there was anything wrong with her mentally. She was a little punch-drunk. She'd been a cham-
pion, in her own way, and then suddenly she couldn't even

get a bout scheduled. Those are her own words, I'm quoting from the report."

"Am I to be allowed to read it?"

"Certain parts. A lot of it is personal."

"To Rose or to me?"

"You're mentioned in it several times."

"In a favorable or unfavorable light?"

Frank seemed uncomfortable. "Well, you know Rose."

"Unfavorable, then."

"Yes. That's understandable. She suffered a great many guilt feelings after abandoning you and the child. In order to tolerate these feelings, she had to convince herself that you were quite the villain."

"I imagine Rose's life teemed with villains."

"They were pretty numerous."

"Any references to those names I told you about that she'd written on the map?"

"Two." Frank untied the tapes on the manila folder. "Phil and Bernard. Phil was the name of her last husband, Philip Lederman. He was killed in a sailing accident a few years ago. He was alone at the time, there was no suspicion of foul play."

"And Bernard?"

"Bernard," Frank said dryly, "was a Pekinese."

"A *dog?*"

"Yes. She had him when she worked on the old United Artists lot. She carried him around everywhere she went, on the set, in restaurants, trains, etcetera. Here are the two references if you want to glance at them."

Dalloway accepted the typewritten pages with a little frown of annoyance. The reference to Bernard was a straight quote from Rose:

"Bernard was the smartest little dog you ever saw. Honest to God, Frank, that dog could read my mind better than you can. Bernie could always tell when I didn't like people, he'd snap at them. Once he bit the headwaiter at the Ambassador. God, it was funny. I had to pay three hundred dollars' damages. I've never set foot in the Ambassador since. It was the principle of the thing—three hundred dollars for a lousy little dog bite. . . ."

Dalloway looked up, still frowning. "This can't be the right Bernard."

"Perhaps not."

"It's only a dog, after all."

"Try the Phil reference," Frank said. "Page 89."

Page 89 began with Frank's own words.

"Patient arrived in a depressed mood, dressed carelessly, hair uncombed. Complained of a sleepless night. Face pallid, respiration uneven. I advised a physical check-up. Patient protested, claiming it was unnecessary, she couldn't afford it, she distrusted doctors, and so on. She seemed afraid. After a time she admitted this.

"Patient: 'I had the screaming meemies last night. I woke up around 4 A.M. and it was dark, pitch dark, and quiet. I had the feeling that I was alone, absolutely alone, that everybody else in the whole world had died and there was just me left in that awful quietness. And then gradually I realized it wasn't so quiet, I could hear the sea. My window was open and I could hear the sea very faintly, that terrible incessant noise, I hate it. It reminds me of Phil. I told you about Phil, didn't I?'

"I said that she had told me he was her third husband.

"Patient: 'Phil went out in his sailboat one day and never came back. The sea got him. It's going to get me if I let him.'

"Note: Patient shows no fear of water in general, only the sea, which she refers to when she is excited as a 'him.' The sea appears to be a God-symbol and a conscience-symbol.

"I asked her why she believed the sea would get her.

"Patient: 'It got Phil. It got him to spite me.'

"I asked her to explain this.

" 'I bought him that sailboat for his birthday. Oh, I'm all mixed up, I can't explain. I was crazy about Phil, he was always nice to me, never played me for a sucker like Hamman and I wasn't afraid of him the way I was afraid of Dalloway.' "

Dalloway closed the report and put it on the nearest table with a decisive little slap. His face, which was normally ruddy, had taken on a purplish tinge around the cheekbones, as if blood vessels were breaking under the skin.

He spoke in a tight, controlled voice. "So she was afraid of Dalloway."

"Oh, you mustn't take that too seriously," Miriam said.

He paid no attention to her, keeping his eyes fixed on Frank. "I'd like to read that report, all of it."

"I'm sorry, you can't."

"Professional ethics?"

"Partly that. Mainly, though, because I think it might be harmful to you."

"I'm not a vulnerable child, you know."

"None of us knows how vulnerable we are until we're tested."

"I've been tested by experts."

Frank didn't reply. He simply replaced the report in the manila folder and tied the tapes.

Watching him, Dalloway realized that it was useless to continue the subject. Frank wasn't merely stubborn, he was right, and the combination was like steel and concrete. Dalloway thought savagely, *he's used to handling mental patients. I must be a cinch.*

He forced a smile on his face, hoping it made him look friendly and unconcerned. "You're right, of course, Clyde. I may be more vulnerable than I think. Naturally, I was curious as to what Rose had to say about me. Funny, after all these years that I should be interested, isn't it?"

77

"You're still interested in her."

"Yes. Yes, I suppose I am."

"So is Frank," Miriam said with a brief, mirthless laugh. "It's all we've talked about for a week now. I'd like a good long discussion about the weather for a change."

"The weather," Dalloway said, "has been perfect. If we suddenly had twelve inches of rain or a tornado, we might work up a lively conversation. As it is"—he shrugged— "what can you say or do about anything perfect? It's the squeaky wheel, like Rose, that gets the oil."

Miriam went and sat on the piano bench, her hands folded on her lap in a limp and resigned way.

"There are," Dalloway added, "other squeaky wheels besides Rose, but so far no one's paid any attention to them except me."

"The Goodfields," Frank said.

"Of course. I talked to Captain Greer about them this morning. He claims that they're more along your line than his. You've seen them?"

"Not the old lady. I've heard about her, though, from Greer."

"You've seen Willett and his wife?"

"Yes. At the inquest and at the funeral."

"What do you make of them?"

Frank smiled. "Well, that's a pretty big question. I haven't formed any conclusions."

"I don't agree. I think that a man like you forms a conclusion every time he even looks at a person. Of course he may change the conclusion later, but he forms one."

"You're half-right anyway. I can't avoid recognizing types of people and of families."

"What about the Goodfield family?"

"It's fairly standard. Much too standard. Dominant mother, rebellious daughter, weak sons."

"And the wife, Ethel?"

78

"Probably picked out by the mother."

"Greer thinks she's feeble-minded."

"She may give that impression now—she's still under Mrs. Goodfield's thumb. When the old lady dies, Ethel will come into her own."

"Willett won't?"

"Afraid not, if he follows the usual pattern. Ethel will simply assume Mrs. Goodfield's role."

"An odd set-up."

"Not nearly odd enough," Frank said. "There are many families like the Goodfields."

"Not many who have a dead woman found in their back yard."

"No."

"I'm thinking it, you're thinking it, we may as well say it. Those Goodfields had better be investigated, from top to bottom."

"By whom?"

"I've done what I could. The trouble is, I can't go around trailing people and asking them questions. I'm too conspicuous for one thing." He gave his artificial arm a contemptuous tap. "For another, I've had no experience in investigation work." Dalloway paused. "You have."

Miriam made a sound of protest though she formed no actual words.

"Why are you anxious to get something on the Goodfields?" Frank said.

"If you'll re-phrase that, I might be able to answer."

"All right. What's your interest?"

"You might call it curiosity."

"I might."

"Or sentiment. Or boredom. Give it any name you choose. I'd just like to find out for certain if Rose was connected in any way with the Goodfields. If she was, maybe Lora was too."

"Was?"

"Was," Dalloway repeated, grimly. "I have a feeling that my daughter is dead."

"Have you any reason for thinking that?"

"One. But it's a good one. She hasn't written to me asking for money. No, I'm not being humorous. Lora is incapable of supporting herself. She's never had a job that lasted more than a day, and in spite of her fancy talk she's as incompetent as a three-year-old." Dalloway paused again and cleared his throat. "I'm willing to pay you liberally for your services."

Frank and Miriam exchanged glances. Frank turned away and looked out of the window. The two boys were wrestling on the front lawn while the little black spaniel yipped furiously at the excitement, not sure whether the wrestling was playful or serious. Happy children, Frank thought. But even happy children needed new shoes and jeans and haircuts.

He knew Miriam was thinking the same thing: clothes for the children, maybe a bicycle for John or a rubber wading-pool for Peter.

"You have," Frank said at last, "touched us in a tender place."

"I was hoping so."

"It's not tender enough, however, for me to accept any compromise with my conscience."

"I'm not asking you to do anything wrong."

"What are you asking me to do and for how much?"

"For a hundred and fifty dollars go up to San Francisco and find out everything you can about the Goodfield clan. The price I'm willing to pay doesn't include any expense account, so you can go up any way you choose—train, plane, car, with or without Mrs. Clyde—depending how much of that hundred and fifty you want to save."

"Frank's always liked walking," Miriam said. She meant the remark to be funny, but neither of the men seemed amused. Money was a serious business, to Dalloway who remembered the times when he hadn't any, and to Frank who had no need to refresh his memory.

"I can't get more than one day off," Frank said.

Dalloway nodded. "One day should do it."

"I'll drive up tomorrow."

"It's Sunday, you won't be able to get much done."

"Why not?"

"The factory will be closed."

"Factory?"

"The Horace Goodfield Doll Corporation. I'd like you to take a look at it, see who's running it and how."

"I know nothing about factories, Dalloway. My business is people."

"People make factories."

"Well, I'll do my best." Frank sounded puzzled. "I wish my instructions were a little more specific."

"If I knew how to make them more specific I wouldn't have to ask you to go. I have a vague, general suspicion about that family. I want it confirmed."

"Or denied?"

"Preferably confirmed."

"Why preferably?"

"I hate to be wrong, that's all." Dalloway made it sound quite convincing. "Well, I must be leaving. I'll hear from you Tuesday then?"

"Yes."

Dalloway's departure was carefully polite. He told Miriam it had been a pleasure to meet such a charming woman, he shook hands with the two little boys, patted the dog's head, and drove off in his Packard with a smile and a friendly wave.

Frank and Miriam looked at each other in silence for a moment.

"Well?" Frank said.

"Well nothing."

81

"You're worried."

"I'm not worried," she said gayly. "I think he's nice. And a hundred and fifty dollars is *very* nice."

"You are worried."

"Oh, don't be so damned subtle about everything! What if I am worried, the world's not going to fall apart, is it?"

"Mine might."

She put both her hands on his shoulders and smiled up into his face. "I love you, too."

The older of the two boys cocked his head sardonically. "Mush, mush, mush."

11

THE SIGN ACROSS the front of the gray concrete building said, "Horace M. Goodfield Doll Corporation, San Francisco, California." Standing stiff and flat-footed on top of this sign was a wooden doll twenty feet high. Years of sun had bleached away her smile and left her hair a dusty gray, and the fog that rolled in from the bay had blurred her eyes. They stared vacantly out at the passing ships, like the eyes of a heathen idol watching without interest or concern its foolish worshippers. The doll's name was printed across her flat, faded chest: Sweetheart.

Frank knew from the noise of machines that the factory was operating, but he had the impression that it would stop at any moment, freeze into immobility like the wooden doll. The building itself bore the marks of neglect, as if no one cared enough about it to replace broken glass or repaint the sills or patch up the holes in the concrete.

The old man sitting in a chair at the entrance gate

matched the building. No one cared about him either. His face was the same color as the concrete, and his eyes had the dinginess of unwashed windows. He looked at Frank, rubbing the arthritis-swollen knuckles of his hands.

Frank noticed that he was wearing a shoulder holster. "You work here?"

"Worked here for twenty-two years." The old man spoke in a monotone. "First I was inside. I painted their faces for them. Delicate work, but I had good nerves. My hands got bad, though. So then they gave me this here chair and this here automatic and says, now you're a guard, Charley. Charley's my name."

"Mine's Clyde. Know how to use the gun?"

"Sure I do."

"Ever used it?"

"Once. A fellow broke in and I shot at him. I missed. Turned out he was a maniac crazy about dolls. They put him away in some place, I heard. It was the first maniac I ever saw, didn't froth at the mouth or nothing, looked as normal as you and me."

"You've worked for the Goodfields a long time, eh?"

"Twenty-two years, like I said. Why, I gave Sweetheart up there her first coat of paint."

"She looks as if she could use another."

"That's what I keep saying, but nobody takes mind of me. Nothing gets done around here any more at all since old Horace died. Not that Horace was any great shakes as a businessman, but he *cared*. He was an artist. Why, single-handed, him and me designed Sweetheart, clothes and everything. Horace," he repeated, "was a real artist."

"What happened after he died?"

"They buried him."

"You have quite a sense of humor, Charley."

"I could always look on the funny side of things."

"Now try looking on the other side. What happened to the factory after Horace died?"

"Nothing happened except one day a guy shows up with a lot of begonia bulbs. Planted a dozen of them in this here very spot where I'm sitting."

"Why begonias?"

"Because Horace left the whole factory, lock, stock and barrel, to his wife, and she thought it'd be kind of pretty to have some flowers growing around."

"Did she take over the factory?"

"Well, for a while she came in bright and early every morning and said hello to everyone. Inside of a week she knew more about the people who worked here than they knew about themselves. Like a mother to them, Mrs. Goodfield was. Only they didn't need a mother, they needed some new machinery and better washrooms and a heating plant that didn't go on the fritz twice a week."

He spat on the ground where the begonias had once been planted. Then he looked up at the wooden doll again, squinting, though there was no sun.

"No sir, poor old Sweetheart don't have much of a future. One of these days the termites will find her and then, phhhtt."

Frank wondered whether the termites hadn't already found her. He said, "Have you seen Mrs. Goodfield recently?"

"She don't come around no more. Lost interest, I guess, when she found out nobody needed an extry mother. Also she got sick, had to rest a lot. That's when she divided all the stock up and gave it to the children."

"Who runs the business now?"

"Who runs it? Everybody runs it. Willett runs it. Jack runs it. I run it. Hell, if you stick around long enough, you'll be running it too. This pie has got so many pinkies in it that there ain't going to be any pie left."

"Is the place losing money?"

"No sir, we get the same volume of business year after

year. Same customers wanting the same thing, a good cheap doll."

"What's the beef then?"

Charley peered at him out of his unwashed eyes. "You a businessman?"

"No."

"I thought not or you wouldn't ask silly questions. A business can't stand still. If it don't move forward it moves back like the tail of a clock. And with a small business like this, it don't take much to ruin it. A few extra taxes here and a few wage increases there, and where are you? Flat on your butt, wondering what hit you. That's where I landed back in twenty-nine. Horace gave me a job. He used to be one of my customers when the wife and me still had the laundry."

The old man lapsed into silence, a puzzled expression on his face, as if he was wondering how it had all happened; where had the years and the laundry and Horace gone, and how did he come to be here, in this chair, with a gun, guarding a senile giant of a doll?

The fog was beginning to blow in from the bay, like dirty gray sheets on a moving clothesline. Somewhere close by a fog horn bellowed. Charley shivered, and turned up the collar of his leather jacket.

"I saw Willett Goodfield and his wife last week," Frank said. "They're in La Mesa, down south."

"So I heard."

"They seem to be living very comfortably."

"That's the only way they know how to live. Yet. Yet," he repeated. "They'll be pulling in their horns one of these days. Wait'll the old lady dies and they got inheritance taxes to pay."

"If she's already given them the stock, there won't be any inheritance taxes."

Charley stared at him with reluctant approval. "By

George, you're right. Never thought of that myself. But there'll be other things, make no mistake about that. When the old lady dies, there'll be a good old-fashioned bust-up. Want to bet on it?"

"Not particularly."

"I'm not a betting man either but I can read the handwriting on the wall. Do you know Shirley?"

"No."

"Shirley's the Goodfield girl. Woman she is now but she was a girl when I first saw her. She's the only one of the family with a head on her shoulders. Takes after Horace, even in looks. But Shirley couldn't stand the old lady. Left home when she was seventeen and got married. She don't come around here no more."

"Why not?"

"No time. She's a widow with four kids."

"Where does she live now?"

"Home."

"Whose home?"

"Horace's place up on Nob Hill. It's a good big place with plenty of valuables and antiques in it. When Mrs. Goodfield left to go traveling around, she didn't want the house to be empty, so Shirley and her kids, they have the first floor, and Jack, he has the second. That way it saves rent, and the valuables and antiques get looked after."

"What's left of them after the four kids get through."

Charley grinned. "My oh my oh my. Wait till the old lady comes back and finds something missing like she did last time. That woman has a tongue that would cut concrete, yes sir, concrete."

The fog horn blew again, its enraged bellow shook the air and frightened the ships at sea.

Following the bellow came the quick slam of a door. A tall, young man in a dark business suit walked briskly down the steps toward the gate where Charley was sitting. The man had curly straw-colored hair carefully parted to disguise the thinning circle on top. He walked as though he took pride in his body and kept it in the best of physical condition, as Mrs. Goodfield kept her valuables and antiques.

Charley bent over and pretended to be engrossed in tying the lace of one of his workboots.

"Charley."

The old man straightened up, making a funny little sound that was barely audible.

"I presume you still work here, Charley?"

"Yes, Mr. Jack."

"I've had to warn you before about standing around talking like this."

"A little talk never hurt—"

"I'm sure your friend here will excuse you while you go on your rounds."

Jack Goodfield gave Frank one sweeping and contemptuous glance, and then marched back into the building like a general who hadn't yet discovered that his army had been cut down behind him.

Charley took out a black and white bandana and blew his nose into it and cursed. Frank, who had heard, and been the object of, considerable cursing, was impressed by Charley's vocabulary.

"Sorry if I caused you any trouble," Frank said. "I came here to see Goodfield, as a matter of fact."

But Charley had apparently lost interest in the whole affair. Getting up, he adjusted his shoulder holster and began to shuffle toward the side of the building. The general still had one man left.

The air inside the building was very warm and dry after the cold dampness of the fog. At the desk where the workers punched the time clock, a young girl was writing a letter on deep mauve stationery. Through the glass partition behind her Frank could see two rows of women at work over a long table. They looked as identical as the dolls' heads they were painting.

Seeing Frank, the girl put down her pen but made no attempt to hide the letter. "Is there anything I can do for you?"

"I'd like to talk to Mr. Jack Goodfield."

"If it's a matter of employment, we're full up."

"It's not."

"All right. That's Mr. Goodfield's office right across the hall. Just walk in. His secretary, Mrs. Hiller, is right there —I think." She added the last two words with a curiously deliberate air, and then she picked up her pen and resumed writing on the mauve notepaper. Before he turned away Frank noticed that she wrote uphill, in a disturbed fashion.

He crossed the hall, unconsciously straightening his shoulders as if to shake off the office he was still carrying four hundred miles from home.

Mrs. Hiller was not at her desk but her name card was: Evangeline Hiller. It was a new and very elaborate name card in a blue plastic container. The rest of the office seemed shabby by comparison.

Frank sat down to wait opposite a blown-up photograph of an office picnic dated in ink at the bottom, July 4, 1932, Muir Park.

The door marked John J. Goodfield opened suddenly and Mrs. Hiller plunged into the room with the reluctant thrust of a diver plunging into cold water. Her body, wrapped in a tight silk jersey dress, was mature and full-blown. Above the shoulders she looked very young and surprised as if she couldn't understand what in the world had happened below. She was flushed, her long, brown hair was mussed and she was breathing fast and hard. It seemed to Frank that she had been running, a lap or two, perhaps, around the building to set a good example for Charley.

To cover her confusion she addressed Frank in a voice that sounded much too genteel. "If you wish to speak to Mr. Goodfield, sir, I'm afraid he just stepped out a moment ago."

"When will he be back?"

"Oh, he won't be back. That is, he won't be back today, I mean. He had an urgent call."

"That's too bad."

"Very urgent." Mrs. Hiller swallowed hard, her whole throat convulsing. "Sickness."

"Whose?"

"Somebody got sick, is all. A friend of Jack's—Mr. Goodfield's."

"And Mr. Goodfield went to soothe the fevered brow?"

"Sure he did. I guess." Mrs. Hiller's gentility had vanished, like a popsicle on the sidewalk leaving a small irregular sticky puddle. "He'll be back maybe tomorrow."

From inside the office came a soft sound like the drawer of a desk or a filing cabinet sliding into place. The girl heard it too. She clutched at her throat as if she was choking, and said loudly, "Maybe tomorrow, maybe the next day. This friend of his is real sick."

Frank wondered if the friend was as sick as Mrs. Hiller looked. "I'm afraid I can't wait that long."

She attempted to disguise her obvious relief by saying, "Oh dear, that's too bad, isn't it? I mean, Jack—Mr. Goodfield will be terribly sorry to've missed you."

"He doesn't know me."

"Well, he—he—just hates to miss people. Anyone."

"A friendly type, eh?"

"Oh yes, very. Now if you'll just leave your name, I'll make sure that he finds out you were here."

"My name's Frank Clyde."

"And your business?"

"I'm a social worker."

89

"A—*social* worker?" Mrs. Hiller's mouth gaped like a hungry carp's. "Oh, I don't believe it."

"Why shouldn't you believe it?"

"Well, because. What would a social worker have to do with Jack? Jack's a millionaire."

There was a brief silence before Frank spoke again in a friendly, reasonable way as if he was addressing a strange child. "Does this look like a millionaire's office to you?"

The girl glanced around the tiny room, biting the edge of her lower lip. "Well, gee, I don't know, I never saw a millionaire's office before."

"Have you seen any office before?"

"Just what do you mean by that? I'm a secretary. A private secretary. I took a course. I graduated."

"Did—"

"With honors. So don't go making any more crumby remarks about me being a birdbrain. I'm sick of being called a birdbrain by a lot of other birdbrains."

"I didn't call you anything. I just wondered if this was your first job."

Mrs. Hiller stuck her head in the air and held the pose. "Don't you go social-workering me, Mr. Social Worker. *I* don't need any."

"Your conception of a social worker is—"

"And don't go saying any dirty words either."

"I'm afraid you misunderstood."

"Oh, did I? Don't tell me I don't know a dirty word if I hear one."

"I'm sure you do."

"Well, that's better." Mrs. Hiller seemed slightly mollified. "And don't tell me I don't know about social workers either. Back when I was a kid we were on relief and those creeps were always coming around to see that we spent enough money on milk. *Milk*, yet. Nobody ever got filled up on milk. Just try it sometime."

"I don't check up on any family finances." Except my own, he added silently.

"*My* finances happen to be swell. This dress I got on cost forty dollars plus tax."

"It's very pretty."

"You think so?" The girl smiled, without meaning to. She was as sensitive to a compliment as she was to a criticism. "I think so, too. It's from Magnin's. I only got it on Saturday at a sale. It was regular $59.95 and the pleats will stay in forever."

Frank wondered which pleats would persist longer, the ones outside Mrs. Hiller or the ones inside. "Is this your first job?"

"In a way. I don't *have* to work. I've got a husband, he's a cook in the army, stationed at Fort Ord. He supports me. And Jack—Mr. Goodfield pays me very well."

Frank didn't have to ask what for.

He said good-bye to Mrs. Hiller and she responded very pleasantly. It was clear that she thought she had given a good account of herself, that she had, in her own fashion, bitten the leg of the social worker who'd come to check up on the milk; and having administered the bite, she felt no further resentment.

Outside, the sheets of fog had coagulated into a flabby gray wall. Moisture condensed on Frank's forehead and ran down his cheeks like cold griefless tears.

Charley's chair stood by the gate looking empty and forlorn.

Frank let himself out through the gate and walked down the driveway, the wall of fog moving always a little ahead of him in a tantalizing way. Before he reached the street, a man's figure appeared suddenly out of the fog.

It was Charley. He was shivering with cold and his leather jacket and peaked cap were dripping wet, but he had a funny little grin on his face.

91

"You find Mr. Jack, buddy?"

"No."

"Want to know why not? He ain't there."

"So I found out."

"He took a powder. Jumped into that convertible of his and beat it like he was shot out of a cannon. Which it's too bad he wasn't. Now I just wonder why he left so sudden-like, don't you?"

"Yes."

"While you were inside there I gave you a little figuring-out in my head. You're a policeman, aren't you?"

Frank was vaguely flattered. He had no idea that he looked in the least authoritative or official. "No, I'm not."

Charley seemed disappointed. "I was hoping maybe you'd come to pick up Evangeline and take her to a detention home. Evangeline. Say, how do you like *that* for the name of a slut. Evangeline." He spit on the sidewalk vigorously. "Wiggles her hips in and out that gate twenty times a day. Gotta go down to the drugstore for coffee, she says. Or gotta have her hair done. Or gotta go shopping. If Mrs. Goodfield knew what was going on, she'd have a stroke. She's real strict about things."

Frank wondered. From what Greer had told him about the old lady, he gathered that she wasn't quite as strict as she pretended.

"The girl's married," Frank said.

"Since when does being married keep a slut from slutting? Since never. To tell you confidential, I got a sneaking sympathy for Mr. Jack. He'll never be the same, mark my words. Well, I gotta go now. It's been nice talking to you." Charley held out his gnarled hand and Frank shook it. "Soon as you came up to the gate I said to myself, now that's a nice open face."

"Thank you."

"You come back again. Maybe by that time I'll have Sweetheart all fixed up pretty like she used to be."

"I may be back."

"You do that."

"Good-bye, Charley," Frank said.

He turned and headed for his car. Sweetheart witnessed his departure without interest.

12

THE NOON TRAFFIC was heavy, slowed by fog and lunch-hour pedestrians, and cable cars that moved up and down the impossibly steep and narrow streets with slow, staggering dignity like drunken duchesses.

Frank drove up Powell Street. With each hill the traffic lessened and the street changed. Cigar and candy shops gave way to hotels and nightclubs and finally apartment houses jammed so close together that they seemed to be one continuous building. There were no lawns, no flowers. Land was too scarce and expensive to use for anything but shelter. People stepped down directly from their vestibules or parlors to the sidewalk, and stepped back up again with no contact with the growing things that were buried under concrete.

What Charley had called the old Goodfield mansion was at the top of the last hill. It may have been a mansion once but now it was curiously dwarfed by the apartment houses that towered above it on each side. It still had its distinction, though—two patches of lawn like green scatter rugs, and, flanking the sidewalk and front steps, a hundred or more potted plants of all colors and all sizes. They lent an air of welcome to the forbidding Gothic door. There was no chime or bell at the door, only a little silver Buddha with jeweled eyes. Frank raised the Buddha's folded arms and let them fall again. They fell with a soft musical twinkle and the little jeweled eyes flashed as if in anger at this invasion of his privacy.

The heavy door opened inward two or three inches and a woman spoke through the crack: "Who is it, please?"

"Miss Goodfield?"

The woman laughed. In contrast to her voice, which sounded tired, her laugh was gay and full of genuine amusement. "Heavens, I almost said yes. That's what comes of returning to the old homestead."

"Sorry I don't know your married name. I'm Frank Clyde."

"I'm Shirley Gunnison, the Miss-Goodfield-that-was, as a maid of ours used to say." She mentioned the maid with intentional casualness as if to make it clear that she hadn't always had to answer the door herself. "If you're working your way through college, don't count on me to help."

"I worked my way through college some time ago."

"Selling subscriptions?"

"Diving for abalone."

There was a pause. Then, "Well, that's *different*, I must say. I don't want to buy any old abalones, however."

But she opened the door wider as if her curiosity, or her desire to talk to someone, had overriden her judgment.

She turned out to be a short stockily built woman in her late twenties. Though there were lines of strain and weariness around her eyes, she seemed essentially a cheerful and gregarious person. Her features were too large for prettiness, but her face and body had a vital quality. Even in the way she stood, with one arm resting on the doorjamb, there was a subtle air of victory, an inconclusive victory after a battle of guerrillas.

She said, "Since you're not selling anything and I'm not buying anything, won't you come in?"

"Thank you."

She stood aside to let him enter. As he passed her Frank was aware of her very careful scrutiny. It didn't fit in with the rather casual way she talked and her informal manners. He wondered whether she frequently invited strangers into her home, or whether he was an exception; if he was, why?

The hall was vast and cold. Its high, narrow windows didn't let in enough sun to dispel the dampness from the corners. It was more like a museum than a place where people lived. Horace's "valuables and antiques" lined the room; everything from a huge bronze statue of the goddess of plenty to tiny coins and medallions in glass cases, and silk prints in lacquered frames on the walls.

"Junk," Shirley said. "Most of it."

"I wouldn't know."

"I wouldn't either. But mother had an appraiser from Gump's up one day and he wasn't very enthusiastic. Come in here, won't you?"

She led him into a small library with a wood fire burning in the grate. There was nothing Chinese or Eastern in the room except a pair of backscratchers lying on a table, tiny ivory hands with sharp, carved fingernails on the ends of two long sticks.

Shirley picked them up with a disdainful glance and put them away in a drawer.

"I don't mind Chinese people but they certainly have some macabre ideas." She sat down on a low, leather hassock in front of the fire. "The children are at a movie today. It's lonesome around here. I've got to the point where I can't stand silence any more."

"Is that why you invited me in?"

"No. I had a reason, though."

"I'd like to know what it is."

Shirley reached in her pocket for a cigarette and lit it before she answered. "Jack phoned from the factory and said you'd probably come here looking for him. He told

me not to let you in and not to answer any questions. So—"
she moved her shoulders in an eloquent shrug—"naturally,
my curiosity was aroused."

"Naturally it would be."

"Are you going to ask me any questions?"

"Are you going to answer?"

"That depends," Shirley said. "I might answer some and
I might refuse to answer others. Jack said you were a detective. Are you?"

"No."

"He's got detectives on the brain. You're the third this
week."

"Why?"

"Why are you the third? I don't know. Maybe he has a
guilty conscience. Or maybe the other two were real."

"Did they come here?"

"No. Jack spotted them downtown and got away by min-
gling with the lunch crowd in the lobby of the St. Francis
and then walking out through the kitchen. That's his story.
I think he went out through the kitchen all right. But as
far as the two men are concerned, they were probably a
couple of convention delegates looking for the lavatory.
After all, why should detectives be following Jack? He
hasn't done anything—has he?"

"I wish I knew."

"Well, if he has, you can bet your bottom dollar he'll be
caught." Picking up the brass poker, she gave the log burning in the grate a vicious little prod. Sparks streamed up
the chimney.

"Your brother lives here?"

"Yes. On the second floor."

"Is he in?"

A slight hesitation. "I didn't hear him come in. He never
comes home at noon. Why?"

"I'm interested."

96

"Why should you be, if you're not a detective?"

"I met Willett Goodfield and his wife in La Mesa. I had to come north on business, so I thought I'd look up Jack and yourself while I was here."

"You mean you took such a profound liking to Willett and Ethel that you wanted to enlarge your circle of Goodfields?"

"Ah—in a way."

"Honestly." Shirley was laughing. "I never heard a sillier explanation."

"I can do better."

"I hope so."

"The fact is, that a woman called Rose French was found dead on your brother's property. You probably know about it."

"Yes. I read it in the paper, and also mother wrote to me about it, or at least dictated a letter to someone called Murphy. It was the first letter I'd had from her in months. Ethel is the one who usually writes."

"What was your mother's reaction?"

"She was thrilled to pieces. Contrary to Willett's opinion, mother thrives on excitement, especially if it brings disaster to someone like a loose woman. She was a loose woman, wasn't she?"

"Not in my opinion."

"Well anyway, mother was thrilled. It seemed to pep her up."

"I don't suppose you still have that letter."

"I don't suppose I'd let you read it if I had."

"I think you would."

Shirley laughed again. "I guess I would. But as a matter of fact, I never keep letters. I chuck them out right away, because I never have time to answer them and I hate them hanging around weighing on my conscience."

"Did you know Rose French?"

"I knew of her. Everyone did." A pause. "I think I'm beginning to see the light. You're trying to connect *us* with *her*."

"It would be an interesting connection."

"Would it?" she said shortly. "Not to me. I have no concern with a woman dropping dead four hundred miles away. I'm just glad that it wasn't mother. I am not," she added, "very fond of my mother, but I like the idea of her living to a ripe old age."

"Why?"

"She keeps Jack and Willett in line. If it weren't for mother, neither of them would go near the factory. Even as it is, things are getting pretty run down. You must have seen that."

"Yes, I did."

"I've thought of taking it over myself. I'm a pretty good business woman, I think. Maybe when the children are a little older, I will. If it's still there and if I care."

She gave her head a sudden, almost violent shake, as if she felt herself sinking into a dream of despondency and had to wake herself up before she sank too far. The existence of the factory, though it was essential to their own existence, seemed to irritate and depress the Goodfields, like a gifted child that had failed to live up to expectations.

Shirley poked at the fire again. Her cheeks had taken on the deep flush of suppressed aggression, and Frank knew now that his first estimate of her as an essentially cheerful person had been too hasty. She had in her all the force and drive that should have been allotted to her brothers. Physically she was a very feminine woman devoted to her children; morally she was the head of the Goodfield clan. It was Shirley who should have been running the factory, keeping Willett and Jack in line, and ordering the new paint job for Sweetheart. As Charley had pointed out, Shirley was the only one with a head on her shoulders.

The head was still here, all right, but Frank had the impression that it wasn't held as high as it used to be.

Shirley lit a second cigarette from the final half-inch of the first. "Well, have I answered all your questions, Mr. Clyde?"

"I have no complaint with your answers. Just the questions. Frankly, I didn't know, and don't know, what to ask."

"In other words, you had no specific object in coming here at all?"

"No."

"Afraid I don't believe that. However—" She rose from the hassock, taking a long, deep pull on her cigarette. It was clear to Frank that she was disturbed, but she covered her nervousness well, keeping her hands active to conceal their trembling, and smiling with her mouth to distract attention from her worried eyes. "You must excuse me now, Mr. Clyde. I don't very often have an afternoon free from the children. I think I'll use it to—better advantage."

She led Frank back through the long, damp hall to the front door. A dismal ending for such a promising beginning, Frank thought, certain that it was the mention of the factory that had changed Shirley's attitude. When the Goodfield children were young, the place must have seemed to them an enchanted toyland, and the great wooden doll, Sweetheart, a symbol of magic and a figurehead of grandeur and privilege. He wondered how often Sweetheart turned up in Shirley's dreams.

The door opened and a gauze curtain of mist blew delicately down the hall and disappeared.

Shirley rubbed her hands together, shivering. "Gloomy climate. It's a wonder anyone stays here. I guess they stay for the same reason as I do, they have to. It's all very well for Willett to travel around the country. But I have children, I can't take them away from their school and their friends. I must give them some kind of continuity in their

99

lives." She seemed to be talking not to Frank but to herself, arguing over a point that she had argued over many times before. "They need security. How can you give anyone security when you have none yourself? But you wouldn't know. You're loaded with the stuff, aren't you?"

The question was deliberately offensive. Frank walked out without answering.

This time it wasn't Sweetheart who watched him leave, it was the little silver Buddha on the front door. His jeweled eyes twinkled. He looked more interested in the departure than Sweetheart.

Shirley waited in the hall until she heard the sound of a car starting. Then she walked briskly down to the end of the hall and called up the wide, marble staircase. "Jack?" Her voice echoed faintly and somberly against the high walls. "Jack."

Jack appeared at the head of the stairs, white-faced and nervous. "Has he gone?"

"He's gone." She watched him with a kind of cynical detachment as he descended the stairs. He was wearing a hat and topcoat, and carrying a Gladstone bag in one hand and a large brief case in the other. "Why all the panic?"

"For God's sake, I told you, he's a detective. He was asking Charley all kinds of questions about me. What did *you* tell him?"

"Oh, I was very ingenuous. Or is it ingenious? Probably both. I pretended I wasn't on your side."

"Pretended. That's a laugh."

"My dear Jack, please stop fluttering like a nervous bride. Where do you think you're going?"

"Away. I can't stand being hounded like this."

"Who's hounding you?"

"Hiller. Evangeline's husband. He's hired detectives to get something on me."

"What a waste of time and money when all he'd really have to do is peek over the transom some time when you're giving dictation." Her smile was full of contempt. "If you must indulge in these sordid little affairs, you must expect to have sordid little men following you around."

He was too disturbed to take offense at her words and tone. "Evangeline says he's got a terrible temper. She says he may kill me."

"Well, if he does I'll do everything in my power to see that he pays the penalty."

"My God, will you quit making a joke of this? I've got to get out of town, I tell you."

"What's stopping you?"

Jack hesitated for a moment, looking down at the floor. "Well, frankly, old girl, I was counting on you for—"

"Well, frankly, old boy, you're not getting any because I haven't got any."

"You must have something."

Shirley laughed. "Must I?"

"What do you do with your money?"

"I feed and clothe my children, which is somewhat more commendable than your practice of feeding and clothing every blonde floozy who walks across your path."

"Evangeline happens to be a natural brunette."

"No doubt you've examined the roots of her hair. Revolting thought."

"Don't you talk like that about Evie. I love her. This is the first time I've ever been in love."

"First time since last Tuesday, anyway. Are you going to take the girl with you, wherever you go?"

"No. She says she can handle Hiller all right."

"I'll bet she can. He probably examines the roots of her hair too."

He was quiet a moment. Then he said, painfully, "You have a nasty tongue."

"It has quite a lot to be nasty about."

"I had no idea until recently that you had become such a—-shrew."

"Shrews are made, not born. Maybe you had a hand in the making, Jack."

"I hope not," he said in a sober voice. "I really hope not."

"As for money, much as I'd enjoy speeding your departure, I'm afraid I can't. Try mother. Or Willett. You and Willett have always been such pals, I'm sure he wouldn't let you down. Except into a nice, deep hole." She turned away, adding, over her shoulder, "I wrote Willett's number on the phone book under mother's name."

"Shirley. Wait."

"Why?"

"I guess I said some unpleasant things. I apologize. I'm sorry."

"Really?" She flashed him a steely smile. "The answer is still no. You're not getting any money from me because I haven't any."

"I didn't mean that."

"Don't be silly, Jack, I know what you meant. I've been on to you since I was three."

"Shirley, listen. Do you suppose—would it be possible to sell some of this museum-ware?"

"Mother would miss it when she comes back."

"If. If she comes back."

Shirley's face had turned a dusty pink. "She'll be back, she's got to be."

"Just don't bet on it, old girl."

"She's *got* to be back," Shirley said again, and stood directly in front of him with her chin out and her feet planted squarely as if daring him to knock her off balance.

Jack took a backward step, propping himself against the banister for support. Though he was two years older than Shirley he had always been a little afraid of her. Even when they were children, she had exercised a power over him which he resented but couldn't understand or explain.

"There's always one way of raising money," he said. "Isn't there?"

"Borrow from the bank."

"I have borrowed from the bank. Ad nauseam. It's reached the point where they lock the place up when they see me coming. No, the bank is out. I was thinking of something a little more drastic."

"Pandering for Evangeline?"

"Don't pretend you don't know what I mean, and don't pretend you don't care. If Willett won't lend me enough money to get to Mexico or perhaps Hawaii, I'll sell my stock in the factory."

"You'll sell that stock over three dead bodies, mine and Willett's and mother's."

"That's an interesting thought, but it's not very realistic. That stock happens to be mine, an outright gift from my unsainted mother."

"On condition that you keep it in the family."

"All right, I'll keep it in the family. Want to buy it, old girl?"

The only sign of her anger was the sudden and violent clenching of her fists. Her voice was steady. "You know I can't raise that much money."

"Perhaps Willett can."

"And if he can't?"

"I'll sell to someone else."

"Mother will kill you if you do that."

"Mother's not in a position to kill anyone."

"I am."

"You're a violent little thing, aren't you?" he said with a lightness he didn't feel.

"I can be, if I have to. You're not selling that stock, Jack."

"No?"

"No. The factory is ours, it always has been and it always will be."

"You're living in a dream."

"It's a good solid dream with an income attached."

"I don't see it that way."

"Then you're a fool. Where would you be without an income? What kind of a job could you hold? Sell your stock and you'll piddle the money away in a year. Evangeline will be wearing mink but you'll be wearing a barrel."

It was calculated to strike hard and it did. Jack was extremely particular about his clothes, and the image of himself clad in a barrel, even a well-tailored barrel, shook him to the very core. All sorts of ghastly pictures ran through his mind: escorting Evangeline to the Top of the Mark and being refused a table because of his costume; trying to board a cable car and being unable to squeeze inside; Evangeline, haughty in mink and diamonds, rejecting him openly in the Embassy Club; small boys and large dogs chasing him down the street, and medium-sized women jeering at him from windows and doorways.

"Well?" Shirley said.

"I—" He wiped the sweat off his forehead with a shaking hand. "I guess I'll phone Willett."

"Do that."

"Maybe if he can't lend me a few thousand to get away until things cool off, he'll let me stay with him in La Mesa for a while."

"Don't count on it."

"After all, blood's thicker than water."

My blood is, Shirley thought. She wasn't sure about Jack's or Willett's. She said, "Actually there's no hurry about your leaving, is there? If this man Clyde really is a detective, that may be exactly what he expects you to do. He's probably parked around the corner waiting for you to make the next move."

"My God. Then what'll I do?"

"Sit tight. He's human, he can't stay there all night. Wait until it gets dark, take your car over to the garage and leave it there, and then first thing in the morning slip out the back way, pick up your car and start moving."

"That sounds all right. In fact—"

"And above all, stay away from Evangeline. Don't even phone her."

"I won't. I mean, we've already said good-bye and all that. She understands, is what I mean."

"I bet."

Now that the decision had been made and the pictures of himself wearing a barrel had faded from his mind, Jack felt quite optimistic. On his way to the telephone in the library, he began to make plans. He would drive down to La Mesa early in the morning by the coast route which was slower but more scenic; lunch at Cambria Pines; and then, possibly around five or six in the afternoon, arrival in La Mesa and reunion, after six months' separation, with good old Willett. Willett would rush out to greet him and with lavish hospitality offer him a haven from the storm or enough cash to seek another haven. Good old Willett.

13

GOOD OLD WILLETT happened to be in the shower when the call came through. At first he tried to ignore Ethel's vigorous pounding on the bathroom door, but Ethel was so persistent that he finally decided it must be something urgent like the house being on fire. He turned off the water and reached hastily for the largest towel on the rack.

"Hurry up and get dry, Willett. Jack's on the phone."

"Jack? Jack who?"

"Your brother."

"Tell him I'm in the shower."

"It's *long distance*," Ethel said in the reverent tone she always applied to long-distance calls, as if they were in some way connected with God. Nobody ever called long distance when Ethel was a girl back in Wisconsin, unless it was a case of death, imminent or established. "I think someone died."

"What?"

"I said, do you know anyone who might have died?"

"Who died?"

"Well, that's just what *I* was asking *you,* dear. I wish you'd hurry up. I hope it wasn't Uncle Harry, he's such a sweet old thing. But then he *is* old, isn't he? Wasn't he?"

Willett stepped out of the bathroom wearing a terry cloth robe and a bilious expression. "Who wasn't old?"

"Uncle Harry, only *I* said he *was* old. You don't even listen to me any more."

"I happened to be drying my ears." Willett walked down the hall with ponderous dignity.

The upstairs phone was in Ethel's bedroom. It was pink to match the ruffled curtains and the skirt on the vanity.

Willett cleared his throat before he spoke. He didn't like talking on a telephone, especially a pink one, and more especially since he was morally certain that Murphy was listening in on the plain black one in the kitchen.

"Hello," Willett said, keeping his voice very soft in the hope that neither Jack nor Murphy would be able to hear him, and everybody would forget the whole thing.

"Hello, Willett, old boy. This is Jack. How are you, fellow?"

"I am well."

"Great. Great. How's mother?"

"She's holding her own."

"Fine. Shirley's right here beside me. She sends her best. She—I— The fact is, Willett, I'm thinking of taking a trip."

"They say Alaska is very nice at this time of year."

"I wasn't planning on Alaska. I was thinking of sauntering down in your direction."

"You mean *here?* You're coming *here?*"

"What's the matter, are you quarantined or something?"

Willett had a wild notion to say yes and then arrange for Murphy to catch chicken pox or, preferably, scarlet fever. "No, we're not quarantined, but—well, we're not settled yet. We're most unsettled."

A long pause, and then Shirley's voice, crisp and quite audible though she was talking to Jack and not into the telephone: "For heaven's sake tell him the truth and quit shilly-shallying like this."

"Jack," Willett said. "Are you there, Jack?"

"Yes."

"What's Shirley talking about?"

"The fact is, I've got to get out of town in a hurry and I'm oof."

"What?"

"Oof—don't you remember?"

Willett remembered. In the days when they were boys at school, Jack had been nicknamed Oof for out of funds, and Willett had been If.

"I thought," Jack went on, "that if I could pick up a couple of thousand from you, I'd go on down to Mexico City."

"Why?"

"I told you, I'm in a spot of trouble. Nothing serious yet, but it might develop if I don't leave town. I've got a couple of detectives on my trail. One's parked around the corner right now. Willett, for God's sake, I need—"

There were sounds of a slight scuffle over the wire and muffled talking. Then, finally, Shirley's voice:

"Willett? This is Shirley. I've sent Jack out of the room. I realize you don't take him very seriously and neither do

I. But this time we have to. He's threatened to sell his stock in the factory."

"He can't."

"He can, and if he gets desperate enough, he will. I thought if he went to La Mesa and saw mother, she'd straighten him out—about selling the stock, I mean."

"Mother's not well. She can't be bothered by things like that."

"She'll be bothered, all right," Shirley said grimly. "And it won't kill her either. I don't think she's quite as delicate as you imagine."

You know everything, Willett thought. *You always know everything.* He said aloud, "Don't send Jack here. Listen, Shirley, we're in a bit of a mess ourselves, about this woman being found dead."

"Why should you be?"

"I don't know, but there's a man in town trying to make trouble for us. He's one of her ex-husbands."

"How can he make trouble for you?"

"Scandal. You know mother can't stand any scandal."

"She adores scandal."

"Not this kind."

"What kind is it?"

"This fellow Dalloway is going around—well, he seems to think that I—we—"

"Hurry up and say it, Willett. This is long distance and I'm paying the bill."

"He seems to think that this woman was murdered—by—by one of us."

"Oh, you're imagining things, Willett."

"No, no, I'm not."

"Good heavens, all anyone has to do is look at you to realize you could never murder anyone."

Willett swallowed hard, twice. "I—that's nice of you to say so."

"I didn't particularly mean it to be *nice,*" Shirley said

brusquely. "Let's face the facts, Willett. Unless you lend Jack some money, he's going to sell his stock."

"All right, all right. I'll send him a check, only keep him away from here."

"Why? What's the matter?"

Willett didn't answer.

"Willett, I asked you what was the matter."

"He's a nuisance, I just don't want him around pestering me."

"By a strange coincidence, neither do I. Wait a minute. Here's Jack now, he just came in." A pause, and then Shirley speaking again in quite a different tone: "You can talk to Willett now if you like, Jack. He says he'd be *delighted* for you to drop in and pick up your money."

"Good old Willett," Jack said with feeling.

Willett hung up, propped his head in his hands and groaned. He stayed that way for a long time, unable to move or even to think clearly. He wished that he could go to sleep for a year, and wake up to find that all the people who annoyed him were dead, the Republicans were in office, and the Goodfield Doll Corporation had tripled its orders and built a new addition.

He was roused finally by the sound of voices floating up through the warm, still air from someplace in the back yard. He dragged himself over to the window seat and gazed down, expecting to see Ethel and Murphy chatting in the patio, making up a grocery list perhaps, or discussing men in general, and him, Willett, in particular. He was well aware that they discussed him frequently, and he often wished he had the nerve to eavesdrop.

There was no one in the patio. It was a windless day; the lily pool was as tranquil as a mirror and the pointed leaves of the oleander, which swayed with the slightest breeze, were still. Yet the glider, where Ethel usually sat with her knitting, was moving slightly. Willett parted the pink ruffled curtains to make sure he was right. Yes, it was certainly moving, as if someone had recently been sitting there or had brushed against it in passing.

The voices were barely audible now, no louder than the buzzing of insects and with the same persistent and threatening defiance.

He was on the point of calling Ethel, whose eyesight was better than his own, when his attention suddenly focused on the lath-house, a yard or so beyond the wall of the garage. The lath-house was in direct sunlight and in the spaces between the laths Willett could see two men standing facing each other. One of them was Ortega, the gardener. The other, half a head taller and looking even at that distance completely in command of the situation, was Dalloway.

14

WILLETT CROSSED the hall, hugging his bathrobe around him as if it was a protective coat of armor. The door of his mother's bedroom was closed and he stood there looking at it for a moment. It seemed to him not like a door but like a high, impenetrable wall which he could neither scale nor break down.

He said, at last, in a feeble voice, "Are you there?"

The answer was a grunt, which Willett rightfully construed as an invitation to enter.

She was sitting on the bed playing solitaire and listening to a ball game. But it was obvious that she was bored and in a bad mood. She gave Willett a sour glance and made no attempt to turn the radio down or off.

She talked above it. "I'm getting damn good and sick of these four walls."

"Yes, I know. I know, but—"

"Why can't I come downstairs?"

"You know why."

"Oh, you make me sick." She jerked her knees up and the table tray crashed on the floor and the cards scattered like confetti. "I can't go on like this, I'd be better off dead."

"Please don't—"

"I've got to see people and do things. You can't keep me shut up in here like a mummy in a case. I'm alive, I tell you, *alive*."

Willett looked grim. "Will you listen to me for a minute?"

"All I do is listen, listen, listen."

"Jack phoned. He's coming here tomorrow. And that's not all. Dalloway's out in the back yard right now. God knows what he's got up his sleeve."

"Dalloway again," she said thoughtfully. "What's he doing?"

"Talking to Ortega."

"It's Monday, Ortega's day off. What's he doing here anyway?"

"I don't know."

"Don't you think you'd better find out?"

"How can I?"

"Just go out there and ask him what the hell he's doing."

"I couldn't."

"You're a big boy now, Willett."

"I tell you I can't. I—it's against my principles, butting into other people's affairs."

"It isn't other people's," she shouted. "It's ours!"

"Even so."

"You have every right to go out there and boot Dalloway off the property. Now go and do it. Boot him off."

Willett looked down at his feet. They seemed singularly

ill-equipped for booting people off property, especially rather large men like Dalloway.

The old lady was pink with excitement. "This namby pamby manner of yours—it's no wonder Dalloway's suspicious. Get in there and fight. Show him who's boss. Fling your weight around a little."

"Do you think that's wise?"

"Listen, Willett, you can't ask for respect, you've got to demand it, with bare knuckles if necessary."

"You mean, *hit* him?"

"Naturally."

"Well, for heaven's sake, he might hit me back," Willett protested. "Besides, a gentleman doesn't go in for that sort of thing, fisticuffs and all that. I mean—"

"You mean you're scared of him."

"Well, what if I am? He's bigger than I am."

"He's only got one arm."

This fact, which Willett had forgotten, cheered him considerably.

The effect, however, didn't last. By the time he reached the bottom of the stairs, the lath-house loomed in his mind as formidable as a lion's den, and the stabbing pain in his back had set in again.

Standing beside the highboy in the hall, he thought the whole situation over carefully and decided that what it needed was a woman's touch.

He found Ethel in the kitchen stacking the luncheon dishes in the dishwasher. When no one was watching her, Ethel moved with speed and efficiency, but as soon as Willett entered the room she resumed her air of languor and her face took on its customary trancelike expression.

"I thought Murphy was supposed to do that," Willett said.

"She wanted to read the morning paper. She says she missed yesterday morning's because I used it to wrap the garbage. I did, too."

"What do we pay her for if she doesn't do anything?"

"She's very helpful about giving advice and suggestions and so on." Ethel closed the lid of the dishwasher and turned on the hot-water tap. She wondered what was the matter with Willett, who was looking hot and fretful like an overfed baby, but she didn't ask. That was one thing about Willett—you never had to ask what was the matter with him, he always told you.

This time was no exception. He explained that Ortega and Dalloway were conspiring in the lath-house and something had to be done about it immediately.

"Why the lath-house," Ethel said.

"How should I know why the lath-house."

"It seems a funny place to conspire, doesn't it." She took a stick of gum from the pocket of her apron, unwrapped it and stuck it in her mouth. Chewing helped her powers of concentration, and they frequently needed help. "Does *she* know about it?"

There was no doubt who *she* was. Both Willett and Ethel always spoke of her with the same mixture of fear and appeasement.

Willett nodded. "I told her."

"What'd she say?"

"She said"—Willet cleared his throat to allow the lie easier passage—"she said you were to go out there and —well, sort of investigate. Know what I mean?"

"I haven't the slightest idea, and why me anyway?"

"She said you do that kind of thing so gracefully and all that."

Flattery was such a rare treat to Ethel that she ate it up raw like caviar. "Naturally I'll do what I can, though I must say I could probably do it better if I knew what it was I was supposed to do."

"Just be firm. Tell them they have no right conspiring in our lath-house. Get the idea?"

"Sort of."

Willett retreated before she could change her mind. When he had gone, Ethel glanced at herself in the mirror over the sink, smoothed her hair and mentally studied her lines: you have no right, Mr. Dalloway, to conspire in our lath-house, so kindly, no, better make it please, so please leave, or how about please vacate the premises. You have no right, Mr. Dalloway, to conspire—

Ethel was flinging herself into her role when the door opened and Murphy came in, dragging the morning newspaper limply behind her. The paper was no longer in very good condition since Murphy had a habit of clipping whatever news items interested her and pasting them in a scrapbook.

Ethel took one look at the mutilated paper. "Willett hasn't seen it. He'll be furious."

"I was merely trying, milady, to prevent a repetition of last night," Murphy said sternly. With her short, bristling, black hair and her small, upturned nose, she reminded Ethel of an aggressive terrier.

"I had to wrap the garbage in something, didn't I?"

"Since you yourself have brought the subject up, milady, I suggest you install a garbage disposal unit. The cost is minimal, say about two hundred dollars."

"I don't think it will sound very minimal to Willett."

"I hesitate to say this, milady, but Mr. Goodfield appears to be living in the past when domestics were treated like slaves. He has failed to develop a social and economic conscience."

Ethel sighed. It wasn't the only thing Willett had failed to develop.

After the interruption Ethel found it difficult to get back into her role, but she did her best. Walking out the back door and across the lawn, her mouth moved in rehearsal: Mr. Dalloway, what do you mean by lurking around our lath-house?

Whatever Mr. Dalloway meant, Ethel was not destined

to learn. The lath-house was empty except for flats of seedlings on the cement floor, and cuttings of pelargoniums and carnations rooting in pots on the long wooden table, and Ortega's gardening tools, sharpened and glistening with oil, neatly placed in a corner.

Her first thought was that the strain of the situation had affected Willett's mind and that he had imagined the whole thing. Then she noticed, beside the bamboo rake, the final inch of a cigar smoldering. She was quite sure that Ortega didn't smoke cigars, since she'd frequently seen him working in the yard with a cigarette hanging from the corner of his mouth.

She called out sharply, "Ortega!"

Almost instantly he appeared from around the corner of the garage. Ethel gave a little gasp of surprise at the abruptness of his appearance. She had not expected so quick a response, and what was even more disturbing was the fact that this was her first direct contact with him. Up to this point Ortega had been just a vague figure moving behind the power-mower or snipping endlessly at the eugenia hedge with a cigarette dangling from his mouth.

She realized now with an odd feeling of excitement which she couldn't or wouldn't identify, that Ortega was a good-looking young man. He was not wearing his ordinary working clothes; instead of levis he wore gray flannel slacks, and instead of a T-shirt a gaudy Hawaiian-print blouse of blue and red. Pointed brown oxfords polished like brass took the place of his heavy work boots.

"You want something, ma'am?" He approached her slowly, his dark bold eyes studying her with an expression of alert suspicion.

"I—yes, I thought I saw Mr. Dalloway out here."

"He was here. He left."

"What did he want?"

"Golly, I don't know," Ortega said with a sudden, ingenuous grin. "He asked questions but I told him I didn't know nothing—anything."

"Questions about what?"

"He wanted to know most how come the dead lady wasn't found before I found her. He wanted to know, didn't you people ever use the patio and wasn't there milk delivered to the back door and didn't you have to pass the lily pond to get to the garage, lots of questions."

"He's very nosy."

"Yes ma'am."

"Did he offer you money?"

"Oh golly, no." Ortega shook his head in vigorous denial.

Ethel was not convinced. She was, in her way, a rather shrewd judge of character, and the first time she'd seen Dalloway at Rose's funeral, she had taken him for a man who was accustomed to buying his way into and out of places and people. She did not despise the type, she merely liked to label it accurately as she labeled the food packages she stored in the deep freeze, and the jams and jellies in the fruit cellar: quince, raspberry, Dalloway, and, on the bottom shelf in the darkest corner, Willett. Unlike Dalloway, Willett would never buy things; he waited until they were bought for him and then complained about the price.

Thinking of Willett had its customary effect on Ethel. She said, quite crossly, "You're not supposed to be working here today, are you?"

"I'm not working."

"What are you doing then?"

Ortega reached down and brushed a speck of dust off his right shoe before he replied. "I'm waiting for someone. If it's all right with you, ma'am."

"There are thousands of other places to wait, surely."

"Yes, ma'am." His tone was docile enough but his jaw

was set and his eyes looked resentful. "Only this is where I'm *supposed* to wait."

"Supposed to?"

"I have a date."

"My goodness, I hate to be unreasonable but our garden seems to be used by everybody but us and for the oddest things. I don't—" Ethel stopped abruptly in the middle of the sentence. "Did you say a *date?*"

"Yes, ma'am."

"Who with?"

Ortega examined the tips of his shoes again. "She said not to tell. She said Mr. Goodfield is full of prejudice."

There was no doubt now who Ortega's date was. "My God," Ethel said with feeling. "You mean Murphy."

"Yes, ma'am."

It was incredible—Murphy with her flighty airs and crisp contemptuous tongue, dating a part-time gardener several years her junior. It couldn't be true and yet Ethel knew that it was, and after the initial shock she realized that the affair was not so unreasonable or strange as she'd thought. To Ortega, Murphy must represent class, the kind of educated and genteel-acting woman he had never dared aspire to; and Murphy, with her peculiar egocentricity, would respond to any man who appreciated her half as much as she appreciated herself.

Yes, it was easy enough to imagine Murphy's attraction to Ortega and her deliberate flaunting of the conventions by meeting him publicly. Murphy did as she pleased, outside as well as inside the house.

"I didn't mean to tell," Ortega said with an uneasy glance toward the house. "She'll be mad. She's got a temper, by golly."

This was news to Ethel who couldn't believe that Murphy would let anyone or anything disturb her to the point of losing her temper.

"Really," Ethel said quite coldly. "Well, that's your problem. My problem is to get a little peace and quiet around here. I suggest that in the future you and Murphy meet somewhere else."

Ortega shrugged. "That suits me, ma'am. Only Ada said for me to wait here for her today, so I'll just wait here if it's all the same to you."

It wasn't all the same to Ethel but it seemed both undignified and futile to argue about it. Murphy had given Ortega his orders, and like a good soldier Ortega intended to obey them, stand or fall.

Ethel returned to the house vaguely disturbed by the encounter and wishing she had someone to confide in. If she told Willett, his reaction would undoubtedly be to fire Murphy, and Ethel had a number of reasons for not wanting this to happen. For one thing Ethel often felt so confused and amorphous inside that she had come to depend on Murphy's hard-boiled detachment. For another, Murphy served both as an ally against Willett and as a buffer against the old lady, taking quite a few of the slings and arrows that would otherwise have been aimed at Ethel herself.

Ethel spent most of the afternoon in Mrs. Goodfield's bedroom playing gin rummy. It was nearly six o'clock when she went down to the kitchen to start preparing supper, feeling rather relieved that Murphy was absent and the meal could be quite simple.

The heat of the sun had begun to decrease and a hint of mist in the air had turned the mountains to violet. Ethel loved to watch the mountains. They changed from hour to hour. In the morning they were gray, and at noon they were green with streaks of brown, and now, just before evening, they seemed to be shrouded in layers of violet-colored chiffon.

Her glance fell on the lath-house. It stood empty, abandoned by the sun and the trysting lovers. But from some place directly behind it, a thin column of smoke twisted skyward like the magic rope of an Indian conjuror.

Ethel's first notion was that Murphy and Ortega were still there, and that Willett, with his perverse talent for doing the wrong thing, might go out into the garden and find them. With a sigh that was half-anger and half-envy, Ethel put down the skillet she had just taken out of the cupboard, and for the second time that afternoon headed in the direction of the lath-house to give Murphy warning.

This time she had no lines prepared. No lines were necessary. Ortega was lying on his back on the grass behind the lath-house, spread-eagled, eyes closed, mouth half-open. Cigarette-butts were strewn all around him, one of them still smoldering.

For one terrible moment Ethel thought he was dead, and her legs felt so weak that she staggered and almost fell on top of him. Regaining her balance, she looked at him more closely and saw the gentle rise and fall of his chest under the gaudy red and blue shirt.

Her voice was high and uncertain. "Ortega? Are you asleep?"

Ortega stirred and smiled slightly.

"You'd better wake up? You'd just better?"

With a sudden unexpected movement Ortega's arm reached out and his left hand grabbed her ankle, and held it, not tightly or cruelly, but in a soft caress. She meant to scream but she felt suffocated, as if Ortega's hand was around her throat instead of her ankle. She had no breath, no strength, no will.

"No," she whispered. "Stop. Help. Please."

Ortega murmured something that she couldn't understand.

"What? What did you say?"

She leaned over so that she could hear him better, and then she saw that he was still asleep. His embrace, his words, were not for her.

"Get up," she said harshly. "Get up, you."

She kicked free of his hand, the toe of her shoe cracking against his wrist bone. Ortega flung himself over on his side with a cry of pain. Groggily, still dazed from sleep, he got up, first to his knees and then to his feet. His flannel slacks were wrinkled, and stained with grass. Around his eyes there were dirt marks like the marks on the face of a child who had wiped away tears with a grubby hand.

He looked first, not at Ethel, but at the sun that was slowly falling toward the sea.

"She never came," he said. "Ada never came."

By nine o'clock that night, when Frank arrived home from San Francisco, at least twenty people knew that Ada Murphy had disappeared.

15

BY NINE-THIRTY Greer himself was on the job, tired, irritable, and inclined to dismiss the whole episode. He would have dismissed it, at least for the night, if it hadn't been for Ortega's insistence.

The fluorescent lights in Greer's office seemed to have dissolved Ortega's tan and made his face look chalky.

"She never came," he said. "Last night when I took her home, she told me to meet her at one-thirty this afternoon in the garden. We were going to go down to the harbor and rent a boat. She's crazy about boats, always wanted to walk along the wharf or out to the end of the breakwater."

The words struck a chord in Greer's mind, and it took him only a moment to put the chord in its place. Rose French had walked along the breakwater several days before her death, according to Mrs. Cushman's report. Many other people walked there too, but in Rose's case it was unusual because she professed to hate the sea, and she certainly hated exercise. Mrs. Cushman's assumption was logical and Greer agreed with her: that Rose had gone to the breakwater not to admire the wonders of nature or walk off a pound or two, but to meet someone.

Greer looked at Ortega with renewed interest. It was quite possible that Dalloway and Frank had been on the wrong track, and that the connection Rose had with the Goodfield family was not with the Goodfields themselves but with Murphy. He said, "Did you ever accompany Murphy to the breakwater?"

"Yes sir, three times."

"Did she meet anyone down there?"

"No sir. Ada's a stranger in town. She didn't know anyone except the Goodfields and me."

"Where did she come from?"

"Los Angeles. She had very good references. She showed them to me one day."

"Do you remember any of the names of her employers?"

"No sir. I just looked at the references to please Ada."

"You and Murphy were going around together—that right?"

"We're going to be married when—when she comes back."

"You're just a boy, aren't you?"

"I'm nineteen," Ortega said stubbornly. "Ada is—she's a little bit older."

Ada, Greer knew, was a hell of a lot older. Aloud he said, "Look, young fellow, I'm no specialist in these affairs but I know Ada Murphy. She's no ordinary servant. She's pretty sharp, she's been to college and probably quite a few other places where they don't give degrees. You're fighting out of your class."

"I've been hearing talk like that all my life. It never changed my mind."

"Has it occurred to you that Murphy couldn't face giving you the brushoff in person, so she just lit out to avoid trouble?"

"Ada would never do that."

"You can't tell. She might have got fed up suddenly with her job or you or life in general and decided to take a bus down to L.A."

"She didn't take a bus," Ortega said with quiet intensity. "All her clothes are still in her room."

It was true. The small closet in Murphy's bedroom—which was at the rear of the house behind the kitchen—was crammed with dresses and uniforms and odds and ends of underwear. In contrast to Murphy's neat appearance, her private habits were slovenly. She seemed to have used the closet as a catchall; anything she'd wanted out of sight, she'd tossed into the closet. Once the door was opened, it couldn't be closed again.

The room was furnished, not with leftovers from other rooms like many domestics' quarters, but with matched maple furniture and chintz drapes that duplicated the design on the bedspread, and a small cherry-red loveseat.

On the loveseat, looking very pale against the brilliant red, sat Ethel. There was no doubt that she was extremely disturbed. She'd discarded her graceful floating movements and vague airs as a snake discards its old skin. Peeled down to her essentials, Ethel presented a different picture to Greer. She wasn't either feeble-minded, as he'd thought at first, or sluggish.

She addressed Greer in a voice sharpened by anxiety. "Well? What do you make of it?"

"I don't know." He indicated the bulging closet with a jab of his thumb. "I don't see how you can be sure nothing is missing, with that mess."

"Because Willett's mother saw her leave. She'd gotten up to go to the bathroom and happened to glance out the window. Murphy was just going down the front walk. She had no suitcase or anything, not even a coat. She just—just *walked away*."

"What was she wearing?"

"One of her ordinary cotton dresses, a turquoise-colored chambray."

"Had there been any disagreement between Murphy and you, or Murphy and Mr. Goodfield?"

"No, not really. Murphy had mentioned something to me about having a garbage disposal unit installed, and I told her I didn't think Willett would agree to it since it isn't our house, after all. She certainly wasn't angry, if that's what you mean. Ortega says she has a temper, but I've never seen any evidence of it. Even when Willett's mother spoke roughly to her, she just smiled in that superior way of hers, as if nothing that anybody else said or did made the slightest impression on her."

"Murphy's the kind of woman who can look after herself," Greer said. "Isn't she?"

"She seems to be. She acts that way. But now—I'm not sure. No one can be sure. *You're* not," she added, "or you wouldn't be here."

Greer made no attempt to deny it. He was not at all sure what kind of woman Murphy was, and even less sure that he'd ever find out. Which was Murphy, the crisp and controlled young woman in the immaculate black and white uniform, or the undisciplined child who tossed her belongings helter-skelter into a closet and closed the door;

the ingenuous and romantic lover who planned trysts in the garden, or the hard-headed realist who had explained to Greer at their first meeting that she'd become a domestic because the job gave her an opportunity to marry the boss?

And now there was still another Murphy, a young woman in a turquoise cotton dress who had walked away and not come back.

Greer's gaze fell on Ethel, who was folded up on the loveseat taking quick, nervous bites at her right thumbnail.

"Everything possible is being done," he assured her. "I have men checking the depots, hospitals, cab stands and so on. My own feeling is that Murphy will turn up some time tonight, wondering what all the fuss is about."

"That's what Willett thinks too. I don't. I think," she added slowly, "that instead of checking bus depots and cab stands, you'd better check Mr. Dalloway."

"Why?"

"Whenever he's around things seem to happen, don't they? Dalloway comes to town and his first wife is mur— dies. Dalloway comes creeping around our yard and my maid disappears." Ethel's voice was rising like a siren. "Maybe she's dead too. Maybe while you're standing there thinking what a charming fellow Dalloway is, he's out somewhere slitting her throat! And you, *you* just *stand* there!"

"Calm down, Mrs. Goodfield. I don't believe Murphy's having her throat slit, certainly not by Dalloway. I happen to know where Dalloway is, right at the moment."

Ethel glared at him, mute and obstinate, as if nothing in the world would convince her that Dalloway was not in some dark alley or grove of trees finishing Murphy off.

"He's over at Frank Clyde's house," Greer continued. "He phoned me before he left."

"Really? Does every Tom, Dick and Harry in town keep you informed where he's going and why and when?"

"Dalloway didn't have to tell me why. I already knew. He hired Clyde to go to San Francisco and check up on the Goodfield family."

"Why, that old goat. The nerve of that old—"

"I told you just so you'd know that Dalloway is as suspicious of you as you are of him."

"We didn't *hire* anybody to check up on him."

"You don't have to. I'm doing it."

"You? Why?"

"Oh, let's just say that suspicion is contagious and I've been exposed." Ethel looked a little mollified, and Greer thought it was a good time to change the subject before she asked any more questions. "Tell me, how did you happen to hire Ada Murphy?"

"Through a want ad in the local paper."

"Her ad?"

"Yes."

"Did you go to her hotel, or wherever she was staying, to interview her?"

"No, she came here. She'd given a phone number in the ad. I called her and she wasn't in. But later she called back and I was—well, impressed by her voice, and her references."

"When she came to see you, did she bring the references along?"

"Yes."

"How many were there?"

"Three."

"Did you keep them or give them back to her?"

Ethel frowned. "Now let me think. We were talking in the dining room—oh yes, I remember. I laid them on the table, and later when I was straightening up a bit, I put them away in the desk drawer, intending to give them back to her when she returned with her luggage. I'm afraid I forgot to, so I guess they're still in the drawer."

"I'd like to take a look at them."

"Why?"

"Oh, curiosity," Greer said lightly.

The references were in three envelopes, two of them large, white, business envelopes, unsealed, and the third a small, square, blue one with a darker blue monogram on the back. The third envelope bore a canceled three-cent stamp and an address: Miss Ada Murphy, c/o The Pines Motel, 343 Lasalle Street, Los Angeles.

The words on the matching blue notepaper inside were written in purple ink in a script so tiny and delicate it was almost illegible:

"Miss Ada Murphy was in my employ as a personal maid for two weeks and is thoroughly efficient and trustful in all respects and I certainly recommend her highly. She is of an even disposition.

Yours very truly,
Luellen di Santi
(Mrs. E. Charles di Santi)
3516 Lakeridge Terrace
North Hollywood."

The other two notes were typewritten:

"To whom it may concern:

The bearer of this letter, Ada Murphy, is a young woman of fine character and excellent reputation. During her period of employment here, she exhibited close attention to her duties and always conducted herself on the highest possible level. Loyalty and integrity are her most outstanding characteristics. I recommend her especially as a nurse and companion to elderly people."

126

It was signed, in a heavy masculine hand, Richard Rob
ertson, III.

The final note was even more glowing.

"Dear Sir or Madame:

My former employee, Miss Ada Murphy, has requested
a recommendation. Nothing gives me greater pleasure than
to comply with this request, inasmuch as Miss Murphy
proved herself an ideal servant in every way, industrious,
courteous and responsible. She was particularly helpful in
assisting with the care of my aged mother who is an invalid
and not easy to please. Miss Murphy showed both patience
and skill in dealing with her. She is a young woman who can
be trusted to cope with any situation in a highly competent
manner.

Harrison L. Macomber."

Mr. Macomber's signature bore a striking resemblance
to Mr. Robertson's. So did his literary style, his inexpert
typing, his choice of notepaper, and his unqualified approval of Murphy.

Greer returned Mrs. di Santi's letter to its envelope. It
was as obviously genuine as the other two were phony.

He looked at Ethel, who was watching him uncertainly,
still biting at her thumbnail. "Did you check these two
references, Mrs. Goodfield?"

"Why—why, no. I mean, they were so good I didn't
bother."

"They should be good. She wrote them herself."

"Oh dear," Ethel said, and again, "Oh *dear*. I hope Willett doesn't find out."

"What's more, I believe they were written especially
for you. Notice that both the letters praise her skill and
patience with elderly invalids, like your mother-in-law.
Tell me, in the advertisement she put in the paper, did
she mention this so-called skill of hers?"

"Yes, but how could Murphy be sure that *I* was going to answer that ad?"

"If I knew how," Greer said, "I might know where she is now, why she went away and if she's coming back."

One of Ethel's hands worked nervously at the arm of the loveseat, plucking out bits of nap from the rough red wool. For a moment she had an almost uncontrollable impulse to tell Greer everything, about herself and Willett and the old lady and the silly doll factory that she wished she'd never heard of.

Then she raised her head and met Greer's eyes. They weren't friendly at all. They were small, accusing eyes without sympathy or tolerance. He wouldn't understand, she thought; he considers me a fool.

The impulse to reveal herself passed like a storm cloud in summer, bringing no rain or relief from the heat. She wished she had enough courage to walk out of the front door, like Murphy, and never come back.

She said, quietly, "Do you think Murphy is alive?"

"I have no reason for presuming that she's dead," Greer replied.

But when he departed a few minutes later, a cold, wet wind swept around the corner of the house and struck him like an unacknowledged fear. Shivering, he pulled up the collar of his coat and wondered where Murphy was, clad for a summer afternoon in her thin cotton dress.

It was ten o'clock.

In Mrs. Goodfield's bedroom the night light was on, its green glow making the whole room look as if it was underwater—the pillows on the bed were stones, and the old lady half-hidden among them, a sea-creature at rest.

But her rest was uneasy. Hearing the opening and closing of the front door, she got out of bed and moved noiselessly across the room in her bare feet.

I feel weak, she thought. *They've kept me in bed too*

long. I must get out and walk around more. My legs are like matchsticks; they used to be quite pretty.

She lifted one of the slats of the Venetian blind and saw Greer crossing the driveway toward his car. The window was open and she wanted to call out to him, invite him up for a chat, to alleviate her loneliness and anxiety. But his car had already rolled down the driveway before the words formed in her throat.

Murphy was gone, and now Greer was gone. She was quite alone.

She put her hand on her heart to stop its wild pounding. *"I've got to go away for awhile,"* Murphy had said. *"You behave yourself like a good girl and I'll be back."*

That was the way Murphy talked to her when they were alone together, in a half-derisive, half-affectionate way which the old lady enjoyed. In front of Willett and Ethel, Murphy was always very respectful, though she frequently winked behind Willett's back, or made a face, or rolled her eyes heavenward.

"I've got to go away for awhile."

That had been at half-past one. Five minutes later she had walked down the driveway, looking very trim and brisk and impatient.

Breathing heavily, the old lady closed the window and locked it. Then, after a minute's hesitation, she went to the door and locked that too.

"Lock your door and windows," Murphy had said.

The locks were flimsy, but they worked. She returned to bed and lay for a long time on her right side watching the second-hand of the clock on the bureau. Its movement seemed to hypnotize her and she fell into a half-doze.

She wasn't sure what awakened her—a troubled dream, the cry of a mockingbird, the flapping of awnings in the wind—but quite suddenly she was fully awake again.

Someone was outside her door. The knob turned, twice, three times.

"Are you there?" Willett said. "Are you sleeping?" A pause. "She's got her door locked, Ethel."

"Then we'll just have to wait. She's not going to run away."

"I don't trust her when she's in one of her moods."

"This is a fine time to think of that."

"You don't suppose—?"

"I'm too tired to suppose anything. I'm going to bed."

Behind the door the old woman stared grimly at the clock wishing that morning and Murphy would arrive.

Morning came, but not Murphy.

16

GREER GOT UP EARLY, made his own breakfast, kissed his wife good-bye, and drove downtown to the white stucco building that housed the local newspaper. In the dusty file room at the rear of the editorial offices he found what he was looking for. The newspaper was dated exactly three weeks before, and Murphy's ad was the first one listed under Situations Wanted, Female:

"Refined, efficient, young woman, well-traveled and educated, wishes domestic service with adult family, preferably as companion to elderly, bedridden lady. Excellent references. Telephone Miss Murphy, 7475."

Greer wrote the number in his notebook and left the building by the rear exit to avoid meeting anyone he knew. He took a lot of kidding from the staff about wanting his picture in the paper, and he had become a little sensitive about it.

At his office he checked the telephone number Murphy had given. 7475 had a multiple listing: the Deluxe Paper

Company, no address, Acorn Products, no address, Marshall Whitney, no address, Factory Sample Shoes, no address, and Personal Services, 103 East Puenta Street.

He picked up the phone on his desk and dialed 7475.

A woman answered on the second ring, in a clear, youthful voice with a professional lilt to it: "This is 7475."

"Is Mr. Whitney in?"

"He's out of town. I expect him back tonight. Will you leave a message?"

"No thanks. How about the Deluxe Paper Company?"

"What do you mean, how about it?"

"Acorn Products—I'm interested in raising acorns."

"Listen, funny man, this is a business office and I don't go for bum jokes so early in the morning."

"It's no joke. I'm trying to contact a Miss Ada Murphy who gave this number as her own."

"I never heard of her," the girl said sharply. "And even if I had, why should I tell you?"

"This is Captain Greer of the Police Department."

"Isn't that just dandy. This is Ingrid Bergman. It's been nice knowing you."

She broke the connection so violently that Greer's ears throbbed. He felt a little angry, not at the girl, but at himself for setting the wrong tone for the conversation.

Puenta Street had been named for the small bridge spanning a creek that had been dry for twenty years. 103 was a two-storied frame house. A line of wet clothes in the rear yard indicated that it was still being used as a house, but the front part had been remodeled and converted into a small office with brick, plate glass and a sign in neon script, Personal Services.

The entire office was visible through the window: on the left side a switchboard, on the right an imposing oak desk. Between the two, facing the switchboard and wearing a pair of earphones, was a young woman with pumpkin-colored hair. She was talking into the receiver and simultaneously writing in pencil on a large yellow sheet of paper. Her face had the rapt expression of someone who is doing several things at once.

When Greer entered she raised her hand by way of greeting and went on talking: "Sorry, Mr. Siebold, I won't have that done until tomorrow. My assistant is home with a cold. Tomorrow at ten, four carbons. Good-bye."

"Miss Bergman?" Greer said.

The girl colored. "Raffin. Irene Raffin."

"I'm Captain Greer."

"I know that now. I checked with Frank Clyde."

"Why Frank?"

"Well, he knows all the nuts in town and I thought that's who it was, some nut impersonating a police captain."

"What did Frank say?"

"He said it was probably you in person all right, because you were trying to find Ada Murphy."

"Frank seems to know more about other people's business than they do themselves."

"That *is* his business," Miss Raffin said with a shrug. "Mine too, in a way."

"I'd like to know more about yours, Miss Raffin."

"Ask me anything. No, hold it a sec. Here comes Frank now."

Greer glanced out of the window and saw Frank crossing the street, squinting in the early morning sun. "Quite a coincidence."

"Oh, it's not a coincidence, I asked him to come. Just to pick up his typing, of course."

"Of course."

"I mean it. I do a lot of typing for the clinic when they're rushed."

"Does Frank usually pick it up at eight o'clock in the morning?"

"He picks it up any time it's ready," Miss Raffin said with a serene smile. "Absolutely any old time."

"I see."

Frank came into the office and the two men shook hands while Miss Raffin watched them, still looking very amused.

"It's a small world," Greer said. "And Miss Raffin seems determined to make it smaller."

Frank nodded, quite seriously. "If you don't want me to stick around, say so and I'll pick up my typing and leave."

"I'm getting a little tired of that typing gimmick. Let's drop it."

"It's not a gim—"

"Drop it."

"All right."

"Miss Raffin," Greer said, "was about to explain her business to me. She appears to be a very versatile young woman. She is the Deluxe Paper Company, Factory Sample Shoes, Acorn Products, Marshall Whitney—have I left anything out, Miss Raffin?"

"Oh my, yes," the girl said briskly. "I'm also Miss Ada Murphy."

"That deserves an explanation."

"You'll get one. First let me tell you that my business is exactly what it claims to be, personal services of all kinds. If you want a baby-sitter, a pair of antique candlesticks, half a beef—or if you're going on a holiday and want your hibiscus watered while you're away, I'll contact someone who'll do it."

"That doesn't explain Ada Murphy."

"It will. I also run a telephone service. Take Acorn Products as an example. They're a firm who handle all kinds of screwy health foods. They have an office down

133

in San Diego, but they can't afford to keep one here, there isn't enough business. There's a little business, however, and that's where I come in. I'm their La Mesa contact. Same with Mr. Whitney, who's an author's agent, and the Deluxe Paper Company and all the rest."

"Including Miss Murphy?"

"Well, she's a little different. When you called I couldn't place her in my mind, but after I talked to Frank I looked up my files. She came in here three weeks ago yesterday. In my kind of business it's awfully easy to get mixed up in shady deals unless you're careful. I'm careful. At least I thought I was. If this Murphy affair turns out bad—"

"Just tell me what happened."

"Well, all right. Like I said, it was three weeks ago yesterday. When she came in, I couldn't figure her at first. She didn't act hesitant or nervous or anxious to please the way most girls do when they're looking for a job. She was very sure of herself, talked pretty fancy using a lot of four-bit words. To impress me, I guess. I'm not easily impressed," Miss Raffin added dryly. "She struck me as a sharp operator. Is she?"

"I'm beginning to think so."

"Confidence racket?"

"Maybe."

"I hope to heaven I'm not going to be dragged into anything that smells. After all, her story was plausible enough: she lived out of town, she was putting a want ad in the paper and she needed a local phone number to use since a lot of people won't go to the trouble of writing to a box number or calling long distance. That sounds plausible to you too, doesn't it?"

"Sure. I don't think it was the truth, though."

"Well, I couldn't be expected to know that," the girl said sharply. "I haven't got X-ray eyes for reading minds. To me it sounded like the truth. Naturally I asked her what kind of ad it was, since my charge would depend on the number of calls she got and the trouble I went to. She showed me a tentative copy that she'd written in pencil. I was surprised. She didn't look like the type for a domestic job. She was far too—well, superior is the word. I couldn't imagine any woman having enough courage to give her orders, if you know what I mean."

"I know very well," Greer said, thinking of his own introduction to Murphy.

"I run a small employment bureau here too, so I asked her if she'd been trained for any other kind of work. She said certainly she had, but this happened to be what she wanted. So that was that. I charged her two bucks for the use of my services."

"What instructions did she give you?"

"I was to make a record of all replies to her ad and call her if any of them were especially good."

"Call her where?"

"I don't know where, but she gave me a phone number. I have it written down somewhere—yes, here it is—22881, ask for Rose."

Frank made a little movement of surprise. But for Greer it was the confirmation of his own theory that the connection between Rose and the Goodfields was through Murphy.

He said, "Did you call 22881 and ask for Rose?"

"Certainly. I gave her the names and addresses of three people who'd phoned about the ad and she said she'd relay them to Miss Murphy. That's about all I can tell you."

"That's enough." He looked at Frank. "Are you beginning to get a different picture of your old pal Rose?"

"No."

"Well, I am. This smells to me like a con game that backfired."

"Rose would never have had any part in a con game. She didn't care about money."

"A lot of people don't care about money until they're broke. Rose was good and broke."

Miss Raffin was busy at the switchboard again, talking in clear emphatic syllables as if she thought all people who used a telephone were deaf or senile. She wheeled around suddenly in the swivel chair and said to Greer, "There's a call for you, Captain. Are you in or out?"

"In."

"You can take it at the desk."

Greer picked up the desk phone. "Greer speaking."

"Jim, this is Daley. I've got some dame on the wire. She insists on talking to you, says it's very important. Shall I put her on?"

"All right."

"O.K. Miss, you can go ahead now."

Greer waited a moment and then repeated, "Greer speaking."

A woman spoke in a hurried breathless way. "I hate to call you so early, Captain, but I thought I'd better tell you before you went to any more trouble."

"Who is this, please?"

"Heavens, that shows how rattled I am, doesn't it. I'm Mrs. Goodfield. Ethel Goodfield." She stumbled over her own name. "You needn't bother looking for Murphy any more. She's home."

"Oh?"

"Yes, she came home late last night. The silly girl never dreamed we'd be worried. You know how girls are."

"I know how some of them are."

"She was just out on a little fling, one of those impulsive little flings."

"I see."

"So—well, I just thought I'd tell you that everything's all right, everything's fine, and you needn't go on looking for her."

"Is she right there?"

"What do you mean, *right* here?"

"In the room with you. I'd like to talk to her."

"Oh no, she's not right here. She's—s-sleeping. In her own room. She's all tired out from her—her little fling."

"I'd like to hear more about this little fling."

"I don't know any more." Ethel's voice was so shrill that both Frank and Miss Raffin could hear every word she spoke as plainly as they could hear Greer's laconic comments.

"She came back last night, eh?"

"Yes. It was very late. Otherwise I'd have let you know before. But anyway, well, everything's just fine now, and I certainly must apologize for all the trouble Murphy's caused you."

"No trouble at all," Greer said with ironic politeness. "I'm just glad to hear she's back. I'd like to talk to her sometime."

"Where?"

"Does it matter where?"

"I only meant it seems silly for you to come all the way out here and go to all this trouble for an idiotic girl. Doesn't it?"

"Perhaps it does."

"Well, I'll let you go now. I know what a busy man you are. I'll—I'll give Murphy a good scolding for you. How would that be?"

"Oh, that would be fine."

"Good-bye now."

"Good-bye, Mrs. Goodfield." Greer replaced the phone and turned to Frank. "You heard?"

Frank nodded. "Yes."

"Murphy's back, everything's fine, and this is the best of all possible worlds. Quite a new twist. What do you make of it?"

"I thought Mrs. Goodfield sounded very nervous. Maybe you ought to go out and see her."

137

"Sure. Sure, maybe I ought to go and see *all* the nervous women in town. Maybe I ought to hold their—"

"It was merely a suggestion."

"Thanks."

"I have another," Frank said. "I'll go out and see Mrs. Goodfield."

"Why?"

"Oh, let's just say that nervous women are my specialty."

"Let's just say that you're the nosiest guy in town."

"All right, put it that way. I have your permission then?"

"Even in this town," Greer said, "you don't need a permit to go calling on a lady."

17

NIGHT HAD LEFT the garden wet, and now, in the early morning sun, every leaf and flower glistened and looked alive. But the house itself seemed dead; all the windows were closed and the blinds drawn tight. At the back door five full bottles of milk stood like pins waiting for a bowler. Beside the bottles a black rubber doormat spelled out Welcome in large red letters.

There was no response of any kind to Frank's knocking. He wiped the dirt off his shoes on the welcome mat and went around the side of the house to the white stucco garage. Looking through the window he could see that there was space for three cars. Only one space was occupied, by a maroon-colored Buick convertible with gaudy maroon and yellow-striped seat covers. Not the kind of car Willett would drive, though he might 'ike to.

"You looking for someone?"

Frank turned around, slowly, to conceal his surprise. He had heard no one, expected no one. The man seemed to have grown out of the shrubbery as silently as a leaf.

"I was looking for Mrs. Goodfield."

"She's not here," Ortega said.

"I remember you from the inquest. You're Ortega."

"Yes."

"I'm Frank Clyde."

"I know. I saw you." Ortega sounded too weary to be interested. His eyes were bloodshot and swollen. A streak of mud zigzagged across one cheek and there was mud too on his levis and his heavy work boots.

"She's not here," he repeated. "When I came to work I saw the two of them drive off in the Lincoln, her and her husband."

"When?"

"Ten, maybe fifteen, minutes ago. They were in a hurry, didn't notice me." He cupped one hand over his eyes as a shield from the sun. "There's something bad going on, very bad. I don't know what."

"I don't know either."

"Last night there was a big quarrel, a hell of a quarrel. If it'd happened down on Mason Street where I live, the cops would of come busting in in five minutes. But out here, no. Rich people like the Goodfields can get away with murder. Maybe they did, too."

"What time were you around here last night?"

"After midnight."

"Why?"

"I thought Ada might've come home."

"And she didn't?"

"No, she didn't. I waited around the lath-house for three, four hours. Ada didn't come home."

"She might be there now."

"She isn't. That's her room over next to the kitchen. I

tapped on her window—we got a special signal. She didn't answer it."

Frank felt a queer uneasiness pricking at his nerves. *You needn't bother looking for Murphy any more,* Ethel had said.

Ortega stuck a cigarette in the corner of his mouth and lit it. The cigarette teetered nervously back and forth as he talked. "We got a special signal, she always answers. See that car in there, the Buick?"

"I saw it."

"This Buick drives up in the middle of the night, and a guy gets out carrying a suitcase and goes into the house. That's when the argument started."

"What was the argument about?"

"Money." Ortega smiled, very slightly. "What do rich people argue about? Money, same as poor people. This man in the Buick wanted money, and him and her, they didn't want to give it to him. The windows were open. I could hear every word."

"Who was the man?"

"They called him Jack. Mrs. Goodfield kept saying, 'My God, we got trouble enough.' And Jack kept telling her she didn't know what trouble was but she was going to find out real quick. I think the two men must have started to take a poke at each other because Mrs. Goodfield screamed."

"Which Mrs. Goodfield?"

"The young one. The old one, she never comes out of her room that I know of."

Ethel screaming, Willett and Jack taking a poke at each other—the picture didn't make sense to Frank. Ethel and Jack were, according to Greer, terrified of the old lady, and Willett was a model of the devoted son. That they should engage in a brawl while she was upstairs sleeping was incredible.

Ortega went on talking and the ash from his cigarette dribbled down on his shirt. He brushed it away with the back of his hand. "Someone must've caught on then that the windows were open and everybody wasn't deaf. Mr. Goodfield closed them and pulled the blinds just the way they are now."

"Was Jack in the Lincoln with them when they left this morning?"

"Not unless he was hiding in the back seat. All I could see was him and her. She was driving. She looked funny. Had her head forward and her eyes glued to the road like she was driving a racing car." He paused, scratching the back of his neck. "They don't use the car much. Most of the time they stay home, never go out at all that I know of. Ada said that some time they went out she'd show me the house, but they never did except to the inquest and the funeral. When they want something they have it delivered or they send Ada. I guess they're scared to leave the old lady for fear she'll have a bad spell."

"I guess."

"Well, I better get to work now; I get paid by the hour." But he still hesitated, pressing the grass down with the toe of his boot and watching it spring up again as if it was made of elastic. "I got to move a bougainvillaea. Moving shocks them, shocks them right to death sometimes. You have to give them vitamin B. But I guess you already knew that."

"No, I didn't."

"It's not important anyway. Ada says I got to better myself, read a lot and learn important things. The trouble is finding out what's important so you can go ahead and learn it."

"That's everybody's trouble."

"Not Ada's. She's smart."

Frank wondered how smart. Watching Ortega shuffle

wearily across the lawn, he had an idea that as far as the boy's welfare was concerned it would be better if Murphy's absence turned out to be permanent.

He went around the side of the house again toward the road where he'd left his car. The back door was still closed and the slats of the Venetian blind squeezed tight, but there were only four bottles of milk lined up on the porch. Where the fifth had been, a small circle of water sparkled in the sun.

Frank walked slowly past the porch, reached the grilled gate that led to the road, turned around and came back. Officially he had no status; and unofficially it was none of his business that there was someone inside the house who wanted breakfast but who didn't want to answer the door or to be seen. There was a possibility that old Mrs. Goodfield was not quite as bedridden as she professed to be, or that Murphy had heard Ortega's special signal and ignored it. But the strongest possibility was Jack.

Frank went up the porch steps trying not to appear quite as furtive as he felt. He had his hand raised ready to knock again when he heard the sudden, loud clanking of an overhead garage door being lifted open hastily and clumsily. He reached the garage just as Jack Goodfield was climbing in behind the wheel of the Buick.

"Wait a minute! Hey, Goodfield!"

"Get out of my way, you." Jack turned on the ignition and pressed the starter switch. But luck—and the fact that the car was in gear—was against him. Instead of going into a steady roar the engine coughed twice and the Buick took three playful leaps forward and stopped with a splintering crash of metal on wood. Simultaneous with the fracture of the garage wall came the fracture of Jack's morale. He sagged forward in the seat, his forehead resting against the top of the steering wheel in a posture of defeat and exhaustion.

"All right, I give up. I give up."

"Are you O.K., Goodfield?"

"Oh sure, I'm great, just great. All right, let's have it. How much do you want?" He got out of the car, slammed the door viciously, and emerged from the garage shaking his head back and forth as if to shake off the painful glare of the sun. "You might as well ask for the shirt off my back. That's about all I've got. And it isn't even a good shirt, it isn't even *clean*. So go ahead, take it."

"Sorry, it's not my size. Besides, my wife doesn't like me to wear white shirts, they're too hard to launder."

"For God's sake, come to the point. You work for Evangeline's husband."

"I have nothing to do with your amours, Goodfield. I work for the Mental Health Society."

"It's too early in the morning for jokes."

"No joke."

Jack turned a little pale. "You mean somebody's gone off their rocker around here? Well, by God, it doesn't surprise me much. Which one is it?"

"I don't know. In fact—"

"Maybe both of them, eh?"

"It's not very likely."

"Likely or not, that's my opinion."

"Based on what?"

"The way they're acting, the way they've treated me. Sure, I arrived late and woke them up. Also, I wanted a small loan and that kind of thing doesn't make you popular. I even grant you that I'm not the most lovable chap in the world. But I'm not absolutely detestable, I'm not completely abominable, I've got *some* good points."

"I'm sure you have," Frank agreed cautiously.

"You wouldn't think so from the way they treated me. You'd think I was carrying bubonic plague. They ordered me out right away, they weren't even going to let me stay the rest of the night, said they didn't have room. Fantastic, isn't it? One's own flesh and blood, and a big house like this. Wouldn't you call that fantastic?"

"I might."

"They just weren't reasonable, considering that all I wanted was a bed for the night and a small loan and a chance to talk to mother about some stock I thought of selling."

"Goodfield stock?"

"Yes. It's mine, it was given to me. Legally, I can do whatever I want with it. I can sell it or I can send it over Niagara Falls in a barrel. I can—" He broke off with an embarrassed little laugh. "I don't know why I'm telling all this to a stranger. You wouldn't be interested."

"I think I would."

"I'm not even interested myself, as a matter of fact. All this business stuff bores me. I wasn't cut out for it."

Frank guided him back to the point. "Did you talk to your mother about selling your stock?"

"Not yet. Last night it was too late, of course, and this morning when I rapped on her door she was still sleeping. I noticed a funny smell in the corridor outside her room."

"What kind of smell?"

"Oh, it reminded me a lot of hospitals and sickness and things like that. I wonder if she's a great deal sicker than they'll admit. Have you seen her lately?"

"I've never seen her. Captain Greer has—he's a friend of mine—and he thought she looked fine. He was pretty captivated, in fact."

"Oh, she can be captivating all right, but she never wastes any of that on her children. Treats us like morons." He paused, stroking his chin with his fingertips. "Speaking of morons, how can you tell when somebody's gone off their rocker? Like Ethel, for instance. Could you tell if she—well, if she suddenly—well, you know—"

144

"I might."

"It isn't just the way she acted last night about my coming here. I'm not stupid enough to believe that anybody who dislikes me is crazy. Some people have their own good reasons for not liking me. But Ethel hasn't. We've always gotten on well. I remembered her birthdays, I took her places like the opera house where Willett refused to go, and whenever any of her relatives showed up from Wisconsin I acted as extra man, took them around Chinatown, things like that. Sometimes it was pretty rough; Ethel has a lot of peculiar relatives."

Frank suspected that Jack's standards of peculiarity were themselves peculiar. Ethel's cousins might have worn the wrong hats or preferred beer to martinis.

Jack went on chewing over his grievance like a dyspeptic steer, trying to make it more digestible. "Yes, you might even say that Ethel and I were pals. It was an awful surprise when she turned on me last night, turned on me like a wildcat—I can see you don't believe that."

"It's difficult. Mrs. Goodfield seems to me to be a very"—*ineffectual* was the word that occurred to Frank but he changed it—"a very mild woman."

"That's what I always thought, until last night. The change in her was downright frightening. Why, I wouldn't stay here now if they got down on their knees and begged me. Dead tired as I am, I'm going on my way."

"You didn't get much sleep?"

"An hour or two. They stuck me in some cramped little room that belongs to the maid—she's away on a holiday—and then first thing this morning the birds started fussing and yipping around. One of them kept tapping at my window—tap, tap, tap. Damned annoying, birds in the morning, especially the tapping kind. I got up about eight-thirty and went upstairs to see if mother was awake yet. I rapped on her door and tried the knob, but it was locked. That's another odd thing, for a sick woman to

145

sleep with her door locked so that no one could get inside to help her if she took a turn for the worse. It didn't seem right, it worried me. People don't lock bedroom doors unless they're afraid, afraid of their own family. And that smell in the hall made me nervous.

"I tried a couple of other doors and they were locked too. Then I looked out the hall window and saw you coming. Right then and there I decided to leave. I couldn't think of a single reason for staying except my mother, and frankly, mother's always been able to look after herself." He stroked his chin again as if the scrape of his whiskers against his fingertips gave him a reassurance of manhood. "I'm not running out on my duty. It's just—I've got troubles of my own, I can't afford to mess around with women who've gone off the beam."

Frank wondered about Evangeline who had never been on the beam, but he didn't bring the subject up because he felt a degree of sympathy for Jack. Like Willett, he was persecuted by his own indecision, because he had never been compelled, or privileged, to make any decisions by himself.

"Avoid trouble," Jack said. "That's my motto. When you see it coming, walk away."

"Unless it's too late."

"Why do you say that?"

"Here's Ethel."

The heavy, black Lincoln rolled ponderously down the driveway like a hearse and came to a stop beside the convertible. Ethel was behind the wheel and Willett was slumped in the seat beside her, his eyes shut, his skin tinged a grayish-yellow. He got out of the car and began walking toward the house, his shoulders heaving with silent retches.

Ethel got out too, and closed both of the car doors carefully before she spoke: "What are you doing here, Mr. Clyde?"

146

"There's no law against a neighborly call, Mrs. Good-field."

"I must ask you to leave. I don't happen to feel very neighborly this morning."

"Other people do. Mr. Goodfield here has been very neighborly."

Ethel wheeled around and faced her brother-in-law. "What have you been telling him?"

"Nothing," Jack said. "Not a thing."

"I don't believe you."

"Now don't go off your—don't get excited, Ethel, old girl."

"What did you tell him?"

"Why, nothing but the truth, old girl: that you weren't very hospitable and I intended to leave."

"When?"

"Right away."

"Good. The sooner the better. I'll get your luggage."

"I already have my luggage," Jack said with pained dignity. "But before I go I must say that—"

"Don't say anything, Jack. Too much has been said. It doesn't help matters."

"Well, I'll just pop in and say good-bye to Willett."

"Don't bother," Ethel said sharply. "I'll say good-bye for you. Willett is not feeling very well. He doesn't want to be disturbed."

"Oh. Well then—" He opened the door of the Buick and climbed behind the wheel, awkwardly, because Ethel was staring at him, her pale eyes cold and suspicious. "Honestly, old girl, if I were you I'd visit a doctor. You're not acting like yourself."

"If I acted like myself, I'd get on a slow boat to Sweden and forget I ever heard the name Goodfield."

"You see, Ethel? That's what I mean. You should visit a doct—"

"For heaven's sake, will you *please go?*"

147

"All right, all right." He started the engine. "Good-bye, Ethel."

Ethel didn't say good-bye. She just watched the convertible until it slid around a curve and out of sight.

Frank was shocked by the change that a few days had made in her appearance. He had seen her twice before: at the inquest, wearing a wispy green silk dress and an expression of complete disinterest; and at Rose's funeral, in a dark suit that made her look very fair and delicate. The fairness was real enough, but her frailty and her unconcern and her benign stupidity were illusory. Perhaps Ethel herself had been taken in by the illusion, did not realize the extent of her passions and her strength and did not want to realize.

"Mrs. Goodfield."

"Please leave. My husband is sick and I have to look after him."

"I'm sorry."

"Why should you be sorry? You're a stranger to us."

"I'm not as much of a stranger as you think."

"I see. Jack's been shooting off his mouth, has he?"

"A little."

"That egghead, that silly, meddling egghead. He doesn't know, he doesn't realize the damage he—" She drew in her breath sharply and it made a tinny sound passing through her throat. "Jack's an awful liar," she added finally.

"It takes one to catch one."

"Then you'd better not catch any, Mr. Clyde. Your reputation might suffer."

"We can stand around all day exchanging beautiful thoughts but it won't get us anywhere."

"That hardly matters to me since I'm not trying to get anywhere."

"I think you're trying on all eight cylinders."

"Oh?"

"But somebody put sugar in the gasoline."

A blank expression crossed her face. "You're beginning to confuse me."

"I don't believe you're confused. I believe you're in trouble, maybe very serious trouble. I'd like to help you."

It was clear that the offer came as a shock to her, that the last thing in the world she expected was sympathy; and when it was offered it disturbed her, softened her emotions and dulled the edges of her purpose. "You're a stranger to us," she repeated. "Why should you want to help? No. No, I don't believe it. That policeman sent you."

"Greer didn't send me."

"Policemen can be so stupid, so terribly stupid. You've got to leave now, Mr. Clyde. You've *got* to. This is my last warning. There's a gun in the house. We have a right to protect our property."

"Where's Murphy, Mrs. Goodfield?"

"We have a right to—"

"Where's Murphy?"

"In her room. Sleeping."

"Jack told me he used her room last night."

"He's lying."

"No, you are. Where is she?"

"I don't know," she said in a whisper. "I simply don't know. If I knew, I'd kill her."

"Why did you tell Greer she'd come back?"

"I had to satisfy him, to keep him away from here."

"Why do you have to keep him away?"

"I was warned."

"By Murphy?"

"Someone called me. I think it was Murphy trying to disguise her voice."

"What was the warning?"

"To keep the police away."

"Or what?"

"Or they'd—I can't tell. That was part of it—I'm not to tell or something terrible will happen to her."

"To Murphy?"

"Not to Murphy. To *her*. Willett's mother."

"You'd better call Greer right away and ask for police protection."

"Police protection? What good will that do?"

"They can put guards around the house."

"Guards around the house. That's funny." She began to laugh quietly to herself, her head bent, her hands cupped over her eyes as if she was looking down into some private joke.

Frank touched her shoulder. "Stop that."

"It's funny."

"No, it's not."

"You wouldn't know. Guards around the house. They could put a million guards around the house. You can't guard something that isn't there."

"What do you mean?"

"Willett's mother was kidnapped," Ethel said. "Last night. Drugged and taken right out of her bed. I don't know what to do. I don't know what to do."

"Call the police."

"I can't. They'll never bring her back alive."

Frank didn't say what he was thinking—that she might not be alive to bring back. "Has any ransom been asked?"

"Asked?" Ethel repeated shrilly. "We've already *paid* it. This morning. That's where we were, leaving the money where they told us. Everything happened so quick. Everything was so quick and yet so planned and deliberate. Even the amount of money they asked for—it was the exact amount we had in the house. Don't you see? It must be someone who knows us, who knows how Willett feels about his mother—someone who may be watching me right this minute. *I don't know what to do*."

This time Frank didn't tell her what to do. He did it himself, went inside the house and phoned Greer.

18

GREER ARRIVED as unobtrusively as possible, by the back road, in an old gray sedan that belonged to one of his sergeants. But in spite of the secrecy the news leaked out that there were policemen around the big house; and where there were policemen there was trouble; and where there was trouble was the place to be.

Maids abandoned their ironing. Gardeners threw down their spading forks. Housewives removed their aprons, applied a dash of lipstick and left junior in the playpen. The mailman paused on his rounds and the music box tinkle of the Good Humor truck stopped in the middle of a waltz. Small boys appeared out of improbable places carrying cap pistols and model airplanes and fat, moist snails and surprised grasshoppers.

For the second time within a week the Goodfield garden came alive with people. They stood in sedate groups and exchanged the wildest rumors in the most plausible manner. The man of the house had gone berserk, strangled his wife and children and shot himself. (Several people had heard the shot, though there was some discrepancy about the time, which ranged from the preceding afternoon to seven o'clock that morning.) There had been a rape, a robbery, a suicide, an explosion. Mr. Goodfield was a well-known mobster (anybody could tell by looking at him), or a banker (same reason). His wife was an ex-burlesque queen (that bleached hair and slinky walk), a society woman (the postman had seen her picture in a newspaper), or a hosiery clerk (one of the housewives had seen a very fair-haired woman working in the hosiery department at Magnin's, and this woman was probably Ethel who had been forced to take a job to pay off the debts of her husband, who was a well-known gambler, as anybody could tell by looking at him).

None of the rumors came close to the story that Willett told Greer. They were in old Mrs. Goodfield's bedroom, Greer pacing the floor and Willett standing in the doorway, his eyes fixed rigidly on the empty bed. From the broken French door that led out to the sun deck a cool fresh wind swept across the room, but the odor of ether still clung to the corners, subtle and tenacious as spider webs. On one jagged edge of the glass door a piece of blue silk was blowing in the breeze like a tiny flag. Greer had noticed the silk but he'd left it, as he'd left everything else in the room, untouched. A special F.B.I. unit was on its way from Los Angeles, and Greer was experienced enough to realize that this unit would handle the physical evidence much better than he could. Psychological evidence was a different matter. The piece of silk was for the specialists; the effect of the piece of silk on Willett was Greer's business.

"I guess—I guess it's part of her nightgown." Willett took out a handkerchief and wiped his face, but within a minute it was damp again. "How did it—how could it get there?"

"I presume she was given the ether while she was asleep —not much sign of a struggle—and then carried out to the sun deck. Her nightgown caught on a piece of glass where the door was broken so it could be unlocked."

"She would have, surely she would have wakened up when the glass was broken."

"Maybe she did."

"She would have screamed for help."

"Not necessarily."

"What does—what are you implying?"

152

"She and Murphy," Greer said, "got along very well, didn't they?"

"Mother despised Murphy."

"Your wife doesn't think so."

"Take her word for it then. I don't see why you're bothering me with these details when Ethel has already told you everything."

"I'd like to hear your version."

"Version," Willett bleated. "My God, man, this isn't the kind of thing you have *versions* of. I can tell you the *facts*."

"All right."

Willett's facts were, with a few exceptions, the same as Ethel's.

He had last seen his mother the preceding evening, Willett said, between nine and ten o'clock. She was feeling somewhat depressed and wanted to be left alone. ("She was in a bitchy mood," Ethel had said, "and told us both to get out and stay out.") At midnight when Willett and Ethel went upstairs to retire, they knocked at Mrs. Goodfield's door intending to say good night. Her door was locked and they presumed she was asleep. There had been no unusual odor in the hall at that time.

During the night Jack arrived.

"We had a drink and a little chat and then we all went to bed."

"That isn't quite what your wife—"

"Ethel," Willett said, "exaggerates."

"Oh."

"Besides, Jack had nothing to do with this affair, this kidnapping."

"Maybe not."

"His arrival was pure coincidence."

"Maybe."

"Naturally you don't know Jack."

"Naturally. But I know Murphy, and I'll eat my badge if Murphy was strong enough to carry a drugged woman out of that door and down that ladder. If Murphy is at the bottom of this, she's sharing the bottom with somebody else."

"Not Jack. I mean—great Scott, chaps don't go around kidnapping their own mothers. Murder, now that might make sense. I've often thought of— But that's getting off the subject."

"All right," Greer said. "You went to bed. Then what?"

"We got the phone call. That is, Ethel did; the upstairs phone is in her room. But the ringing woke me up, it was around seven o'clock, I think. I heard Ethel talking, arguing with someone. Arguing upsets me. I got up to put a stop to it. I found Ethel standing right in this doorway and there was a terrible smell of ether coming from somewhere. 'We've got to pay it,' Ethel said. I didn't know what she was talking about. I went into mother's room. It was just the way it is now and m-mother was gone."

Tears welled in Willett's eyes, magnifying the irises so that they looked ready to pop out of their sockets. Greer wasn't sure whether the tears were caused by mere annoyance or by genuine grief at his mother's disappearance: the rejected boy crying for his mother who had died or been divorced or merely gone off to an early matinee at the Bijou. Greer wondered gravely if there would ever be any more matinees for Mrs. Goodfield. Though he had spoken optimistically to Ethel and Frank and Willett, his own feeling was that the old lady was dead, that whoever conceived such a drastic plan in the first place would take drastic measures to avoid being caught. It was easier to dispose of a dead woman than to conceal a reluctant and protesting live one.

"It was all so sudden," Willett said. "So shockingly sudden. The demand for ransom came before we even knew she'd been taken away. They asked for three thousand dollars."

"They?"

"Murphy. Ethel said it sounded like Murphy, not the voice so much as the words. Murphy has a way of talking."

"What were her instructions?"

"She said that my mother was in safe hands and would be returned, providing we paid the money promptly and didn't inform the police or anyone else of her disappearance. Ethel agreed. She had to. She acted *right*—I don't care what your viewpoint is—Ethel acted *right*."

Greer didn't argue. "I hope so. The money was to be paid in cash?"

"Yes."

"You had that much cash in the house?"

"Exactly that much. I'd been to the bank yesterday afternoon and drawn it out to lend to Jack. He'd phoned me in the morning from San Francisco and asked me for a loan."

"Anybody else know about this?"

"Ethel, of course. And my mother. Oh yes, and Shirley, I guess. She's my younger sister."

"And Murphy?"

"I didn't confide in Murphy," Willett said. "Ethel did sometimes, but not about important things like money. Just," Willett added rather wistfully, "about things like me."

"Was Murphy in the house at the time the call came through from San Francisco?"

"I think she was downstairs."

"There's another telephone down there?"

"Yes."

"Then I think we can assume that Murphy was listening in."

"I—yes. If you say so."

"Is something troubling you, Mr. Goodfield?"

"I—it's this damned smell. It's making me ill."

"We can leave in a minute. First, I want to know if your mother ever used that desk in the corner."

The desk was very small, almost child-sized. On it was a bowl of faded iris dripping purple, a fountain pen with its top off, and a piece of paper that had been crumpled and smoothed out again. The paper bore the words, written in a shaky, hesitant hand: "I'm getting scared. I have a premonition." The letters were crudely formed as if the person who'd written them had forgotten how to write correctly or had never learned.

"She used the desk," Willett said. "Sometimes she wrote letters, not often."

"Is this her handwriting? Please don't touch the paper."

"I can't tell. Her handwriting changed a lot during her illness. I—I suppose she wrote this, though I can't understand why."

"Did she go in for premonitions?"

"Premonitions, astrology, fad diets, anything to pass the time. She got bored lying in bed day after day."

"What would she have to be scared about?"

"N-nothing."

"Were you and your wife and Murphy her sole contacts with the outside world?"

"I don't like the way you put that. You're implying that Ethel and I are culpable. We're not. But I know who is. I know whose fault it will be if my mother is never brought back alive. Your fault, Captain Greer. Yours alone."

"I don't agree."

"You think Ethel and I were wrong to pay the money," Willett said passionately. "Well, I think you were wrong to interfere like this, to spoil our chances."

"Cooperating with criminals is always wrong. I hope you don't learn that the hard way, Mr. Goodfield."

Greer locked the bedroom. Then they went down the

wide staircase together, walking in step but as far apart as possible, as if to emphasize their unity of purpose and their separateness of minds.

"You paid the ransom," Greer said, "at the time and place specified?"

"Yes. Our instructions were very definite. We put the money in a paper bag, drove down to the breakwater and walked out about a third of the way. There's a big rock there on the channel side covered with mussels. At exactly a quarter to eight I put the paper bag on the rock. The tide was coming in."

"The timing was very close."

"Very. We almost didn't make it. No more than forty-five minutes elapsed from the time of the phone call till the time we left the money on the rock." Willett leaned against the banister as if he found his body suddenly and intolerably heavy. "Even if we had wanted to—well, think it over a bit, we didn't have time. Everything moved too fast, don't you see?"

Greer saw. Speed and moderation were the elements that made the kidnapping unusual and, possibly, successful. There had been none of the delays common to such cases: Willett and Ethel were not forced to wait for a ransom note, raise a large amount of cash and then wait again for instructions about the payoff. Such delays would have given Willett a chance to think the matter over in a reasonable way. As it was, the ransom was already paid before he emerged from a state of shock, and the tide had covered the tracks and tracings of the kidnapper before anybody started to search for them.

A neat and simple payoff. At seven-forty-five in the morning the breakwater was usually well-filled with people, mostly fishermen, men, women and children carrying their bait or their lunches in paper bags. One more paper bag, one more fisherman, would hardly attract attention. Was that fisherman Murphy? Everything pointed to her

—her disappearance, the amount of money demanded, the voice on the phone, the knowledge of Willett's psychology and the advantage taken of his weakness, the fact that the old lady had made no outcry—everything pointed, almost too clearly, to Murphy. Murphy was, Greer thought, too shrewd a woman to leave such a blazing trail, and besides, she was not strong enough to have handled the actual kidnapping by herself. There were two possibilities: either someone had helped her, or someone sufficiently intimate with her to share her knowledge of the Goodfields was using her as a dupe. But Murphy would never willingly be used as a dupe, she was more likely to use someone else; so Greer was left with the disturbing thought that Murphy, as well as the old lady, had been kidnapped. Yet this picture of Murphy as a victim was distorted in his mind because it did not coincide with his own impression of her.

"Everything moved too fast," Willett said again in an aggrieved tone as if speed was always being used unfairly against him in one way or another.

He followed Greer into the dining room. The room was long and narrow with windows on three sides. The drapes were still drawn closely over two of the windows. The third was open and in front of it stood Ethel staring out at the people on the lawn, her face white with strain and anger. It was as if all her resentments—against the Goodfields, the doll factory, the police, the kidnappers, and, inevitably, Willett—had been fused together and were now directed against the curiosity-seekers in the yard.

She spoke in a harsh voice, one hand pressing her throat. "Look at them. Look at them, ruining everything, not even knowing, not even *caring*. What do they expect, a floor show?—a hanging?"

"I'll send them away," Greer said.

"They won't go."

"They might. I'll give them a story. I only wish," he

added dryly, "that I could give them a story as good as some of the ones I get."

When he had gone Ethel looked at Willett. "What did he mean by that?"

"How should I know?"

"It sounded as if he thought we were lying."

"Well, weren't we?"

"I lied very little." She watched Greer cross the lawn, and then she slanted the slats of the blind so that Greer and the people were shut out and only the sun came in. "What do you think will happen if he finds out everything?"

"You know what will happen. We'll be ruined."

"Maybe it won't be as bad as you—"

"Don't kid yourself, Ethel."

"Well, all right then, we'll be ruined. If we're going to be ruined anyway, let's at least be cheerful about it. I can always go out and take a job." After a time she added wistfully, "Wouldn't it be kind of fun, Willett, to start all over again, without the factory and your mother and Jack —just you and me—wouldn't it be kind of fun?"

Willett didn't answer and Ethel interpreted his silence as acquiescence.

"You're not old, Willett. Why, you could even go out and learn a trade, be something real, like a carpenter, maybe. Your mother told me you always enjoyed hammering nails into things so maybe carpentry would be just—" She looked at his face and added hastily, "Well, of course you don't *have* to be a carpenter, dear. There are lots of other things, a mechanic, or a bricklayer— Your mother said you were very neat about piling up your blocks when you were a boy, and piling bricks is practically the same thing, isn't it, except for the glue in between?"

"It's not glue."

"Or a farmer, Willett. That's it, we could have a dairy

farm. You've always been very good with dogs and you could probably handle cows quite— You don't like that idea, either?"

"Don't be silly."

"Silly. Yes, I guess I am." She stared at him, blankly, all her wistfulness gone and nothing in its place. "Willett."

"I won't listen to any more of this nonsense."

"I was just thinking, Willett," she said very softly. "It just occurred to me, maybe they'll teach you a trade in prison."

Willett's plump face seemed to come apart like an overdone chicken at the touch of a fork. "They can't send me to prison. They can't send me to prison. Not unless—"

"Not unless they send me, too? Oh, they will. I'm sure of that. Only I won't mind it quite as much as you. I've been in prison for years, with a cantankerous old woman as warden and a nasty little doll factory as a whip."

"The doors were never locked. You could have walked out."

"Oh sure, I could have. But I didn't. I always had hopes that you and I would be free, that she would—"

"Would what?"

"Die."

Willett stared at her. "You wanted that for a long time. You *willed* it."

"Maybe."

"Sometimes I think you're a bad woman."

"Sometimes I think so, too," Ethel said, quite mildly. "Maybe prison's just the place for me."

"Stop this talk about prison, do you hear me? We may be ruined financially, morally, but they can't send us to prison. We still have the letter. Haven't we?"

"I guess so."

"You *guess* so! I told you to put it away in a safe place."

"Well, I did. Behind that fruit picture in my room."

"Go and get it."

"Why? It's safe there. No one would think of looking behind a picture."

"That's the first place they'll look."

"Who will?"

"The F.B.I.," Willett said.

"Why should they search *my* room? *I* haven't—"

"Go and get that letter."

"Well, all right." She went to the door, hesitated, and swung round again with a swish of silk. "Willett?"

"Yes."

"If they're really going to search my room, I think I'll tidy up my drawers a bit. I wouldn't want them to think I'm a creature of messy habits."

"You haven't time."

"Oh. Well, then, I'll just explain to them that my mother-in-law has been ill and my maid disappeared, so naturally my drawers aren't quite—"

"*Ethel.*"

"Well, all right," Ethel said with dignity. "I was just leaving."

The letter was where she had put it two weeks ago, behind an oil painting of a bunch of grapes and two dusty-looking tangerines. Across the front of the unsealed envelope were the words, *To Whom it May Concern,* in Mrs. Goodfield's handwriting. Ethel knew it was Mrs. Goodfield's handwriting because she had been there, in the old lady's bedroom, when the letter was written:

"*Sit down, Ethel. And stop fidgeting.*"

"*Sorry.*"

"*This blasted pen. Haven't we a decent pen in the house?*"

"*It works if you use it sideways.*"

"*If you use it sideways. That's typical. That's absolutely typical of what happens when I'm not up and around to manage things. Nothing works unless you use it sideways.*"

"Sorry."

"To whom it may concern," the old lady wrote, sideways. "In the event that my son, Willett Peter Goodfield, is implicated in any way with my death, I wish to make the following statement to clarify the facts."

Downstairs the front door chime sounded with raucous shrillness, not like a bell announcing the arrival of guests, but like a burglar alarm arousing the household against intruders.

Ethel folded the envelope and tucked it in the front of her dress. It was the one place in the house where she was reasonably sure that the F.B.I. wouldn't search.

19

NEWS OF THE KIDNAPPING spread quickly across the town and by noon it had reached the corner of Fifth and Anacapa and an obscure druggist by the name of Lopat. Leaving his wife, brother-in-law and two cousins in charge of the drugstore, Lopat set out on foot for the police station four blocks south. He had visited the station several times before, usually to explain certain lapses in his narcotics records, but this time his conscience was clear and his step blithe.

Lopat was nobody's fool and he knew perfectly well that most people didn't use ether for dry-cleaning any more, especially people with class like Mrs. Willett Goodfield.

He greeted Greer with a broad and virtuous smile. "Afternoon, Captain."

"Hello Lopat. What's on your mind except larceny?"

"My, my, you're quite a kidder, Captain. Ha, ha."

"Ha, ha. Let's have it. Got your license back yet, Lopat?"

"Naturally."

"Better watch that brother-in-law of yours if you want to keep it."

"Manny? Oh, Manny's changed, he's off the stuff, never touches it."

"That isn't how I heard it."

"You guys are prejudiced. Manny's a good boy, maybe a little loose in his ways, but a good boy."

"If he gets any looser he'll fall apart."

"Now, now, Captain. Here I come to do you a favor and right away you start making wise. I'm hurt."

"What's the favor?"

Lopat leaned across the desk, confidentially. "I heard an old lady was snatched."

"You did, eh?"

"You don't have to admit anything, Captain. Let me do the talking."

"Go ahead."

"Last night around suppertime a lady comes into the shop and asks for some ether. For dry-cleaning a couple of dresses, she said. Well, that was legitimate. In this state you can't buy ether to do away with a sick cat or anything, but you can buy it for dry-cleaning. You don't even have to sign for it like in some states. So I sold it to her."

"How much?"

"What she asked for, six ounces."

"What was she, a midget or something?"

"That's what I asked myself. She was small, all right, but she wasn't a midget. And she wasn't the type who'd do her own dry-cleaning either. She had class, real class."

"What's your idea of class, Lopat?"

"I don't like how you say that, implying I've got no taste in women. You can't judge my taste in women by my

163

wife. I've got very good taste in women—the best—I've just never had a chance to indulge it, is all."

"So?"

"So I'm telling you this girl had class. Classy name and address, too."

"If she didn't have to sign for the stuff, how come you know her name and address?"

"She told me, right off the bat. You know how some of these society dames are—they walk into a store and even if they're just going to buy two noodles they've got to announce themselves. Well, that's what she did. I am Mrs. Willett Goodfield, she says, of 2201 Ventura Boulevard."

Greer attempted to conceal his surprise, but he wasn't quick enough to fool Lopat.

Lopat grinned slyly. "A friend of yours, Captain?"

"I've heard the name."

"Has she got class, like I said, or hasn't she?"

"She's loaded."

"There, you see? Maybe my taste in women isn't so bad after all, eh?"

"Change the record, will you, Lopat?"

"I didn't put it on. You did. You implied that my taste in—"

"Forget about women and go on with your story," Greer said, "or next year you might not even get a dog license."

"You don't have to talk so tough. After all, I came here of my own free will to do my duty as a citizen. Just because my brother-in-law, Manny, gets in a little scrape now and then is no reflection on me. Is it O.K. if I smoke in here, Captain?"

"As long as you don't smoke the same brand as Manny."

"Aw, the hell with Manny. So he's a bum. So that doesn't make me a bum, does it?"

"No."

"That's better. I like to be appreciated." Lopat lit a cigarette, scraping the match against his thumbnail. "I keep

164

my ear to the ground, and that way I catch a lot of dirt. Like about this snatch. How I heard it, the names got a little mixed up—Goodyear instead of Goodfield—but I added two and two and here I am."

"Think you can identify this Mrs. Willett Goodfield?"

"Sure I could."

"Good." Greer flipped the switch of the com box on his desk. "Daley? Get me a copy of that picture just going out on an APB."

"An APB," Lopat repeated. "She's really flown the coop, eh?"

"You figure it out."

"I'm trying."

"Don't strain yourself. At your age it shows."

The picture was brought in, a small, candid shot of a young woman in profile looking into the window of a store.

Lopat gazed at it a long time with the air of a connoisseur. "She's not dolled up the way I saw her last night, but that's Mrs. Goodfield for sure. Not a very good likeness of her, though."

Greer agreed. The picture had been taken by Ortega without the knowledge of the subject; and it wasn't a very good likeness of Ethel Goodfield because the young woman looking into the store window was Ada Murphy. Ortega had lent Greer the picture earlier in the day, handing it over with pained reluctance as if he realized that all he'd ever have of Murphy was a creased snapshot and a few fading memories.

Lopat passed the picture back across the desk and Greer looked at it again, for the twentieth time that day. The features were clearly Murphy's, the posture and the haughty tilt of the head unmistakable.

"She's a nice-looking girl," Lopat said. "Funny she'd do a thing like that."

"Yes."

"What gets into some women, I wonder? They got every-

165

thing, looks, class, money, only nothing's ever enough." Lopat broke off with an embarrassed little laugh. "Didn't know I went in for philosophy, did you, Captain?"

"No. It's quite a shock."

"Well, I do. I'm what you might call a real philosopher, a guy who figures out what's the matter with the world and then doesn't do a damn thing about it."

"What *is* the matter with the world, Lopat?"

"People, Captain. Just people."

Greer rose, heavily. Some days he felt his weight, some days he did not. This afternoon he felt massive and inert, like a stone imbedded in mud at the bottom of a river. "Daley will take your statement in the next office and you can sign it."

"All right."

"Thanks for coming in, Lopat."

"Don't mention it, Captain. On the other hand, don't forget it either. The next time you send a couple of your boys to pick up Manny, see that he gets roughed up a little. Nothing that'll show—the wife would blame me, always does. Just see the kid gets a lesson, understand?"

"I think so."

"And if any reward is offered for this old lady that disappeared—well, you know how tough it is these days to operate a small business like mine."

"See that it stays small, Lopat. Go reaching out too far and somebody'll slap your wrist."

"I'm not reaching. A little reward money, that's different. A soft buck is a soft buck. Just don't forget me, is all I ask."

"I won't."

"Well, so long, Captain. Don't think it ain't been charming."

"I'll try not to." He flipped on the com box again. "Daley? Vince Lopat wants to make a statement. Four carbons, and send one of them right out to Barrett. I think he's still at the Goodfield house."

"He's still there," Daley said. "He phoned in a few minutes ago. One of his boys found some new evidence he wants you to look at."

"O.K. Make up Lopat's statement and I'll take a copy of it down with me."

"Don't I get any lunch?"

"Chew a couple of paper clips."

"Oh, for—"

"And cheer up, Daley. Another nineteen years and you can retire on a pension and have lunch every hour on the hour."

"By that time they'll be feeding me through a tube. Malted milks and raw eggs."

"By that time nobody'll be able to afford steaks anyway."

"Captain—"

"You have your orders."

"Yes sir."

Greer reached for his hat.

Barrett let him in at the front door of the Goodfield house. "You got here fast, Captain."

"It's not far. What's the news?"

"About the old lady, none. No trace of her. But certain other things have come up. A couple of maps."

"What kind of maps?"

"Ordinary kind they give away at service stations. Road maps. Come on upstairs and I'll show you."

Barrett led the way up the wide staircase and down the hall to Mrs. Goodfield's bedroom. He was a small man with an oversized head that gave him a faint resemblance to a cartoonist's version of a man from Mars. Barrett had started out as a doctor, switched to medical jurisprudence, and ended up with the F.B.I. as an expert on paper; paper of all kinds, from its origin in the forests of Quebec, North Carolina, Oregon, to its final form, a dollar bill, a newspaper, a child's toy, a will, a crumpled wad in a garbage can or a bit of ash in an incinerator.

The paper this time was in the form of two maps. One of them showed all forty-eight states and a fringe of Canada and Mexico; the other was a more detailed map of California with four inserts containing the street layouts of Los Angeles, San Diego, Sacramento and San Francisco.

"Carbonaro found them wedged between the headboard of the bed and the mattress," Barrett said. "I can't see that they have any connection with the kidnapping but I thought you might be interested."

"I am."

"Apparently the family traveled pretty extensively. Notice the routes and the stopovers are all marked in ink."

Greer noticed more than that. In the left-hand margin of the California map were two penciled, vertical lists: American League—New York Yankees, Washington Senators, Chicago White Sox, Cleveland Indians, Detroit Tigers, Philadelphia Athletics, St. Louis Browns, Boston Red Sox. The second column was headed National League, and underneath it were listed the Brooklyn Dodgers, Pittsburgh Pirates, Cincinnati Reds, Chicago Cubs, Boston Braves, Philadelphia Phils, St. Louis Cardinals, New York Giants.

The margins of the other map were also crammed with writing. They contained a variety of names and dates and comments: Phil, Sept 27. Cleve, Oct. 8, Gary, Oct 14, Paul and Minnie, Oct 29. Pierre, Nov 13, Billings, Nov 20 (cold) S.L.C., Nov 30, Vegas, Dec 5, Tucson, Dec 10 (Palace Hotel, Redlands Hospital), Col Sprs, Feb 19 (Westcott Clinic, Dr. George Sampson, diet, complain), L.A, May 2, Town House.

Greer folded the maps and put them in his pocket. There was no doubt at all that they were Rose's maps, the same ones that Mrs. Cushman had seen in her room and that had disappeared after her death. A birthday memo, Mrs. Cushman had called the writing in the margin. It was a memo, not of birthdays but of cities. Greer still did not know what the writing meant or even if Rose herself had done it. But he was sure of one thing, that he now had conclusive proof that Rose had been involved with the Goodfields, had probably been a visitor in this very room.

She may have died here, Greer thought. *They may both have died here, Rose and old Mrs. Goodfield.*

Yet it was Mrs. Goodfield herself who had most vehemently denied knowing Rose, and denied that Willett knew her. "I've never allowed Willett to have any truck with actresses," she had told Greer. "I explained all about actresses to him when he was eighteen."

Maybe, Greer thought grimly, the explanation wasn't good enough for Willett, and he had to find out for himself.

"Any ideas about the maps?" Barrett said.

"Quite a few. I'll check first and tell you later."

20

GREER RETURNED to the main floor. There was no sign of the Goodfields in any of the front rooms but from the back of the house came a sound that Greer couldn't identify, a loud whirring accentuated by little periods of silence. Greer followed the sound down the hall and through a swinging door into the kitchen.

Ethel was seated at a small built-in table that folded

down out of a wall between two windows. On the table was a portable electric sewing-machine and Ethel was bent over it with intense concentration.

The noise of the machine had covered Greer's entrance, so he stood and watched her for a minute, surprised by her speed and efficiency. She had her long fair hair pinned back tightly out of the way, and in place of the trailing silk housecoat she'd had on in the morning, she wore a plain cotton dress with the sleeves rolled up. Greer had the impression that he was seeing Ethel for the first time without costume or disguise and without the mask of idiocy she assumed for self-protection.

"Mrs. Goodfield."

She bent her head toward him with the alert inquisitiveness of a bird. "Oh, it's you. Have those other men gone yet?"

"No."

"I wish they'd go. They're making Willett nervous. But then everything does, doesn't it?"

"I wouldn't know."

She sighed. "I suppose you have to interrupt me?"

"Yes."

"I've been sewing. That is, I haven't been sewing anything in particular, just practising up in case—well, you never know what will happen, do you. I think every wife should be prepared to go out and take a job."

"Are you going to take a job, Mrs. Goodfield?"

"No, but it's nice to be prepared in case worst comes to worst. So I thought I'd practice up on my sewing. I used to do a lot of sewing back home. I even made all my brother's shirts. So I thought, if worst comes to worst—"

"Do you think it's coming?"

She looked at him blandly, assuming the mask again. "One never knows."

"Sometimes one has a rough idea."

"I don't follow you. I'm not a bit subtle. Ask Willett."

"I intend to ask Willett quite a few things. And you too."

"I've answered a thousand questions already today. Who does everybody think I am, Einstein?"

"What I think," Greer said, "is that you're an accomplished liar."

"I consider that an insult."

"You consider it correctly. It is an insult."

"And if I'm such a liar, why do you keep asking me questions?"

"I'm hoping you'll change your attitude and cooperate." Greer took the maps out of his pocket and unfolded them. "Ever see these before?"

Ethel hesitated slightly before answering. "Of course. They belong to my mother-in-law."

"Is this her writing in the margins?"

"Whose else would it be? They're her maps. She kept them as a souvenir of the trip, I guess."

"What trip?"

"I told you we've been traveling for the past six months, mother, Willett and I."

"Why?"

"Why do people travel? To see things and places."

"For enjoyment, in other words."

"I—yes, you might call it that."

"Was it enjoyable traveling with a bedridden invalid?"

"It was hell," Ethel said flatly. "Just plain hell. But she wanted to travel, so we had to."

"It couldn't have been very pleasant for her either. Why did she insist on it?"

"I don't know."

"Is it possible that she had a very good reason for visiting these various places, Philadelphia, Cleveland, Minneapolis, and so on?"

"She never had to have a reason for doing anything. If she wanted to do it, that was enough."

"Why did she consider it important to make these memos of dates and places? Take a specific example: Tucson, Dec. 10, Palace Hotel, Redlands Hospital. Did anything significant happen to Mrs. Goodfield in Tucson? Did she go to visit anyone, friend, relative?"

"She went into Redlands Hospital for a week for a rest and a checkup. The results of the checkup weren't good at all. I wanted to come home but mother refused. We went on to Colorado Springs and she entered a clinic there."

"Why didn't she stay in the hospital in Tucson?"

Ethel's expression remained blank, but there was a thin, white line of anger around her mouth. "I told you, if she wanted to do something, that was enough. She never gave reasons. She didn't have to, she was boss."

"This checkup she had in Tucson—it showed she was gravely ill?"

"Yes."

"And still she refused to go home?"

"She refused."

"Is it possible," Greer said, "that she was looking for someone?"

Ethel turned and looked out the window. "Practically anything is possible, but it doesn't make much sense, her looking for someone all over the country in her condition. Who would she be looking for?"

"Some relative, perhaps. She was aware of her approaching death—she talked to me about it—and she may have wanted to make another will to include some relatives that she'd lost touch with."

"She hasn't any. We're her relatives, Willett and Jack and Shirley and I. As for making another will, that would never have occurred to her."

"You're positive?"

"Of course. She had nothing to leave to anyone, not a thing."

"I understood she was fairly well off."

"She was once. She gave it all away to her children quite a while ago."

"Why?"

"Why?" Ethel repeated with a dry little smile. "I guess she didn't want any of us to sit around waiting for her to die."

It seemed logical enough, and yet Greer had a feeling that it was not the true explanation. From what he knew and had heard of old Mrs. Goodfield, sensibility was not one of her characteristics. She was a hard woman with an iron will which she enforced on others by moral and financial pressure. Was she so sure of her moral force that she could afford to give up the advantage of financial pressure? And what kind of moral force was it that could compel free adults like Willett and Ethel to forego their own wishes and escort on a countrywide tour a woman who was gravely ill?

They were not traveling for enjoyment, Greer thought, *but for a purpose.*

He was certain that Ethel knew the purpose and was a part of it; equally certain that she would never tell. The maps were involved in some way. They were the connecting link between Rose and the Goodfields, and this suggested to Greer the possibility that Rose was the person Mrs. Goodfield had been searching for on her travels. But he had no evidence to support this theory; there was even evidence against it. Rose had not been in hiding. It would have been easy enough for anyone who seriously wanted to locate her to do so, either through her old studio connections, or, as Dalloway had, by a newspaper item. Why, then, should Mrs. Goodfield have been looking for Rose in Philadelphia or Minneapolis? Another and even more unanswerable question arose: if Mrs. Goodfield had wanted to find anyone, why hadn't she hired a detective instead of undertaking the difficult task herself?

He said finally, "There's nothing more you'd like to tell me?"

"Oh, but there is. I'd like to tell you a lot of things, I'd like to tell you the whole messy story of my life." She laughed, sharply, as if it hurt. "But I'm not going to. It's so futile, don't you see? There's nothing I can do for my mother-in-law now, nothing I can do for anybody, really. I'm completely, utterly, absolutely useless. My sole function is to shut up and play dead like a possum and I don't even do that very well."

"Well enough. You had me fooled for awhile."

"I ruin things by talking too much, don't I? I can't help it, I'm lonely, I like to talk to people. Normal people. Not Goodfields. For years I haven't talked to anybody but Goodfields, and all they ever cared about was their stinking money and their stinking hides. Well, now there's a lot less money and a lot less hide."

"What happened to the money?"

"Nothing drastic. It just keeps getting less. And less. The factory's going downhill and nobody seems able to stop it. Neither Jack nor Willett could operate a popcorn stand without losing their shirts."

"Thank you, Ethel," Willett said from the doorway.

She was not startled. She didn't even turn to look at him. "You're welcome."

"What have you been telling this policeman?"

"The story of my life."

"Is it as dull as you've always led me to believe?"

"Duller. Much, much duller. Especially the last ten years. I wouldn't wish the last ten years of my life on a dog."

"I suggest that if you can't control your emotions in front of strangers, you go up to your room."

"You suggest. Well, I suggest that you go jump in the lake. There's a lake back home near the farm, only a small

174

lake but it has a quicksand bottom. When you go down, you stay down. So *I* suggest—"

"Ethel, are you drunk or something?"

"I'm something but I'm not drunk. I wanted a drink, I went to get one, only there isn't any."

"That's absurd. I bought a whole case of Scotch when we moved in. What happened to it?"

"*I* suggest that you ask your old lady."

"Don't talk like that." He advanced on her, his chubby hands clenched into fists, held tightly against his ribs. "She couldn't have— She never left her room."

"She didn't have to. She sent Murphy to get it for her."

"When?"

"How should I know when? All I know is, the liquor's gone."

"Ortega might—"

"He's never been inside the house."

"Murphy took it for herself, not for—"

"Let's not kid ourselves."

"But she promised."

"Her promises aren't worth the oxygen they use up."

"Ethel, I've got to talk to you alone." He took a tentative step toward Greer. "Would you excuse us, Captain? We—this is a private matter, nothing to do with your investigation. Would you mind if we just stepped out for a minute?"

"Go ahead. I'll wait here. I have to make a phone call."

"The telephone is right there by the—"

"I see it."

"I—come on, Ethel."

She didn't move.

"Ethel, please."

He stretched out a hand to touch her shoulder. With a swift, neat movement she ducked out of his way and strode ahead of him through the swinging door. The door swung shut in his face. He pushed it open again, slowly, as if against the pressure of Ethel's weight.

Greer went over to the telephone and dialed a number.

A man's voice answered on the fifth ring. "Hello?"

"Dr. Severn?"

"Yes."

"Jim Greer. Are you busy?"

"I'm not in the middle of an autopsy if that's what you mean. I'm always busy."

"Have you got your notes handy on the Rose French case?"

"Why?"

"I'm rechecking."

"Why all this sudden new surge of interest in poor old Rose?"

"What do you mean, *all?*"

"I've had several calls about her this morning, one of them from the local paper, the other two anonymous. And Frank Clyde's right here in my office now. You know Clyde, he's one of the Psych boys."

"The name," Greer said, "sounds familiar."

"A lot of people seem to be getting back to the idea that Rose was murdered. You, too?"

"I tell you, I'm just rechecking."

"Well, you heard my testimony at the inquest. I'm not changing it."

"I'm not asking you to."

"You know how I work, Greer. I commit nothing to memory; everything is written down on the spot. I've done over two thousand autopsies, counting those I did in the army."

"I realize all this. So?"

"So I repeat, it's my conviction that Rose died a natural death that was, to be blunt, overdue. Probably the only thing that kept her alive with a heart in that condition was the fact that she was slender, had no excess weight to haul around. She certainly had at one time—there were un-mistakable evidences of obesity. Very likely her physi-cian spotted her heart condition and put her on a rigid diet. Speaking of diets, Greer, it wouldn't be a bad idea if you—"

"All right, all right. Starting tomorrow."

"No need to get huffy about it. Wait a minute, Clyde wants to talk to you."

"Put him on." Greer waited, tapping the stem of his pipe against the phone. The noise sounded like the rattle of bones. "Clyde? I thought you had a living to make."

"I worked this morning," Frank said. "These are my lunch hours."

"Hours?"

"I'm taking a little extra time off."

"It seems to me you've been taking a lot of extra time off. Better watch it or they'll toss you out."

"They can't toss me out until they have somebody to toss in."

"You're invaluable, are you?"

"No. Merely valuable."

"Well, you're not so valuable to me, Clyde. You might just as well carry on with your own job and let me do mine."

"You may regret those words," Frank said. "I found out something very interesting this morning about a friend of yours."

"Who?"

"Mr. Dalloway."

"Spill it."

"Not over the phone. Why not pick me up and we'll pay Dalloway a visit?"

"It's that interesting, is it?"

"I think so."

"I'll be there in twenty minutes," Greer said.

21

IT WASN'T twenty minutes, it was fifteen; and Greer had to wait. He parked at a red curb and pressed on the horn, hard and long.

Frank came hurrying out of the side door and climbed into the front seat of the car. "Why all the noise, Greer? This is a hospital; people are sick in there."

Greer made a sound of disgust. "People are sick out here too."

"What's the peeve?"

"I'm sick of liars. I've heard them all, fat liars, skinny liars, blonde liars, cross-eyed liars, the whole caboodle."

"How about one-armed liars?"

"Them too." He pulled away from the curb carefully, letting none of his impatience spill over into his driving. Cars were to Greer what people were to Frank: each was different and each commanded respect. "What's the story on Dalloway?"

"Do I tell it my way or yours?"

"Tell it any damn way you please."

"All right. This morning I was looking over my files. I have to give a report next month to the state board about the progress the clinic has made during the past year— how many patients we've handled, how many cures and commitments, etcetera. One of the files I came across was that of a man called Rudolph Fenton who was discharged as cured about six months ago."

"Only it turns out that he's not cured and his name isn't Fenton, it's Dalloway, and—"

"Nothing like that at all." Frank smiled. "The man's

cured and his name's Fenton, and he comes from a little town in Arkansas called Boulder Junction. Does that ring a bell?"

"Not loud."

"Rose was born in Boulder Junction. So was Fenton. I looked the town up in the atlas I keep in my office. The population, as of three years ago, was about three thousand."

"And?"

"I figured that in a community that size everybody would know everybody else's business, so I went down to see Fenton this morning at the glass factory where he works. He's a pretty old man but his memory's good."

"He knew Rose?"

"Both of them, Rose and Dalloway. In fact, Fenton claims that he was the first person at the scene on the night Dalloway was shot. That's how Dalloway lost his arm. It wasn't caught by a buzz-saw, as he told me. It was amputated because the elbow bones were crushed by the bullet."

"Who fired the shot?"

"I'm afraid," Frank said with some regret, "that Rose did."

"Any details?"

"Some. Neither Rose nor Dalloway made any secret of the fact that Rose joined up with a circus. According to Fenton, there actually was a circus in Boulder Junction that night. Not a Barnum and Bailey production as Rose liked to pretend later on, but one of those shoestring circuses with a trapeze act, an elephant, a couple of moth-eaten lions, half a dozen jugglers. Rose went to the circus alone. Fenton claims it was her first night out after the baby was born. This makes her subsequent behavior more understandable. A great many women feel trapped after they have their first child, especially talented and ambitious women like Rose. Most of them eventually adjust themselves, in one way or another. Rose didn't. She adjusted the circumstances. Nobody knows exactly what happened during Rose's little visit to the circus, whom she met or what kind of hook and sinker she swallowed. But the results of the visit were pretty drastic. She came home and told Dalloway she was leaving him, that she had a job with the circus as a dancer. Dalloway objected. There was a quarrel—one of many, I gather—only this time Dalloway's .32 Smith & Wesson came into the picture. There was a struggle over the gun and Dalloway got shot in the elbow. Rose didn't even wait around for the sheriff to arrive. The next day when an investigation was made, Dalloway took the blame and the whole episode was hushed up. It was hushed up so completely that even in later years when Rose became famous and practically every detail of her past was written up in newspapers and magazines, the shooting of Dalloway was never mentioned, according to Fenton. Shortly after the incident Dalloway took the baby, Lora, and left town."

Greer shrugged. "All this is fairly interesting, but it proves nothing against Dalloway."

"It gives him a reason for wanting Rose dead."

"Men don't usually wait thirty-two years for revenge unless they have difficulty finding their victim. Dalloway couldn't have had that difficulty. Rose was famous for years. Nearly everybody in the country knew where she was, including Dalloway. He'd have had no trouble getting revenge then."

"Maybe he didn't want it then. The thought of revenge might not have occurred to him until two months ago when Lora disappeared. His theory was that Lora came west to locate her mother, and the idea of Rose being reunited with Lora after her years of complete neglect might have been the final straw for Dalloway. So he came here on a mission, to find the two women who had deserted him."

"And found them?"

"Maybe," Frank said. "Maybe he did."

The desk clerk was a prim tight-lipped man with large, pale eyes magnified by a pair of thick, rimless bifocals. His eyes moved constantly as if in a desperate attempt to see over or around the lenses. With difficulty they focused on Greer for a second, slid to Frank, paused, and then rolled upward and around and back to Greer.

"Yes sir?"

"You have a Haley Dalloway registered here?"

"Yes, but—"

"I'd like to speak to him."

"Mr. Dalloway is not seeing anyone today, sir. He left word that he did not wish to be disturbed."

"Oh." Greer took his badge out of his pocket, showed it and slipped it back in, all in one swift, practiced motion. "Go and disturb him."

"I—I can't."

"Try, like a good boy."

"He's not here. He checked out an hour ago." The clerk's eyes made a wild tour of their sockets. "I would have said so right away, but I didn't know you were co— I didn't realize you were officers. Mr. Dalloway was a very special guest, very generous. When he asked me to tell a little white lie for him, well, how was I to know he was in trouble with the co—officers?"

"What's your name?"

"Ryan. Billy Ryan. There's no law against little white lies. If there was a law against little white—"

"Did Dalloway make up his mind quite suddenly?"

"This morning. I got his plane reservations for him by phone—two seats through to New York."

"Two?"

"Yes sir, he asked for two, I got him two."

"What flight?"

"Thirty-seven. If it's anything urgent, you should be

able to catch him. The limousine that picks up our passengers for the airport just left a few minutes ago."

"With Dalloway?"

"No sir. Mr. Dalloway left by himself in a cab."

The airport was on the main highway ten miles north of the city. Because traffic was heavy, Greer drove with the siren open. Conversation was impossible and neither of the men attempted it until the airport was in sight and the siren expired with a whimper.

Greer spoke first. "This is a pretty stupid move for a smart guy like Dalloway. Running away is the surest way to get chased, as any cat knows."

"Maybe he didn't expect to be chased."

"In that case we'll give him a surprise." He parked the car, and the two men walked toward the small, oval building that served the airline as ticket office, restaurant and waiting room. There was no large passenger plane in sight, though a group of people was already waiting at the locked gate to go aboard. Among them was Dalloway wearing dark glasses and a hat pulled down low on his forehead, and carrying a brief case in his ungloved hand.

Greer squinted. "See him?"

"Yes."

"I don't. Where?"

"Behind the fat woman in the green dress. I think he's spotted us, too."

From overhead came the distant drone of plane engines as Greer and Frank made their way through the lineup of people.

"Say, quit shoving," the fat woman muttered. "Land, it's just like in the last war, everybody lines up, everybody shoves, everybody—"

"Sorry, madam." Greer thrust past her and faced Dalloway. "Going somewhere?"

"Yes."

"I'd like to talk to you first."

"Sorry," Dalloway said calmly. "My plane's leaving."

"There'll be other planes."

"This happens to be the one I have a reservation on."

"Better cancel it. You've just had a change of plan."

"Have I?"

"Come on, Dalloway."

The waiting room was deserted except for a small, black kitten which lay purring in the sun on a window ledge.

Dalloway sat down on one of the long wooden benches, his brief case across his knees. He still appeared very calm and detached. Too calm, Frank thought, considering the irascible temper Dalloway had displayed in the past.

"Your decision to leave," Greer said, "came pretty suddenly, didn't it?"

"I am accustomed to making quick decisions and acting on them."

"Tell me, Dalloway, who was the second plane ticket for?"

"When I'm going on a long journey I always buy two tickets. It ensures me privacy."

"Kind of expensive, isn't it?"

"I am willing to pay for certain small luxuries."

"All right. Now let's have the truth."

Dalloway smiled. "As a matter of fact, the truth doesn't sound much better."

"Give it a whirl anyway."

"Very well. I met a lady last night. In a bar. It was one of those things, mutual attraction and interests and all that. Unfortunately, when she sobered up this morning, the attraction was no longer mutual and she didn't want to go east because it gets too cold in the wintertime."

"And the lady's name?"

"I wouldn't want to injure her reputation, Captain."

"You're still in there pitching, Dalloway, but you've

lost your control. You're wild. You might even walk a run in."

"I don't understand baseball slang very well, but I gather you don't believe me."

"That's good gathering. Now, try again. Who was the second plane ticket for?"

"It was bought," Dalloway said, "for a lady who changed her mind."

"Did you get your money back on the ticket?"

"No, I decided to keep it. For sentimental reasons."

"I'd like to see it."

"Sorry." Dalloway was still smiling but his hand tightened on the brief case he held in his lap. "Sorry, Captain, I can't quite recall where I put it."

"Mind if I look through your brief case?"

"Certainly I mind. You have no right to search me or my property without a warrant."

"I can get a warrant. That's doing it the hard way, Dalloway, hard for you."

"I don't know what you mean."

"While I'm getting a warrant, I'll want to know where you are, and in order to know where you are I'll have to book you. Know what I'd book you for?"

"No."

"Suspicion of murder."

"You're crazy. I didn't—murder anyone. I didn't even know anyone was murdered."

"New evidence has turned up in the case of Rose French." It was a lie, but Greer told it with utter conviction as if he believed it himself.

"Evidence against whom?"

"You, for one."

"Anyone else?"

"You don't seem to be very worried about yourself, Dalloway. Who *are* you worried about?"

"No one." Patches of purplish-red spread across Dalloway's cheeks and the bridge of his nose. "I have no personal concern with this sordid affair. For a time I was curious about Rose's death, and I suspected that the Good-fields were implicated. As Clyde here can tell you, I hired him to do some checking up in San Francisco. Nothing much came of it. I decided that my efforts were futile and I might just as well return home, since there was nothing further I could do."

"Your part in this business sounds very noble and innocent. Which surprises me because I don't figure you for a very noble or innocent man, Dalloway."

"People with small minds usually get a great many surprises in their lifetime."

"Okay, Dalloway." Greer's voice was tight with rage. "Give me another surprise. Hand me that brief case."

"I won't hand it to you. If you want it, take it by force. Clyde will be a witness."

"Please leave me out of it," Frank said uncomfortably.

"You wanted to be in on everything," Greer snapped. "You're in. Don't squawk about it."

"I don't like to be a witness to anything illegal."

"You're not going to be a witness, Clyde. Take Dalloway's brief case and open it."

"For crying in—"

"Now."

Frank reached out and took the brief case from Dalloway's lap, handling it cautiously as if it was full of snakes.

The big plane was coming down for a landing like a giant bird with tired wings. Dalloway turned and watched it bitterly as if the plane intended to leave without him, to desert him as Rose had, and Lora had. He said, "Open the case, Clyde. It's not locked. The Captain here wants to be surprised and I think he will be. Tell me, Captain, what do you expect, a shipment of counterfeit money?— a cache of heroin?—smuggled diamonds?"

"I'm not expecting anything," Greer replied flatly.

"Then you'll certainly be surprised."

"Try me."

Frank opened the brief case and removed the contents item by item, setting each item carefully on the bench beside him: two current magazines, a *Los Angeles Times,* a toothbrush and tube of paste in a special travel case, a clean white shirt, a pint of bourbon unopened, and a brown paper bag, the top folded down and sealed with scotch tape. The bag was fairly heavy and there was a sharp clink of metal when Frank put it down on the bench.

"Please accept the paper bag, Captain," Dalloway said, "with my compliments."

"What is it, a home-made bomb?"

"A home-made bomb. Yes. Yes, that's what it is, in a way. I didn't make it myself. It was handed to me for safe-keeping. I was quite wrong, of course, to accept the responsibility, I see that now. But at the time I thought that I could perhaps take the money and send it back to its rightful owners without incriminating myself or anyone else."

"What money, and whose?"

"I don't know who it belongs to, but the amount is three thousand dollars and some silver." Dalloway rubbed one of his cheekbones where the blood vessels had broken, leaving the skin tattooed with tiny purplish crosses. "I am not prepared to say anything more at the present time."

"So you don't know who the money belongs to?"

"No. I intended to find out, as I told you. I assumed—I suspected that there might be some—well, some slight illegality as to its source."

"How *slight?*" Greer emphasized the word sardonically.

"I don't know."

"Then I'll tell you, Mr. Dalloway. For that three thousand dollars a sick old woman was kidnapped."

"No. My God, no, I don't believe—it can't be, *can't*—"

"Drugged and taken out of her bed and held for ransom. The ransom was paid early this morning, but the woman is still missing."

"This is terrible, a terrible thing." Dalloway held a handkerchief against his trembling mouth. "Who—who was the woman?"

"For a man who was attempting to skip town with the ransom money, you're acting very innocent."

"I am innocent."

"You didn't know about the kidnapping, you don't know who the victim is. I'll bet you don't even know how you happened to get hold of that ransom money. Maybe a tall, dark stranger handed it to you on the street. Or maybe you got it from that lady you met in the bar last night?"

Dalloway had regained some of his control. He said quietly, "I'd prefer not to answer any more questions until I see a lawyer."

"Your preferences don't weigh very heavy with me. Where's Mrs. Goodfield?"

"I don't know."

"Where's Ada Murphy?"

"I have no idea. I'm not familiar with the name."

"Are you familiar with the face?"

"I—well, she might be someone I've seen around town somewhere and don't know by name."

"I think you know her," Greer said, "very intimately. I think you helped her with her crazy scheme, took charge of the ransom money and arranged for two seats on flight thirty-seven going east. The second plane ticket was for Murphy."

"You're telling me, not asking."

"I'm not asking, because the answer's so obvious."

"Not to me. I don't recall any Ada Murphy among my acquaintances."

"Try refreshing your memory." Greer took from his billfold the picture of Murphy gazing into the store window. In the unposed snapshot Murphy's characteristics stood out with sharp distinction. Her posture was arrogant, her face determined, as if she had spotted in the store window an object that she wanted and meant to have at any cost. "Recognize her, Dalloway?"

"No," Dalloway whispered, and then, realizing that his voice was barely audible he cleared his throat and said again, "No."

"She's not the lady you picked up in a bar last night? And she didn't give you this three thousand dollars to keep for her or split with her?"

"No."

"You're a liar, aren't you, Dalloway?"

"No. I want a lawyer."

"You're not even a good liar. A good liar has sense enough to admit facts that can be proven. I can prove this woman's identity."

"Not through me."

"No. In spite of you."

"I want a lawyer."

"Your needle's stuck," Greer said. "Besides, I don't carry a supply of lawyers in my pocket like lifesavers. Come on, Dalloway, have another look at this picture. Here, take it right in your hand and study it. Has she changed much since you've seen her? Put on a little weight, maybe?—showing her age a little more? How old is she now, Dalloway? How many years since you left Boulder Junction?"

Slowly, wordlessly, Dalloway crushed the snapshot in his fist and threw it over his shoulder. It struck the window sharply and fell on the floor like a stunned insect.

"How many years since you left Boulder Junction, Dalloway?"

There was no answer.

"It must have been tough for you being both a mother and a father to a girl like Lora. You have my sympathy."

"I wouldn't touch it with a ten-foot pole," Dalloway said. "You—"

"Watch your language, mister, or you're going to have to depend on your age to get you out of here in one piece."

Dalloway repeated the words with deliberate emphasis.

"I warn you, Dalloway."

"You talk a good fight."

Frank stepped between the two men. "Take it easy. There's a lady coming."

The lady, a platinum blonde wearing enormous jeweled sunglasses, teetered into the waiting room on four-inch heels. She was obviously in a hurry, but the high heels and the sunglasses held her back; she couldn't balance herself properly and she couldn't see too well in the gloom of the waiting room after the bright sunlight outside. She hesitated, peered with nervous uncertainty at the three men and then made her way with little running steps toward the exit door.

Greer reached the door before she did. "Wait a minute, please."

"Just what do you think you're doing? Get out of my way. That's my plane. I'm late."

"You're later than you think, Murphy."

"My name's Johnston."

"The wig is becoming, but a little theatrical. Where did you get it—from Rose?"

"Let me out of here."

"You'll get out but not through that door."

"You can't stop me."

"Try me."

But she didn't try. Instead, she reached up, slowly, and took off the jeweled sunglasses. She looked first at Greer, then at Frank, and finally at Dalloway.

It was Dalloway she addressed. "You lousy stool pigeon."

Dalloway got up and walked toward her in an easy, sauntering way as if he was going to greet an old friend. "What did you call me, my dear?"

"I suppose you've blabbed everything."

"What did you call me?"

"You heard me. Surely you're not deaf as well as cripp—"

The word was never finished because the flat of his hand struck her across the cheek. The force of the blow staggered her but she didn't fall, didn't cry out. Only the gradual reddening of her cheek indicated that anything had happened.

"Would you care to repeat the epithet, Lora?"

"I don't mind," she said with a little shrug. "You're a lousy stool pigeon."

Dalloway struck her again. This time Greer tried to stop him but he wasn't fast enough. Lora fell against the door. Still she made no outcry, gave no indication of the blow. It was as if he had lost his power to hurt her and she derived a certain pleasure from having him try and seeing him hurt himself instead.

She picked herself up. Her wig had slipped a little so she took it off entirely, yanked it away from her real hair with a spill of bobby pins and tossed it on the floor.

Dalloway watched her. His face had gone livid and he was swaying slightly as if on the verge of collapse.

"Think how tough you could get if you had two arms," Lora said. "As it is you merely bore me."

Dalloway covered his eyes with his one hand. "What did I do, what have I ever done to deserve you?"

"You not only deserve me, you made me. I am your little girl, strictly your product. Maybe I should have it tattooed across my back, Made By Haley Dalloway."

"I can't—Lora—"

"Let's not get maudlin. Things are bad enough." She turned to Greer. "I suppose you're going to arrest me."

Greer nodded.

"Him, too?"

"Yes."

"What's the charge? Against me, I mean."

"Kidnapping. Extortion. Felonious assault. Forcible entry. And maybe murder."

"I haven't done any of those things, not really."

"Really enough for me," Greer said. "Shall we go?"

"I don't seem to have a choice right now. But I'm not worried. None of those charges will stick."

"We'll see."

"If I committed a murder, where's the body? If I kidnapped anyone, where's the victim? If I extorted money, where is it?"

"In your father's brief case."

"That's *his* brief case, not mine. Really, Sergeant—"

"Captain."

"Sergeant, Captain, what's the difference? You're just a cop."

"I'll try to show you the difference some day."

"Lora, for God's sake," Dalloway interrupted. "Don't antagonize him."

Lora looked very surprised at the notion that she could antagonize anyone. "I'm not."

"Cooperate with him. Whatever you've done, admit it. Tell him what he wants to know."

"Such as?"

"Such as," Greer said, "where's Mrs. Goodfield?"

She answered without hesitation. "I don't know. I haven't seen her for some time."

"What time?"

"Oh, about noon yesterday, or a little after."

"What happened?"

"Nothing happened. She had a grouch on and didn't want to talk."

"Did you do anything to help the grouch?"

"What do you mean?"

"Ethel Goodfield claims there's quite a bit of liquor missing."

"Oh that," Lora said casually. "Sure, I took her up a bottle when she asked me to. She got the blues sometimes just sitting around in her room."

"A case of Scotch dissolves a lot of blues."

"I drank with her sometimes when she asked me to. We had some laughs together."

"Where is she now?"

"I told you I didn't know."

"Where were you at six o'clock last night?"

"Six? I guess I was having dinner."

"You were in a drugstore at Anacapa and Fifth, buying six ounces of ether under a false name."

"If you know, don't ask."

"Where were you during the early hours this morning, say between three and six?"

"You tell me."

"You were in Mrs. Goodfield's bedroom. Why?"

"I was in a jam," Lora said. "I was sick of the whole business. That's why I bought that ether—I thought perhaps I'd kill myself. But then it occurred to me that the old lady might lend me some money to get out of town and start all over again."

"How did you get into the house?"

"Walked in. I had a key to the back door."

"How did you get into the bedroom?"

"Same way. Walked. The door wasn't locked."

"Mrs. Goodfield was sleeping?"

"Mrs. Goodfield," Lora said dryly, "was gone."

The big plane was taking off, rising slowly into the air like a gull heading out to sea.

"Maybe you don't believe that, eh, Captain?"

"I don't."

"I knew you wouldn't. But it happens to be true. She was gone when I got there."

"How did the room look?"

"Look?"

"The windows, for instance."

"They were closed. Locked, in fact."

"Your story's full of holes," Greer said.

"I can plug them."

"What with?"

"Just paper." She took a folded piece of stationery out of her purse and handed it to him. "When I went into the bedroom, the old lady was gone and this was on her desk. There was another paper there too, all crumpled up as if she'd been practicing what to say. I smoothed it out to read it but I left it there and took this instead."

Greer unfolded the paper and read Mrs. Goodfield's last message to her son: *Willett, can't stand this kind of life so am leaving. Don't worry, everything will be all right, you can trust me. Will let you know later where I am but don't look for me and I mean it.*

22

No one believed her, but Lora Dalloway stuck to her story for the rest of the afternoon. At five-thirty she was served a light supper in the cell adjoining Greer's office, which was reserved for special prisoners. Greer had a pot of coffee and a canvas chair brought in for himself. He had questioned Lora at the airport, in the car, in his office, and he thought this rather drastic change of atmosphere might affect her veracity.

It didn't. She seemed quite at ease in the cell, ate with good appetite, and repeated her version of the facts.

No, she did not know where Mrs. Goodfield was or why or how she had left. She had bought the ether in a fit of despondency but had changed her mind when the idea occurred to her of borrowing money from old Mrs. Goodfield so she could leave town.

"What kind of jam were you in?" Greer asked.

"Oh, you know, personal troubles."

"I don't know. You tell me."

"Well, in the first place there was Ortega breathing down my neck, wanting to get married and start raising children. *Children*, yet. Makes me sick to think of it. Ortega's all right, he has a nice build, but he's just a boy. Anyway he was getting hard to handle. I thought it was the strategic moment to disappear. You can't always trust these Mexicans—they don't put as much value on human life as we do."

Even though he thought he was beginning to understand Lora, Greer was startled by the inconsistency of her mind. She seemed to consider it logical to run away from Ortega's possible violence, yet at the same time plan violence against herself; to speak of the value of human life and yet to ignore its value. Her words and her emotions had little connection. They flowed separately and in opposite directions, and only occasionally did they touch as they had during the meeting with her father in the airport waiting room.

He said, "Ortega's a nice boy. I think you could have handled him all right. He's very fond of you."

"He adores me," Lora said sharply. "So what? I hate being adored. I hate that feeling of *responsibility*. It makes me want to hit out at people."

And at yourself, Greer thought. But he didn't say it. Instead, he sipped at his coffee and waited for her to continue.

194

"The second reason was my father. Naturally I knew he was in town, but I had no idea he was so close on my trail until yesterday. I looked out of the window and there he was in the garden talking to Ortega. I was furious. All my life he's been doing that."

"Doing what?"

"Hovering over me, treating me as if I were a four-year-old, trying to make me stay home and live his kind of life. I can't stand his kind of life. I need excitement, change, fun."

"Is that your idea of fun and excitement, taking a job as an ordinary servant?"

"I wasn't ordinary. And yes, it was fun, in a way, watching Ethel swallow that milady stuff and Willett inflate like a balloon when I called him sir. I got some laughs out of it. Talk about a pair of dimwits, those two really deserve a prize."

Greer glanced pointedly at the barred window. "Your own mammoth intellect has managed to land you in jail."

"It will get me out."

"You're confident."

"Just wait until Willett comes. He'll explain, arrange the necessary bail, and so on. He is coming? You gave him my message?"

"Yes."

She leaned forward eagerly, like a child about to hear a favorite story. "What did you tell him?"

"What you asked me to—that you wanted to see him and that your real name was Lora Dalloway and you were Rose's daughter."

"How did he react?"

"He seemed startled, genuinely startled."

"Oh, it was genuine, all right," she said, smiling, pleased with herself. "He had no idea who I was. I played my role to the hilt."

"Beyond the hilt."

"I don't consider you an authority on acting."

"You don't have to be an authority to recognize schmalz," Greer said. "You're like your mother in that respect. I saw one of her old movies on TV last week—she couldn't ask the time of day without flinging herself all over the screen."

"That's not true. My mother was a wonderful actress. I could have been too, if I'd had any chance."

"That's the story of your life, is it? You never had any chances."

"Not real ones. Dalloway hemmed me in."

"So you decided to come west and find your mother. Where did you go first?"

"I've told you all this."

"Tell me again."

"I landed in L.A. I was broke, so I took a job for a couple of weeks to earn some money for clothes. I'd left most of my clothes behind and I didn't want to meet my mother looking like a bum. I thought—I was under the impression that she was quite wealthy."

"You must have had a shock."

"I did. That awful boarding house—that slatternly Mrs. Cushman—I could hardly believe it. And mother looked terrible, old and haggard and half-starved."

"Was she glad to see you?"

"Glad enough. I didn't expect her to dissolve with joy. We got along all right, not as mother and daughter but as two people with something in common—we both needed money."

"You only paid one visit to the boarding house?"

"Just one—the first. After that we met other places, in cafés or on the breakwater."

"Why?"

"Rose wasn't keen on acknowledging me as her long-lost daughter; it put her in too bad a light. And frankly, I wasn't very keen on being acknowledged. I kept on using the name Ada Murphy. It's such an earthy, ugly name, no one would ever think it wasn't real."

"What did you and your mother talk about when you met?"

"Oh, things in general," she said with a vague wave of one hand.

"Nothing in particular?"

"No."

"She didn't tell you about a job she was offered?"

"No."

"She was apparently on her way to start that job when she died. In fact, she may have decided to stop in at the Goodfields' to say good-bye to you."

Lora blinked. "Yes, I've thought of that. It seems likely. She knew where I was working."

"Did she know why you were working there?"

"Why? Why does anyone work? For beans and coffee."

"You deliberately planted yourself in the Goodfield house. Don't deny it. We have the evidence of Ethel Goodfield and Miss Raffin of Personal Services. Why go through all that fancy footwork to land a mediocre job?"

"I heard that the Goodfields wanted someone to help look after the old lady."

"Where did you hear it?"

"From Ortega. I met him down on the beach one day surf-fishing. We got to talking about the new family who'd just moved into the Pearce estate where he worked."

"And Ortega told you all about the Goodfields and how they needed a companion for Mrs. Goodfield?"

"That's right."

"It's not right at all," Greer said. "It's not even close. Neither Willett nor Ethel Goodfield had any real contact with Ortega until after Rose's death. He came certain days a week and did his work. His salary was included in the rent the Goodfields paid; they had no personal contact with him or interest in him."

197

"He knew all about them anyway."

"You're going to stick to that story?"

"Like glue." She had finished eating her supper. She put the tin tray on the floor and wiped her mouth with a handkerchief. "By the way, where's my father?"

"He's being held for questioning."

"That's absurd. Not that I care about him, but he had nothing to do with that money. I've explained all that."

"Explain it again."

"Very well, if you insist. I went to the Goodfields' house around three in the morning. I'm not sure about the time —I'd bummed around the town all night, went to a movie and walked around and had a few drinks. The drinks made me feel better, more hopeful. I wasn't so keen on killing myself. I'm not really the suicidal type. I get depressed but I bounce right back again."

"In fact, you bounced right over to the Goodfields'."

"Yes, to borrow money from Olive Goodfield. I knew she didn't have much, if any, but I was certain that there was cash somewhere in the house. I'd heard Willett talking to Jack over the phone about the loan Jack wanted, and after the phone call Willett went to the bank. I put two and two together and got three thousand dollars."

"You intended to borrow it all?"

"I thought I'd try to. After all, she and I were quite close, closer than anyone realizes. The only trouble was that when I got there she was gone. I'd walked three whole miles in the middle of the night for nothing. My feet hurt and my head ached and I was cold and hungry. It's funny how the mind can function brilliantly sometimes when the body is all worn out."

"Vice versa is even funnier," Greer said.

"What I had was a marvelous idea. You just don't appreciate it because it wasn't strictly legal."

"It wasn't even remotely legal. You faked a kidnapping."

198

"What else could I do?"

Greer realized the futility of trying to answer her. Like her mother, Lora had a psychopathic streak in her nature that made moral self-judgments impossible. What she thought was brilliant, what she did was right. Later on, when the brilliance faded and the rightness turned wrong, she could admit her mistakes. But at the time of action her course always seemed inevitable; she steered straight for her objective whether it was a harbor or a floating mine.

"I still had the bottle of ether in my purse," Lora went on. "It didn't take me long to arrange the room, the windows and the piece of silk from her nightgown caught on the broken glass. At the last moment I opened the ether and sprinkled it around the bed. Then I went downstairs and out the back door to the garage. I carried the extension ladder around to the sun deck outside Mrs. Goodfield's bedroom windows."

She gave Greer a bright wasn't-I-clever glance. Greer turned away, feeling a cold dislike flowing like ice water through his veins. "Did you have any concern about Mrs. Goodfield, what had happened to her?"

"Why should I? If she wanted to run out, it was her own business, not mine. I merely took advantage of it."

"I see."

"I went back to town and checked in at some crummy hotel for a couple of hours' sleep. I gave the night clerk a story about having a quarrel with my husband and walking out, and he wasn't suspicious. Shortly before seven I got up and phoned Ethel from a pay phone in a restaurant. Everything went smoothly as I planned. It wasn't until after I'd picked up the ransom money that I began to get nervous. I realized that Ethel couldn't keep her mouth shut, and that every cop in town would be looking for me. As soon as the stores opened up I bought a pair of sunglasses. Then I saw this blonde wig on a dummy in a

199

beauty parlor window. I gave the proprietor a story about wanting to borrow it to play a gag on my husband. He swallowed it. It's amazing how unsuspicious people are when you pretend to confide in them.

"I felt a lot safer with the wig and the sunglasses, but not safe enough. I still had the money on me, and I still had no way of getting far enough away from town. The police would be sure to be covering the ticket offices and I'm not the type to hitchhike. So I made my big mistake. I went to see my father." She laughed, a throaty laugh that splashed across the cell and dripped venomously down the wall. "God, what a happy reunion that was. The old boy acted like a cross between Jesus Christ and Simon Legree."

"He agreed to help you, though."

"Oh sure. I played it with tears and violins and promises. Poor Dalloway is a sucker for all of them, especially the promises. He agreed to hold the money for me—I told him I won it on the horses—and to buy two plane tickets to New York. I was to meet him at the airport. I did. You know the rest."

"Are you willing to sign a statement?"

"I told you before, no. I'm not signing anything."

"Why not?"

"It's very simple. I might want to change my story and then it wouldn't look so good if there was a signed statement contradicting me."

"It won't look so good anyway."

"Oh, I don't know. If the case goes to court it will be your word against mine, and I can be pretty convincing."

"You can be dangerously candid."

This pleased her. "I've always been candid, like my mother."

"I suppose you know that your mother was under treatment for some time at the Mental Health Clinic."

"Nonsense. She wasn't under treatment. Frank Clyde,

a friend of hers, worked at the clinic. She went there for laughs."

"You have," Greer said, "more in common with your mother than you realize."

"You didn't even know her."

"Frank has a file on her a mile long."

"Files don't live and breathe. You didn't know Rose," she repeated. "That wonderful vitality she had—nothing could get her down, nothing. She could pitch."

"Towards the end she was pitching empty wine bottles into left field."

"Nonsense." Lora glanced at her wrist watch. "It's time Willett was here. I can't wait all night."

"I'll see if he's arrived yet."

"You're very kind. You're so kind it makes me wonder."

"Wondering," Greer said, "is good for a girl like you."

23

BARRETT WAS WAITING in Greer's office smoking a long black cigar that smelled like burning wool.

Greer opened the window. "Hear much?"

"Nearly every word. Fine acoustics."

"What do you think?"

"About the kidnapping? She's right. There wasn't any."

"Sure?"

"I was sure before. Now I'm certain sure. I've sent Woody and Carbonaro back home. I thought I'd stick around here for a couple of days, see if the climate clears up my sinusitis."

"If I smoked weeds like that all the time, I'd have sinusitis too."

"I don't smoke them all the time. A friend of mine happened to have a baby, his eighth. You don't buy the same quality cigar for the eighth."

The two men sat down, Greer behind the desk, Barrett in a straight chair tilted against the wall, holding the cigar carefully as if he was afraid it might explode.

"I'm aware," Barrett said, "that you would have found out everything we did. I'm glad you didn't. Having your boys messing around would have made things a lot tougher for us. As it is, the evidence is clear. First, the ether. Woody used a reagent on the sheets and pillow slip and the ether was undoubtedly sprinkled around haphazardly as the woman claims. Next, the piece of blue silk caught in the glass door. It was cut with a scissors, not torn, and the door was broken from the inside not the outside. Then there's the matter of the sun deck. It hasn't been used for months, not a single print or mark on it, just a few bird droppings. Then the ladder. It was propped against the railing of the sun deck as she says, but it never held any weight, the grass underneath is barely dented. In fact the whole thing is nothing more than a badly planned hoax."

"Olive Goodfield's disappearance is no hoax."

"I realize that, but I think she disappeared voluntarily. I examined the farewell note she left, the one Miss Dalloway gave you at the airport. The handwriting is undoubtedly the same as the handwriting in the margins of the two maps, but in the case of the note there are indications that she was under emotional stress: discrepancies in spacing and pressure and certain distortions of letters. I'm convinced she left the house of her own free will and with what she considered good reason."

"It must have been a compelling reason to make a woman who was an invalid pick up and leave like that in the middle of the night without luggage and, as far as I know, without money."

"She was afraid. Fear is a compelling enough reason. Whether it's rational or irrational. Perhaps something happened to precipitate her decision, perhaps nothing happened."

"Something happened," Greer said. "Her son Jack arrived from San Francisco, but I can't see any connection between that and her disappearance."

"You can't, but maybe she could." Barrett rose and butted the cigar in an ashtray. "I've done quite a bit of work with the Missing Persons Bureau in L.A. People disappear for some very strange reasons. I remember one young man who was gone for two years because he didn't want to wear a tie his mother had given him for his birthday and he didn't have enough nerve to say so. When we finally caught up with him in Spokane, his mother had died. It turned out fine. He's married now, has a good job and two kids."

"What's the moral, that we should all be born orphans?"

"The moral is, don't buy birthday ties." Barrett went to the door, grinning. "See you later. You know where I'm staying."

"Yes."

"I'd like to see you break this case, Jim. Good luck."

"Thanks."

The door closed.

Greer looked at his watch. Nearly six. He was going to be late to dinner again. Pot roast, May had promised, flavored with plenty of garlic and braised onions. He tried to imagine the pot roast waiting for him at the table, but the vile odor of the cigar still clung to the walls and his tongue and the roof of his mouth tasted only the acid bitterness of too much coffee.

"Pot roast," he said aloud, but the image, the smell, wouldn't come. He knew perfectly well he'd be lucky if he got a couple of fried eggs by ten o'clock.

"Sorry, we're all out of pot roast," Frank said from the

doorway. "How about a top sirloin with a double order of French fries?"

"It's no joke." Greer sighed. "Other men can get home for meals. Postmen, plumbers, cement finishers, auto mechanics, they're all sitting down right now feeding their fat faces. Did you bring Goodfield along?"

"Yes. There was no trouble, he wanted to come."

"What did he say?"

"As far as I can tell, he believes the kidnapping is real, all right. He's almost hysterically anxious to find his mother. I'm not sure that it's filial devotion, though. Looks more like anger to me."

"Who's he mad at?"

"See for yourself."

"All right, bring him in."

Frank opened the door. "You can come in now, Mr. Goodfield."

Red-cheeked, red-eyed, Willett swept into the office as if there was a strong wind pushing at his back. "Where is she? Where is that lying, deceitful, two-faced little monster?"

"You'll see her in a minute. Sit down."

"The impudence. The treachery. After all we put up with from her. She never did an hour's honest work. I'm incensed, that's what I am, incensed, and I'm not a man to get incensed without reason."

"Sure, sure. But—"

"When I think of the way Ethel cooked and scrubbed and washed dishes while that lazy little viper sat around and sneered. Sneered. At *my wife*. And the paper—the way she mutilated the evening paper before I had a chance to see it. Cut whole sections right out of it. And all the time I was putting up with that kind of thing she was plotting behind *my back*."

"When I talked to you this morning, you didn't seem quite so angry with her."

"That was before I found out she was Dalloway's daughter. Imagine the two of them plotting, scheming together—"

"What was the object of their scheming, do you think?"

"Money," Willett said tersely. "My money. They abducted my mother and—"

"They didn't."

"Pardon? What—did you say?"

"They didn't abduct your mother. She left of her own accord."

Willett sagged heavily against the desk, hanging on to the edge of it with plump fingers that looked pale and boneless as worms. "My God. Why didn't you tell me?"

"I didn't know until a short time ago. She left a note addressed to you. Murphy—Miss Dalloway removed it when she arranged the kidnapping setting."

"Let me see the note."

"It's in the lab right now. I can tell you what she said, approximately. She stated that she was leaving because she couldn't tolerate her life and that you were to trust her, not to worry, and above all, not to look for her."

There was a prolonged silence. Frank lit a cigarette, Greer looked carefully at a picture on the wall that he'd seen a thousand times before, Willett pressed a white silk handkerchief tightly to his mouth as if to hold back a stream of words that might have spurted out like blood or bile.

He spoke through the handkerchief, his voice muffled and hoarse. "She had no right. No *right*. The *injustice* of it. Never cared about anyone but herself. I always treated her well, too well. I should never have, never, never have listened to—"

"Sit down, Mr. Goodfield." Greer pushed a chair towards him.

But Willett was too distracted to sit down. "It's incredible that she'd do a thing like this to me after all I've done. You're sure she wrote that note?"

"Yes."

"You're *positive?*"

"Yes."

"I—then, there's nothing for me to do but to accede to her wishes. I know my duty. If she doesn't want me to look for her, I won't."

"I know my duty too. I'm going to find her."

"No. Please. You don't understand, Captain. She'll be upset if you go against her wishes, she'll be furious."

"If the day comes when an old woman's anger can set me off course, I'll turn in my badge."

"I am not afraid for myself," Willett said quietly, "but for her. She's ill. The least shock might be fatal."

"So far she's proved pretty durable. That case of Scotch didn't go up in smoke. Nor, for that matter, do ordinary invalids take off in the middle of the night and disappear. No, Mr. Goodfield," he added with a sardonic smile, "I don't think a shock is going to kill her."

"It's useless to argue with you."

"Quite useless. Every policeman in town is looking for your mother, has been since this morning."

"I see. Well, in that case, there's nothing more to say."

"Not on that score." Greer leaned across the desk and spoke into the com box. "Daley? Come in here, will you?"

A minute later Daley appeared, a pink-cheeked, blue-eyed young man with an air of gentleness that made him irresistible to women and infuriated his wife. "Yes sir?"

"Take Mr. Goodfield in to see Miss Dalloway. See that they're left alone."

"Alone? You mean—"

"I mean, alone."

"I heard you, sir. Only it seems to me that it would be contrary to official reg—"

"Daley, when you get to be a Captain, you may run this place the way you want to. Meanwhile."

"Meanwhile, yes sir."

Willett followed Daley through the side door, glancing back over his shoulder as if he wanted to change his mind and go home again.

Frank crossed to the window and threw his cigarette out onto the patch of lawn below. "I agree with Daley. You're being extraordinarily lenient."

"I'm generous. I want them to have a nice heart-to-heart chat."

"Have you got the cell wired?"

"No. If they speak up clearly I can hear them through the wall, but something tells me they're not going to. Be quiet and listen."

Frank listened. He heard the sharp clank of the cell door as it opened and closed again, and then Daley's voice: "I'm afraid I have to lock it, sir" . . . "There's no danger of fire, everything's fireproofed" . . . "Yes sir, I know you're a taxpayer. So am I." A silence, followed by Lora Dalloway's voice, brisk and incisive: "When are you going to get over pulling that taxpayer routine? Every boy with a paper route is a taxpayer in this day and age."

"Goddam you," Willett said. "Where is she?"

"Wouldn't you like to know."

"Tell me or I swear I'll—"

"Don't swear anything. My patience is thin. So are the walls. That cop isn't as fatheaded as he looks. I was put in this cell because his office is right next to it. I heard you when you came in, so *he* can hear us now. Understand?"

Willett apparently understood. Although he began talking again, his words were indistinct, mere nonsense syllables like a speech played backward on a tape recording.

"Let them talk," Greer said, sounding relaxed and contented. "They should have lots to say to each other. Then it'll be my turn."

"Greer—"

"How's Miriam?"

"Fine," Frank said. "Listen—"

"And the boys?"

"Fine."

"Glad to hear it."

"Greer, I don't think you should leave those two alone together in there without even trying to find out what they're talking about."

"I know what they're talking about. And I want them to be alone together. The cosier they get, the better."

"What's the gimmick?"

"Nature," Greer said. "Human nature. That's the gimmick."

"See that it doesn't explode."

"Take two people who hate each other and mistrust each other and yet want something from each other and you get an explosion. Or a deal. I kind of think," he added after a moment, "that it'll be a deal."

24

IT WAS A DEAL.

Seven-thirty, and outside the window in Greer's office hung the sea haze that preceded darkness. He pressed the wall switch and the fluorescent ceiling lights flickered on, giving Willett's skin a moist, greenish phosphorescence.

"Sit down," Greer said. "Finish your talk with Miss Dalloway?"

"Yes. Yes, I did." Willett sat down, first looking carefully at the chair as if he thought Frank or Greer might pull it out from under him. "A very satisfactory talk, as a matter of fact. Certain doubtful points were cleared up."

"Indeed?"

"I was rather hasty in judging Miss Dalloway, I'm afraid. After giving the matter some thought I'm convinced that her part in this affair was the result of a mere girlish impulse."

"Going after three thousand dollars tooth and nail is a little more than an impulse and Miss Dalloway is a little more than a girl."

"I don't propose to argue," Willett said with a decisive shake of his head. "Miss Dalloway has explained everything to me and offered to make full restitution. Under the circumstances I refuse to prosecute or sign any complaint against her."

"I see."

"Furthermore, I refuse to appear in court as a witness against her."

"And Mrs. Goodfield?"

"My wife will also refuse when I explain the situation."

"What is the situation?"

"Miss Dalloway acted on impulse and is willing to repay the money."

"She hasn't got the money." Greer smiled. "I have."

"That's merely a technicality. It's not your money, it's mine."

"You may have to go to court to prove it, Mr. Goodfield."

"That's ridiculous, you know it's my money."

"How do I know? I got it from Dalloway."

"It's mine," Willett repeated like a child. "It's my money."

"Would you be willing to tell a judge or jury just how you're so sure that it's yours?"

"I—no. No. It's a private matter between Miss Dalloway and me."

Greer didn't argue the point. "So you're convinced that

Miss Dalloway should be let off and any charges against her dismissed?"

"What are the charges against her?"

"So far, none. I merely held her for questioning."

"You've questioned her?"

"Yes."

"Then she may leave?" Willett said. "You're letting her go?"

"Sure. She can go."

"Well, well, I must say that's very decent of you, Captain, very civilized."

"I'm as civilized as hell," Greer said.

"Dear me, I'm quite overwhelmed. I didn't expect such immediate cooperation."

"I am also as immediate and cooperative as hell."

"Ha, ha," Willett said painfully. "I must tell that to Ethel. I—you're not just fooling about releasing Miss Dalloway?"

"I'm not fooling, no, indeed. Of course, I'd like her to stay around town."

"Oh, she will. Right at my house."

"Good. I'll go and tell Daley to get her things out of the safe." He left the room, closing the door behind him.

Willett glanced rather timidly at Frank. "He's rather a decent chap for a policeman."

"Yes."

"His taking such a reasonable attitude was quite a surprise to me."

To me, too, Frank thought.

"You don't suppose he's got something up his sleeve?"

"Oh no, not at all."

Willett was silent for a time. Then he said in a resigned voice, "I'm sure things will work out somehow."

"What things?"

"Oh, everything. Life is very difficult, problems leaping out at you from all sides. Take a man, an ordinary chap like myself, nothing special about him one way or another, what's he going to do when he finds himself in a spot?"

"Try to get out of it."

"Exactly. He must act. He must take the aggressive role. Within the law, naturally."

"Naturally."

"Even if some of the laws aren't fair."

"Which laws, for instance?"

Willett looked stubborn. "Never you mind."

At the switchboard in the receiving room Greer was talking to Daley. "Where's his car?"

"Half a block down on Garden Street, facing north, '47 Lincoln, black sedan, plates 62X895."

"Two tails should be enough. Goodfield's not very bright and the woman is cocksure. I'll drive my own car and Shaeffer can use that souped-up jalopy of his. Right?"

"Check."

"O.K., hand over her stuff. I'll take it to her. Oh yes, and tell Clyde he can come along for the ride."

"Why?"

"I like to have a psychiatrist around. Then if I go nuts, I'll be the first to know."

"I should never have asked."

"Next time, don't," Greer said. He had a better reason for wanting Frank to come along, but he didn't tell Daley or even Frank himself.

Lora Dalloway was waiting to be released, her hands curled around the bars of the cell, her face peering out expectantly like a monkey's. At some point in the past hour she had decided to switch roles, from the hard-boiled sophisticate to the sweet and wistful country girl.

Greer unlocked the door and swung it open. "All right, you can leave."

"You mean I'm free?"

"Like a bird."

"Oh, that's wonderful. Gee, I just can't thank—"

"Play it straight," Greer said. "Here's your stuff, wallet, key ring, wrist watch, and three dollars and eighty-seven cents in cash. Sign this receipt, please."

"What name shall I sign?"

"How about Eleanor Roosevelt's, just to make it more interesting?"

"You know damned well what I meant. I've been going under the name of Ada Murphy so I thought—"

"Sign your own name."

"You don't have to be so grumpy about it." She signed the receipt, Lora Eloise Frances Dalloway, and handed it back to him. "Now what?"

"You can go through that door to my office where the faithful Willett awaits you."

"It sounds too easy. What's the catch?"

"No catch. I'd just like to know where you're going, so I can get in touch with you if necessary."

"I'm going home—that is, to the Goodfields'."

"To resume your job?"

"That's right."

"Very magnanimous of Goodfield to take back a woman who just rooked him of three G's."

"He knows I didn't mean it. It was an impulse."

"A girlish impulse, in fact."

"In fact, yes."

"You'd better watch both the impulsiveness and the girlishness, Miss Dalloway. Neither is very becoming at your age."

"Your cracks don't bother me." She went into his office, slamming the door behind her so violently that the walls shook.

Greer left by the side entrance. His car was parked about twenty yards behind the black Lincoln, with the engine running and Frank in the front seat looking a little worried.

"Listen, Jim. It's nearly eight o'clock."

"I know it." Greer got in behind the wheel. "So?"

"Miriam expected me home an hour ago."

"Miriam's a nice girl. How is she, by the way?"

"You asked me that before."

"I did? Well, it just goes to show how my thoughts dwell with her. A very fine girl, Miriam, admirable."

"Cut it out, will you?" Frank said. "Where are we going?"

"I don't know."

"You must have some idea."

"What are you so concerned about? For a solid week you've been horning in on this case, hanging around, getting in my hair. Now when the time comes for you to make yourself useful, you want to back out because you're afraid you'll catch hell from your wife."

"How am I making myself useful?"

"You'll see," Greer said. "Here they come now."

Lora and Willett came down the front steps of the building, Lora walking briskly and a little ahead of Willett like an older sister impatient with the slowness of her little brother. At the curb she paused to wait for him and the two of them stood silhouetted by the headlights of an approaching car. The car passed and they crossed the road and got into the black Lincoln.

It was obvious from the beginning that neither of them expected to be followed. The Lincoln went directly to its destination, a dilapidated two-story building on Third Street with a green neon sign across the entrance which said tersely, Food. Inside, a fat Mexican was sleeping at the counter, his right hand still holding a half-empty beer bottle.

Willett parked at a yellow curb and Lora Dalloway got

out and walked swiftly around the side of the building and up an open flight of stairs that led to a narrow balcony circling the second story.

"Part of the place is the old Pico adobe," Greer said. "The top was added later, converted into studios that are rented out to artists."

"What kind of artists?"

"All kinds, mostly bad."

Lora paused at one of the arched doors on the balcony and pounded on it with both fists. The door opened inward and a woman stood outlined in the lighted arch, an enormous woman with clipped gray hair. She wore green plaid slacks and a white turtleneck sweater and she had a cigarette tucked behind her left ear.

Lora went inside and the door closed, but not for long. Within a minute she came out again and hurried along the balcony and down the steps. Before she got into the Lincoln she looked carefully up and down the street as if it had occurred to her for the first time that someone might be following her. Her eyes slid past Greer's car without hesitating.

"Think she spotted us?" Frank asked.

"If she did, she covered it up nicely." The Lincoln pulled away from the curb and Greer followed. "Did you recognize the woman in the green plaid slacks?"

"I've seen her around."

"Name's Billy McKeon. Between gin bouts she makes puppets and paints scenery for the various little theatre groups."

"What possible connection could she have with Mrs. Goodfield?"

"I'm hoping Lora Dalloway will tell us that."

At the next stop light Willett braked the Lincoln, made a careful hand signal and turned right onto Anacapa Street.

Greer leaned back, relaxed and smiling.

"For cripe's sake," Lora said. "Can't we go any faster?"

"I don't like to drive fast. Besides, it's against the law."

"Against the *law*. You kill me, you really kill me."

"I'd like to." Willett made the statement without emotion of any kind. "I'd like to see you dead."

"Don't get nasty. I might get nasty right back at you, and then you'd never find her."

"I don't expect to anyway."

"We'll find her."

"She could be five hundred miles away by this time."

"Well, she isn't," Lora said crisply. "Billy McKeon saw her this morning."

In the dim light of the dashboard Willett's face had a luminous pallor. "Is she—was she all right?"

"Alive and kicking."

"You know what I mean."

"Certainly she was all right. She bummed some food and a package of cigarettes. She wanted to stay there but Billy wouldn't let her. She's superstitious."

"Can the McKeon woman be trusted?"

"Trusted to do what?"

"Not to call the police."

"Billy wouldn't call the police if someone had a knife at her throat. Turn left at the next corner."

Once again Willett made a careful signal before turning. "Didn't she tell this McKeon woman anything, where she was going, when she'd be back?"

"Nothing."

"Did she have any money with her?"

"Where would she get any money?"

"From you."

"I *didn't* give her any money."

"Thank God for that. It means she can't be very far away."

215

"I told you I don't think she intended to go far. She just wanted to throw a scare into us. And," Lora added with a bleak little smile, "she did."

"I'm not exactly scared."

"You exactly are. Don't kid me. You won't look any better in stripes than I will."

"It's all your fault, not mine."

"*My* fault. Listen, mister, don't make me lose my temper. Stick to the facts. *I* just came into the middle of a very fancy little game you'd rigged up by yourself."

"I didn't, I didn't. It was her. *She* did it!"

"Well, don't get hysterical. And for Pete's sake watch the road, do you want to get us killed?"

"I don't care. It may be the only way out."

"Well, it's not the only way out for me!" Lora screamed. "I've got a future."

"Have you?"

"What do you mean, have I?"

"You didn't think so much of your future when you were buying that ether."

"I had a fit of depression, that's all. I couldn't see my way clear."

"Now you can?"

"With your help, I can. I need your help and you need mine. We're a sort of mutual aid society."

Willett took his eyes off the road for a second and stared at her. "How much are you going to try and swindle out of me?"

"I want the money you promised my mother plus a little extra for myself."

"I never promised your mother any lump sum. I couldn't afford to then and I can't now. That three thousand dollars was the last cash I have in the world. I'm at the end of my rope."

"You've got the kind of rope that stretches."

"What do you mean?"

"I mean," she said carefully, "your stock in the doll factory."

"That must never be touched. I'll go to prison, I'll kill myself, before I disregard my mother's wishes."

"Why?"

"Because they're sacred to me."

"Oh nuts."

Willett's jaw clenched. "They are. You wouldn't understand about human feelings."

"Forget about feelings and let's get back to factories. Ethel says you're not even interested in the doll factory, and what's more she says it's losing money and the place is falling apart."

"Ethel knows nothing about business. The factory is not losing money and it's not falling apart. It simply needs recapitalization and a firm hand."

"Yours?"

"I'm certainly going to try. I've had very little chance to take care of the business this past year because I've been traveling around with mother."

"Maybe that was her idea."

"Pardon?"

"Nothing. Skip it."

They were passing through the oldest section of town where front parlors had become little grocery stores or antique shops, and bright new gas stations rubbed shoulders with shabby-looking mansions that had been converted into boarding houses or two-room apartments.

Traffic was heavy and sluggish, slowed down by pedestrians ambling across the streets and children on bicycles and dogs of every size and shape and breed and mixture of breeds. These dogs were different from the dogs in the other parts of town—they had seen everything, and having seen everything, they were not so curious or so friendly.

They moved in and out of traffic, skillfully, knowing which cars to step in front of and which to avoid, using their right of way with more insight and consideration than the pedestrians. Lora turned and looked out of the rear window. "Greer is still with us, six cars back."

"What will we do?"

"I know this neighborhood. There's a Texaco station in the next block. Drive in very slowly and I'll duck out and hide in the rest-room. Then you can lead Greer around for awhile while I walk over to the house. It's only half a block from the gas station."

"I can't lead him around all night."

"Give me half an hour."

"You don't even know for sure that she's at the house."

"Where else would she go if she was broke? She'll be there, all right," Lora said grimly. "She'd better be."

"I can't drive around all night," he said again.

"You don't have to. Just go home. That will give me a chance to talk to her. Then if things work out we'll take a cab and meet you at home."

"I hope—"

"Here's the station. Turn in."

He turned in, very slowly, passing within two yards of the Ladies' Rest Room. Lora jumped out of the car while it was moving.

She was quick, but not quick enough.

Both Frank and Greer spotted her in the three seconds that it took her to reach the door. But instead of stopping the car and waiting for her to come out Greer pressed on the accelerator.

"Aren't you going to follow her?" Frank said.

"I don't have to. I know where she's going. So I think we'll get there first and surprise her."

Half a block down the street Greer turned into a long narrow driveway, drove to the end of it and switched off his car lights.

Within five minutes Lora Dalloway went past the drive-way and up the geranium-lined sidewalk of the house next door.

25

THE HOUSE WAS old but in better repair than most of its neighbors. The wooden steps had been rebuilt and the paint on the four Doric pillars that supported the ve-randa had been touched up. A twenty-watt bulb lit up the framed sign on one of the pillars, Room and Board, Ladies Only.

Lora pressed the doorbell and then stepped back so that she could get a better view of the front room through the window. Under a blue-beaded chandelier three middle-aged women were playing bridge at a large, old-fashioned, round table. One of them, a plump brunette in a faded blue housedress, was talking and eating potato chips out of a cellophane bag.

Lora rang again and at the second ring the door was opened by a thin pallid-faced woman about forty.

She spoke in a hushed, sibilant whisper like a librarian. "Yes?"

"I was passing by and happened to see your sign."

"*My* sign? Dear me, it isn't *my* sign, I just board here." The woman laughed deprecatingly, making it clear that while she might have to live in a boarding house she'd certainly never stoop to running one. "There's no vacancy anyway, that I know."

"Oh."

"There was a room vacant for some time, but only this morning someone came and rented it, an elderly woman.

I haven't seen her myself. She doesn't come down for meals and I hear she's not going to. In fact, what I heard is that she's a little—you know, in the head." She touched the side of her own head lightly with one forefinger. "Poor soul."

Lora murmured, "It happens in the best of families."

"It does for a fact. Only it seems to me that a respectable boarding house isn't quite the place for such people. I said to Blanche—that's Mrs. Cushman, the landlady—I said, great Caesar, Blanche, haven't you enough to do without taking on the burden of carrying trays up and down stairs? Poor Blanche, she just can't resist trying to help people. Sometimes I think it's a weakness rather than a strength."

"I suppose you're right."

"Well, I must go back to the game, I'm dummy this hand. Sorry there's no vacancy, it would be nice to have a few younger people around. Maybe you'll try again?"

"It looks like a well-run place."

"Oh, it is. I've lived here since the beginning of the spring semester—we have loads of fun."

"I'd like to leave my name with Mrs. Cushman."

"That's a good idea. Just a sec and I'll call her. Oh, Blanche. Blanche? Come here, will you? Someone to see you."

The plump brunette in the blue dress came into the hall, still holding the bag of potato chips as if she didn't trust the discretion or appetite of her friends in the front room. When she saw Lora she put the bag on the seat of the hall rack and wiped her hands unobtrusively on the back of her dress.

The thin woman looked at her questioningly. "Did we—?"

"We lost," Mrs. Cushman said.

"Oh dear."

"It wasn't my fault, Madeleine. You had no cards."

"If you only wouldn't bid so *wildly*."

Madeleine returned to the game, shaking her head in sorrow at the folly of wild bidding.

Mrs. Cushman, too, shook her head. "I can't stand a bum sport."

"Nor can I."

"After all, it's only a game."

"You don't play for money?"

"No."

"I do," Lora said. "I play for money."

Mrs. Cushman began to look a little uneasy. "That's very interesting, I'm sure. I—are you selling something?"

"No."

"If it's a room you want, sorry, we're all filled up."

"As of this morning, in fact."

"That's right."

"Who moved in here this morning?"

"I can't see it's any of your business."

"It's my business, believe me," Lora said. "What room is she in—the front room on the left—Rose's room?"

Mrs. Cushman was breathing heavily and noisily through her mouth. "It isn't Rose's room any more. Rose is dead. Her stuff was all taken out days ago. I've got a perfect right to rent it again."

"Who rented it?"

"Say, I don't like the way you're acting, young woman. You better get out of here."

"I'll get out after I see your new boarder."

"You can't see her. She's sleeping. She wasn't feeling so well."

"She'll feel a lot worse when the police arrive."

"Police?"

"The police are looking for her. So am I. I got here first."

"Yes," Mrs. Cushman said heavily. "Yes, I see you did. You're Rose's daughter, aren't you?"

"Yes."

"I should of guessed it right away. There's a resemblance around the eyes and mouth. You're not as pretty as Rose was in her youth."

"My mother's looks never did her much good."

"No." Mrs. Cushman turned with a sigh and started up the steps, leaning her weight on the banister. "No, they never did."

The door of the front room on the left was closed. On the other side of it someone was humming softly and off-key.

Lora looked grimly at Mrs. Cushman. "Sounds happy, doesn't she?"

"She *is* happy. Seems like a cruel shame to bust it up."

"She'd bust it up herself if nobody else did."

"You want me to stick around?"

"I can handle her myself."

"I feel," Mrs. Cushman said, "I just feel like crying, I do. She came to me for help, poor soul. I didn't know the police were after her. How was I to know?"

"I wish you'd go downstairs."

"Well, all right, but you got a real rude way of expressing yourself. Like your mother."

"I'm tired of being compared with my mother."

"Yes." Mrs. Cushman headed for the stairs. "I can see you are."

On the other side of the closed door the humming had stopped. A woman's voice, husky and slightly slurred, called out, "Who's there? That you? Blanche?"

"Yes," Lora said.

"Come in."

"I'm coming." She went into the room, closing the door swiftly behind her as if she was afraid that the older woman would make some protest or outcry.

There was neither. "So you found me. Aren't you smart!"

"You're potted."

"The cup that cheers, Murphy, old girl, the cup that—"

"You can stop calling me Murphy. Everybody knows." She picked up a black wool coat that was lying across a chair. "Put it on."

"Why?"

"Every cop in town is looking for you. We've got to get out of here."

The old woman chuckled and clapped her hands like a delighted child. "They'll never think of looking *here*."

"I thought of it."

"That's because you're so smart. I said that before, didn't I? You're smart."

"Put your coat on."

"All right, all right, don't nag." She struggled out of the rocking chair, using her arms like a tightrope walker to keep her balance. "Who's potted? I'm not."

"Hurry up. Willett's waiting for us at home."

"Is he—mad?"

"What do you think?"

"All right, let him be mad. I can be mad too." She managed to get the coat on by herself. Lora didn't offer to help. "Murphy, listen. I've got an idea."

"Don't even bother to tell me."

"Listen. Let's not go back to that house at all. Let's run away."

"Where?"

"Oh, anywhere. Mexico City."

"How are we going to get there, hitchhike?"

"I don't want to go back to that house. It's depressing. I can't bear it, the two of them *watching* me all the time." But even while she was protesting, she was buttoning her coat getting ready to leave. "How much longer will I have to stay there?"

"Two months, maybe a week longer than that so nobody will get suspicious."

"And then?"

"Then you see a lawyer. Willett will bring him out to the house, and you'll make a will."

"I haven't anything to leave."

"It isn't the bequests that are important, it's the fact that— Oh, for heaven's sake, we've gone into this a dozen times before. We haven't time right now. Where's your purse?"

"On the bed."

"Did you bring anything else? A hat?"

"No."

"Come on, then." Lora took her by the arm. "You feel all right?"

"I wish I was dead."

"You can't die for two months yet."

"I wish I was—"

"Stop acting like a baby. Wait." Lora paused in the middle of the room and listened. From the hall came the sound of heavy footsteps, men's footsteps, punctuated by the sharp clicking of a woman's high heels on the hall linoleum.

Then Mrs. Cushman's voice, swollen with tears: "That's the room. They're in there, both of them. How was I to know anything was wrong? Frank, you tell him, tell him I only did my duty, so help me."

"It's the police," Lora said rapidly. "Now listen. You don't know why you ran away. You didn't remember a thing until you suddenly recognized me. I persuaded you to go home. Got that?"

"I didn't remember a thing. Not a thing."

"That's right."

Lora crossed the room and opened the door, adjusting her face to what she hoped was an expression of innocent surprise. "Why, it's Captain Greer. Isn't this a coincidence? I was just going to call you and tell you that I'd found her."

"Thoughtful of you," Greer said. "Come in, Frank."

Frank came in, looking pale and embarrassed.

"You've been in this room before, haven't you, Frank?"

"Yes."

"When was the last time?"

"The last time was after Rose's funeral."

"And the time before that?"

"It was a week ago last Sunday."

"What was the occasion?"

"Mrs. Cushman called me and asked me to come over and see Rose and try and straighten her out."

"Did you straighten her out?"

"No," Frank said gravely. "I guess not."

Greer didn't look at the two women or give any indication that he realized they were still there watching him. "Rose was more than a patient of yours, wasn't she?"

"I considered her a friend."

"You knew her well? Very well?"

"I thought I did. As things turned out, I was wrong."

"How have things turned out, Frank?"

"Say, what is this anyway?" Lora said. "If you two want to have a private conversation, have it some other place. I have to get Mrs. Goodfield home. She's not well." She took the older woman by the shoulder. "Are you?"

"No. I'm not well. I can't remember anything."

Greer didn't even turn his head. With his eyes still fixed on Frank he repeated the question: "How have things turned out?"

"You know how. Why do you ask me?"

"It's more fun to hear it from somebody else."

"All right. Things have turned out, well, very oddly."

"Let's get back to Rose. After you left her that Sunday, you heard from her again?"

"Yes. She phoned me the next afternoon around three o'clock."

"At the inquest there was considerable doubt about the time on the part of the Sheriff."

"Not on my part. It was the middle of the afternoon. I couldn't swear to that at the inquest because the evidence was all against it, but I can now."

"You had still further news from Rose?"

"Yes. A postcard came the following morning, Tuesday. No message on it, just a rough pencil sketch of a rose."

"What was the postmark time on the card?"

"Six o'clock. You saw it yourself."

"According to the evidence, Rose was dead three hours before she telephoned you and several hours before she mailed that postcard. You heard Dr. Severn testify to that?"

"Yes."

"Did you believe his testimony?"

"Yes."

"Do you believe it now?"

"No."

"Severn also testified that Rose was suffering from an incurable enlargement of the heart, and that the only reason she had not died before was because she managed to lose a great deal of weight by rigorous dieting. Does this fit in with what you know of Rose?"

"No. She never dieted. She boasted about being able to eat anything and not gain a pound. I didn't recall this at the inquest but I checked my file on her this morning and then I went directly over to Dr. Severn's office. He confirmed his own testimony. Within the past three years or so the dead woman had been extremely overweight."

"You don't think Severn is a liar, do you?"

"No."

"Think he made a mistake?"

"No."

"Some mistake was made. Who made it?"

"I'm afraid Rose did." For the first time Frank looked

226

directly across the room at the two women. "I don't believe she realized the gravity of the situation. Her emotional responses were frequently very childish. I think she considered the whole thing as a game or as a play with herself in the leading role."

"Who wrote the play?" Greer said.

"I don't know."

"Miss Dalloway, perhaps you know?"

"Of course I do." Lora went over to the window and looked down at the street below, listlessly, as if what the people on this street were doing—or any other street—didn't interest or concern her. "Mrs. Goodfield wrote it. Every line, every stage direction, she wrote."

"Why?"

"Money. Some people will do anything for money, even after they're dead."

"Mrs. Goodfield is dead?"

"She's dead, all right. I saw them carry her out the back door, the three of them, Willett and Ethel and Rose. They tried to put her in the Lincoln. They intended to drive her away and let her be found some place else. But she was too stiff by that time; they couldn't get her through the car door. God, it was funny. It wasn't so funny at the time, but now when I think of it, it strikes me as hilarious. There were the three of them, Willett bawling and Ethel hysterical and Rose with a load on—there they were, trying to push that skinny little dead woman into the car. You don't find it amusing, Captain?"

Instead of answering, Greer glanced at the other woman. She was clutching the black wool coat around her as if it were a tent to hide inside. "Did *you* find it amusing?"

"No." She spoke in a whisper. "How can she talk like that? It was terrible. She was so *stiff*. I didn't know people got so *stiff*."

Lora started to laugh. She didn't turn, she just stood

227

looking down at the people on the streets, laughing softly to herself. Greer told her to stop and she stopped, immediately. It was as if her laughter meant nothing to her anyway, it was merely a way to pass the time, a sound to fill a vacuum.

Greer said, "You couldn't get the dead woman into the car?"

"No," Rose said. "Then Willett broke down completely and we had to send him back to the house. Ethel decided we couldn't carry out the plan, that we'd have to leave her in the garden. So we put her in the chair by the lily pool. Or tried to. She wouldn't stay in, she was so—so brittle. Like glass."

"She died at noon?"

"Yes, at noon. In her bed. But we had to wait until dark to arrange—things."

"You spoke of a plan. Whose plan?"

"Mrs. Goodfield's. It was all her idea. Don't blame the others."

"The 'others' include you, Rose?"

"I didn't mean any harm. I didn't even want to do it; I wouldn't listen to her at first. It was such a crazy scheme, and I couldn't understand the reason for it. The next time I met Lora I told her about it. She was looking for a job anyway, so she decided to plant herself at the Goodfields' and find out more about them and exactly what the set-up was."

"And she did?"

"Yes, she kept me posted. The next time Willett phoned and asked me if I'd made up my mind, I told him yes, I'd do it. I couldn't see anything really *wrong* about it, not at first."

"And later?"

"Later, I began to get jittery, cooped up in that room all the time with Ethel and Willett watching every move I made, listening outside my door. They were jittery too, worse than me, I guess. With Mrs. Goodfield dead there was no one to, well, to pull us together. It was like carrying out a conspiracy with the chief conspirator missing and the reason behind it not very clear, not to me anyway. Then came the payoff, a double payoff. Dalloway started hanging around the house and Jack Goodfield was on his way. I realized I had to get out of there, fast. I was good enough to fool strangers like you, but I knew I couldn't fool a man who was supposed to be my son. And Dalloway, I was afraid Dalloway would recognize me even after all these years. Ethel kept telling me that Jack could be taken in quite easily, because he hadn't seen his mother for some time and her illness had previously caused great changes in her. But I didn't believe her. I was scared. Lora hadn't come back and I was all alone. I waited until Willett and Ethel went to bed and then I put on my coat and sneaked out. I left a note for Willett."

"Why?"

"I didn't want him searching for me right away. I had to have time to think, figure things out."

"And have you figured things out?"

"I guess not. But I know I never meant to do anything wrong. It still doesn't seem to me that what I did was *exactly* wrong. I didn't harm anyone, cheat anyone. All I did was lie a little, pretend to be a woman I wasn't because the woman died too soon."

"Too soon for what?"

"For the deadline. She had a deadline. I'm not trying to be funny; that's what it *was*. Mrs. Goodfield explained the details to me, but I didn't pay much attention. I'm not," she added, with a conciliatory little smile, "much of a business woman."

Greer was not conciliated. "You were paid for your part in the fraud?"

"I hate that word fraud. It sounds—"

"You were paid?"

"No. No. I wasn't."

"Expect me to believe that?"

"Well, naturally. It's true. They didn't pay me. They were going to when it was all over. Not a lump sum, because I didn't want it that way and they couldn't afford it anyway—but just a little each month." Rose's eyes were wide and wistful. "It would have been nice for my old age, wouldn't it?"

"Dandy."

"You don't suppose there's still a chance that I'll get it?"

"I don't suppose."

"Oh well, something will turn up." She looked across the room at Frank. "Frankie?"

"What do you want?" Frank said.

"You're mad at me?"

"No."

"You haven't spoken a word to me. You must be mad."

"No."

"Disappointed, then?"

"A little disappointed, maybe."

"Oh, what the hell, Frankie, I didn't mean to do anything wrong. It could happen to anybody."

"But especially to you."

Rose was delighted by this observation. "That's the honest-to-God truth, Frankie. I attract disaster."

Lora turned and addressed her mother coldly: "There wouldn't be any disaster, there wouldn't even be any trouble if you hadn't phoned this guy long after you were supposed to be dead. What a brain wave that was. You—"

"How was I to know she was dead? Ethel didn't tell me. All she said was to come on over to the house. I didn't realize there was any great rush about it. So I took my time, I phoned Frank, I bought the postcards and sent him one, little things like that."

"*Little* things like that. For Pete's sake, you're a birdbrain, a *birdbrain*."

"Look who's calling who a—"

"Ladies," Greer said, pleasantly. "It's time to be leaving."

Rose clutched the black coat around her again, her hands working nervously at the cloth. "Where are we going?"

"To pay a visit to the Goodfields."

"I don't want to. I've had enough of them."

"It's possible," Greer said, "that they've had enough of you, too. But you're each going to have a little more."

26

THE DRAWING ROOM was warm and humid and the heavy mahogany and gold satin furniture seemed to smother its occupants with excess. There was too much of everything in the room, too much sun and furniture, too much gilt and crystal, too many mirrors, too many people.

At the huge picture window that framed the mountains, a bluebottle fly buzzed, flung himself against the glass, paused, and attacked again with renewed fury and desperation.

Ethel watched the fly, engrossed, feeling so much empathy with it that she would have liked to pick up the fire tongs and smash the window and let the fly go on its way. If it gets away, she thought, if it escapes, where will it go? What will it do? If I got away, where would I go? What would I do?

Suddenly the bluebottle swooped across the room and out of the open door, directly, as if it had known all along which way to get out and the fussing at the window had been only play. With its departure Ethel felt a certain loss.

She wanted to follow the bluebottle right out of the house, wing along beside it, gay, reckless, without a past, without a future, without Willett.

She became aware gradually that the policeman, Greer, was talking, not talking actually, but reading aloud from the letter he held stiffly in both his hands. Everyone was watching him, listening attentively—even Willett, though by this time Willett knew the letter by heart. He'd read it over and over again as if he'd been trying to memorize it like a catechism.

"—the event that my son, Willett Peter Goodfield, is implicated in any way with my death, I wish to make the following statement to clarify the facts. With my limited knowledge of the law, I am not certain what credence is given to the written statement of a dying woman. I can only hope it will be full credence. I swear that these statements are true, and that my mind is functioning clearly, perhaps too clearly. If I did not have such real understanding of my children and such bitter awareness of their inability to look after themselves, I could die in peace like an ordinary woman. I cannot. The enclosed pages will explain everything. I wrote them as they happened and I swear they are the full truth.

Olive Regina Goodfield

It is May the fourth. Today my search ended. Months of searching, all over the country, and today, just when I was about to abandon hope, I found her, on a street corner waiting for a traffic light to change. Her name is Rose French. The physical resemblance to me is not perfect by any means and she is younger than I, but her coloring is the same, and the bone structure of her face, and our sizes are identical. I have come to the end of a long journey.

May 7. She is stubborn. That, too, we have in common. But her stubbornness is not as great as mine because there is not the same urgency behind it. I talked to her this evening again. She came out by bus; Willett did not bring her. I want no one to see her with Willett or on these premises, not even the new maid, Ada Murphy, whom Ethel hired yesterday. Hiring the maid was entirely Ethel's idea. She meant it to be a surprise for me. It was. She couldn't have done a more stupid thing, under the circumstances. The only course for me to follow is to refuse to have anything to do with Murphy. That way she won't know the difference when the substitution is effected. As it will be. Rose French is getting very curious, and the smell of money is beginning to tickle her nostrils.

May 9. The arrangements were completed last night, and this afternoon I gave Rose her first coaching. She is an excellent mimic and I enjoyed the afternoon tremendously. I no longer have many pleasures and turning a stranger into oneself is amusing. I see now how I must appear to others, to Willett and Jack and to poor Ethel who hates me and is so ashamed of her hatred and jealousy because she thinks it is abnormal. It is not abnormal at all. If our positions were reversed, I would certainly hate her with equal vigor. As it is, I like Ethel and her essential honesty, and I appreciate her bungling little kindnesses. I have often regretted my decision that she should marry Willett. She deserves a better fate.

Willett and Ethel looked at each other across the room and spoke in silence:

"Do you, Ethel? Do you deserve a better fate?"

"No. No, of course not."

"Yes, you do. Yes."

"Not really. Everything's going to be all right, dear, all right."

Greer had turned a page and was reading again, softly and slowly and without emotion as if he didn't intend to be overheard and was merely forming the words with his mouth like an inexperienced reader.

233

May 12. Tonight we had a preview, Willett and Rose and Ethel and I, though I didn't count. I was only the audience. I lay in bed and watched. Willett was himself and Ethel was herself, but Rose was me. I rather enjoyed it and I have a suspicion that Ethel did too. But Rose was nervous and Willett broke down completely and cried and kept asking me why, why we had to go through with this terrible thing. For the fiftieth time I told him why. I explained it to all three of them. Willett did not need an explanation. What he wanted was reassurance; he wanted me to say, no, no, Willett, I'm not going to die. I could not say it. I wish I could.

May 13. After last night's emotional tension I am very tired and I am beginning to wonder if my plan will work out. For months I have lived with the *idea* of it; the actual execution is a different matter. There are difficulties which I didn't anticipate. Willett, for one. I have made him swear on the sacred Book that he will carry out my plan, no matter how many misgivings he may have about its legality. Both in mind and heart he is reluctant, but he has sworn. If the time should ever come when these pages are read by an agent of the law, I repeat, this plan is mine alone. Willett and Ethel are acting under compulsion; any blame or criticism must be given to me.

The other difficulty is Rose. I suspect that she drinks, and I know that she has a faulty memory. Since she is to become me, she must learn and learn accurately what I have been doing lately and where I have been and what my little hobbies and weaknesses are. Dependence upon the radio during these last years has made me a baseball fan. Rose is very bored by the game. She simply cannot remember which teams belong in which leagues. Nor can she remember dates and places. I had Willett bring home some road maps and Rose wrote notes in the margin, making a little game of it. I believe this will help her memorize more readily. Our personal relationship is not a friendly one. She respects me, and I am dependent upon her. She is *me,* and she will be me longer than I will. In its macabre way, the situation is amusing. I cannot laugh out loud, my breathing is uneasy, but I can smile inside. I can weep inside, too. Life these days swings from farce to tragedy and back again, back and forth, with all of us clinging to the pendulum like squirming little puppets. When I look at Willett and see his torment, I almost choke with tears. And then quite suddenly Ethel comes up with one of her exquisitely inane remarks and back goes the pendulum again. It will never stop. One of these days I will release my hold on it, but the pendulum itself will go on swinging and so will Ethel, Willett, and certainly Rose, who swings more violently than anyone.

May 16. This afternoon I went over with Ethel and Willett the details of my plan for what may be the last time. It is, in essence, a simple one. Some people will consider it only as an attempt to defraud the government. Others will see it as I do, an attempt to protect my children from what I consider unjust claims.

I am not by nature interested in business and finance. Interest was thrust upon me by two events: first I inherited all of my husband's stock, and second, I learned from my doctor approximately three years ago, that I had a bad heart condition which might prove fatal at any time. I told no one about it. Instead, I went directly to my husband's lawyer. I had everything I owned divided into three equal parts and given to my children—an outright gift, no strings attached.

But there were strings, invisible strings which I discovered later. I will try to explain them simply. According to law I was allowed to give away to each of my children, or anyone else, up to thirty thousand dollars by cash or its equivalent, free of gift tax. Sums beyond that are subject to gift taxes. They are not high and the children managed to pay them without sacrificing any of their stock in the factory. The factory is their livelihood. None of them can support themselves, not even Shirley. She is clever enough, but she has to look after her four children.

For a while I felt quite pleased with myself, believing that the division of my property had accomplished a number of things which I thought desirable: there would be no squabbling over money after my death, and above all, the factory would still belong to the family and would continue to support them comfortably if not luxuriously. I became resigned to the idea of my death, because I thought my children's future was taken care of. I had nothing to leave to them; they would not have to pay a penny of inheritance taxes which I consider exorbitant and in certain cases quite unjust.

It was about a year ago when I discovered that my sense of security about the future was founded on ignorance. It happened quietly as important things often do, quietly and without warning. Shirley and I were at home and Shirley was reading one of those obscure second-hand books she likes to collect.

Suddenly she looked up at me and asked me how I was feeling.

I told her I felt quite well, all things considered.

"Your sticking to your diet, aren't you?"

"I'm half-starved all the time," I said sharply. "I've lost seventy pounds."

"Have you been to the doctor lately?"

"Last month."

"What did he say?"

"He said I was doing better than he expected."

"You mean there was an improvement in your condition?"

I told her the truth. "There was no improvement, no. I'm simply not disintegrating as rapidly as he thought I would."

"Do you suppose you'll live for a year?"

It was an odd question, but I was not surprised. Shirley

is an odd girl, unemotional, except where her children are concerned. "Would you care if I didn't?"

"Care? It's not really a matter of caring."

"What is it a matter of, then?"

"Taxes."

"Taxes. What are you talking about? What's that book you're reading?"

She told me, then. I won't attempt to reconstruct her words. I will explain it more personally, as it affects me. If I live another two months, to the middle of July, it will be exactly three years since I divided my property among my children. Three years—that is the arbitrary legal time limit. If I live that long, everything will be well. If I don't, the property I gave away will be presumed to have been given in anticipation of death, and under those circumstances it will be taxed not as a gift but as an inheritance. This would not apply to accidental deaths or ones that could not be foreseen. But it applied to me. I had disposed of my property in anticipation of death. My doctor knew it; it was a matter of record. A funny law, isn't it? If I lived three years, not a day more, it would indicate that I hadn't anticipated death. Yes, it's quite a funny law.

"This is awful," Shirley said. "Don't you see?"

"I see."

"I can't afford to pay inheritance taxes without selling some of my stock. You know what that means."

I knew. Little by little, they'd sell. Little by little, other people would take over the factory. How well I knew.

Shirley was watching me with that half-grim, half-humorous expression she often wears. "I guess you'll just have to hold out for a year, won't you?"

"Yes, I guess I will."

"Do you think you can?"

"Of course."

No, Shirley, I didn't think I could. But there were ways.

Devious ways, perhaps. That's why I couldn't ask you to be a party to them, you or Jack. It had to be Willett—he loved me more.

The bluebottle fly had returned to the window with a rush of wings, its vigor unabated. Ethel watched it, but she no longer felt it was a part of her. Its incessant buzzing seemed silly, its energy without purpose, and the reckless charm of its existence an illusion.

Willett loved her more, she thought. Yes, it's true. He loved her too much. I didn't have a chance while she was alive. Now she's gone, and when this is all over perhaps the factory will be gone too, and Willett and I can start a new life.

Greer turned a page.

May 18. I am very weary but somehow more hopeful to-night. Everything is settled. Rose is ready to move in at a moment's notice if anything should happen to me. Ethel has kept the maid, Murphy, out of my room so she will not suspect any substitution when it is made. *If* it is made. I feel so hopeful that I'm almost convinced it won't be necessary. If it is, however, Willett has his instructions. In the middle of July it must be established that I am still alive, perhaps by means of some legal action like a will. There should be no trouble about the difference in signatures. Illness has already changed mine so much that I can hardly believe it is mine. Even now, as I write, I look at this hesitant, shaky script and despise it.

So much for that. On July, the fifteenth, I will be alive, perhaps really, perhaps apparently. Willett and Ethel will then return to San Francisco and resume their life.

But what of Rose?

She's the problem. Obviously she cannot continue to be me forever. She cannot take my place among my friends and family, in my home. Even if it were remotely possible,

I couldn't stand the idea of it. No. Rose must die. She must die as me. If I die as her, she must die as me.

Once or twice lately I have caught her looking at me queerly. I believe she knows what I am thinking. When she is sober, there is fear in her eyes, but I have no sympathy to waste on such a woman. Rose has seen much life, many beds; why this childish greed for more?

I was amused, at first, by her mimicry. No longer. It has become more cruel and cunning and exaggerated as if she is saying to me, *see this irritable and autocratic old woman? It is you.*

Yes, I have come to despise her. But I am not sure which I am despising, the Rose who is Rose or the Rose who is me. Rose. I dislike the very name. That old song keeps running through my head: *The last rose of summer left blooming alone, all her lovely companions have faded and gone.*

Rose hates to be alone. She should join her lovely companions.

May 19. Murder. The word occurred to me in the middle of the night. I woke up with it on my lips. Then I went back to sleep, and when I woke up again there were church bells ringing. The incongruity amused me. Murder and church bells.

It is Sunday. Murphy had the day off so Rose came out this afternoon. She had been drinking, using alcohol to dissolve her fear. But it wouldn't dissolve. It has become too hard and dense; a diamond of fear, nothing can dissolve it, nothing can make a mark on it.

She sat by the window, mute and morose.

"Talk to me," I said.

She shook her head.

"Why won't you talk to me?"

"I've been talking."

"Oh, you have? To whom?"

"A friend of mine. You don't know him. His name is Frank."

239

"And did you talk quite frankly?" I smiled at the pun, expecting that Rose would smile too.

"I never talk frankly any more. I talk like you, pretending to be frank but never saying the truth."

"You find that unpleasant?"

"I hate it."

"You hate me too, Rose. Don't you?"

She wouldn't answer.

I spoke to her again in a soft, friendly way: "Perhaps you hate yourself, too, Rose. We are almost twins."

She sat all huddled up in the chair, watching me, hugging her knees as if for warmth and comfort.

"Practically twins," I repeated. "Come here. Stand beside my bed, look into the mirror. What do you see?"

She came and stood beside my bed and looked into the mirror on the door.

"What do you see, Rose?"

"I see two dreadful old women," she said quietly, and picked up her coat and left.

The door closed behind her, and its mirror sprang back at me like a beast out of ambush.

I could not take my eyes away. The dreadful old woman fascinated me. Surely it was not I. I had picked up my coat and walked out of the door. I could hear my own footsteps on the stairs.

"Ethel," I said. "Ethel, Ethel, Ethel!"

When I became conscious again, Ethel and Willett were bending over my bed. I felt quite cleansed, pure. My body was light as a bird's, my mind extraordinarily clear. There was nothing it could not have solved in that moment, no mathematical formula too involved, no problem too difficult.

I said, "Willett, I must talk to you alone."

"You mustn't talk. I've sent for the doctor."

"Cancel it."

"No. No, I can't, I won't."

240

"Cancel it," I said. A doctor. I didn't need a doctor. My mind was so clear and bright. There was nothing it could not solve.

"The doctor will help you," Willett said.

I called him a name, just a quiet little name, and he went downstairs and canceled the doctor's call.

When he came back up again, he sat on the edge of my bed and his breathing sounded hard and painful.

"Willett, you love me?"

"Yes, mother."

"You would do anything for me?"

"Yes."

"When the time comes," I said, "when the time comes, Rose must disappear."

"I know that. It's all been arranged. She has promised—"

"Promises are only words, only air going in and out of the lungs and shapes of sounds in and out of the larynx. Promises are nothing, Willett. You understand?"

"They're all I have."

"You must have more. You must have certainty."

"There aren't many certainties in this world."

"There are two," I said. "Death and taxes."

"You should be resting, mother."

"Death and taxes," I repeated. "She's not a good woman, Willett. It isn't as if she were. No one will miss her. No one will care."

"I don't know what you're talking about."

"She's a dreadful old woman, really. Haven't you noticed? Don't you hate the way she looks, the way she talks? Don't you think she's dreadful?"

"No. *No.*"

"Those eyes, mean, hard, little eyes. They would be better off sealed."

"Mother—"

"Seal them."

"You're not rational, mother."

241

"Make Rose a certainty. Seal those horrid, little eyes."

Willett looked at me with such sadness. Then he got up and leaned over me and pressed his hand on my forehead and touched the lids of my eyes. "Go to sleep, momma, you're tired."

I am tired. But I must not sleep. I must plan. Willett thinks I am losing my mind. He doesn't understand, he hasn't looked into that mirror, he hasn't seen what I have. Tomorrow I will show him what springs out at me when the door closes. Tomorrow he will see that dreadful old woman . . .

But tomorrow was too late.

She went to sleep with the pen in her hand, and the sound of church bells in her ears, and in the morning she did not awaken.

The drawing room was still hot, still humid. There was too much of everything in it, too much sun and furniture and gilt, too many mirrors.

Ethel looked at Willett across the excess of everything and spoke to him without words: *Take it easy, old boy. Everything will be all right. You still have me.*

27

THE FRONT LEFT, second-floor room of Mrs. Cushman's boarding house was beginning to look normal again. Rose's clothes were strewn across the bed, a tomato and half a dozen oranges were ripening on the window-sill and Rose herself was rehanging her pictures on the wall. She had on a red plaid dress that Ethel had given to her. The dress was two or three sizes too large and made her resemble a scarecrow, a fact which Rose used to her own advantage.

"Look at me," she said. "Just look. I've lost pounds."

Mrs. Cushman looked, and said with feeling, "You poor thing."

"I damn near starved."

"We'll feed you up real nice, Rose. Don't you worry, you've got some good years in you yet. And just to think not more than a week ago I went to your funeral."

"Was it nice?"

"Real nice. The minister said some lovely things about you. Better than you deserve, if you'll pardon my tactlessness." Mrs. Cushman's eyes narrowed in thought. "As a matter of fact, it seems to me you always get a little better than you deserve."

Rose did not take offense, because she couldn't afford to; but she tucked the remark away in a corner of her mind for future reference and rebuttal. "Things have," she admitted, "turned out very well."

Mrs. Cushman stood quietly for a moment, torn between her desire to see justice done and her desire to remain the friend and confidante of someone who was very nearly murdered and who'd already had a funeral.

Justice won. "It don't seem right that nobody was arrested."

"You have a small mind," Rose said crushingly. "Extremely small."

"Small mind or no small mind, somebody should of been arrested."

"They couldn't get enough evidence to take into court. Besides, we've all suffered enough."

"I wonder."

"When I think of myself imprisoned in that room, hungry, chained to the bed, practically—"

"Huh."

"Well, if you're going to be unpleasant about it, Blanche, I've a good notion to pack up my bags and leave."

"You haven't got anywhere to go."

"Oh, haven't I? Well, I'll have you know that Dalloway is yearning to have me back, and Lora wants me to share an apartment with her, and Ethel offered me a job in San Francisco, and Frank and Miriam would be delighted if I—"

"That last picture's not straight, the one from *Golden Girls.*"

Rose straightened the picture, brushing off a speck of dust with the sleeve of Ethel's plaid dress. She said, with a sigh, *"Golden Girls.* Ah, that was a production. Remember it, Blanche?"

"I remember."

"Those were the days. I was married to Hamman then, Dwight Hamman. God, what a skunk he turned out to be, a real crook if I ever saw one."

"You saw more than one," Mrs. Cushman said pointedly. "And more than *saw,* too." From the kitchen below came the sound of the supper bell. "Chained to the bed. *Huh.*"

"Morally, I was."

"Justice ain't been done."

But justice was vast, evasive, misty. You could not talk to it, play canasta with it, invite it for a cup of tea. Besides, there was the vague possibility that everyone had indeed suffered enough.

The two women went down the stairs to supper arm in arm, with justice following at a respectful distance.

On the couch in his own parlor Captain Greer was enjoying his after-dinner nap. His stomach was full and his dream was sweet: he had arrested all of them—Rose and Willett and Jack and Ethel and Dalloway and Lora, yes, even Miriam and Frank—and their sad, pleading faces were looking out at him from behind steel bars.

Greer smiled in his sleep.

ABOUT THE AUTHOR

Margaret Millar was born in Kitchener, Ontario, Canada, and educated at the Kitchener Collegiate Institute and the University of Toronto. In 1938 she married Kenneth Millar, better known under his pen name of Ross Macdonald, and for over forty years they enjoyed a unique relationship as a husband and wife who successfully pursued separate writing careers.

She published her first novel, *The Invisible Worm,* in 1941. Now, over four decades later, she is busily polishing her twenty-fifth work of fiction. During that time she has established herself as one of the great practitioners in the field of mystery and psychological suspense. Her work has been translated into more than a dozen foreign languages, appeared in twenty-seven paperback editions and has been selected seventeen times by book clubs. She received an Edgar Award for the Best Mystery of the Year with her classic *Beast in View;* and two of her other novels, *The Fiend* and *How Like an Angel,* were runners-up for that award. She is a past President of the Mystery Writers of America, and in 1983 she received that organization's most prestigious honor, the Grand Master Award, for lifetime achievement.